DARK SHADOWS AT
CENTRAL TERMINAL

STEVE BANKO

NFB Publishing
Buffalo, New York

This book is dedicated to a great basketball player, an even better mayor, and one of the best friends anyone could have. This is for Tony Masiello who loves Buffalo more than anyone I know.

PREFACE

I HAD NO SOONER finished work on my first novel, <u>For No Good Reason</u>, when people started asking me when I would write another. Well, here it is – another.

<u>Dark Shadows at Central Terminal</u> is equal parts a mystery I concocted and a paean to the city of my birth and a city I love. In telling this story, I've incorporated several of the people and places that deserve to be front and center in any tale about Buffalo. Of course, those mentioned in this book are my favorites and friends but they may not be yours so, to you, I say - write your own story. We all have one.

The catalyst for the book was actually voiced one day in Mayor Tony Masiello's office in City Hall, shortly after Tony had been elected. We were wrestling with some thorny budget issues and somehow the matter of Central Terminal came up. At that time, no one had viable plans for effective reuse of the landmark and there was no money available to demolish it. We diverged from the budget issues for a few minutes to offer suggestions, real and imagined, to deal with the terminal. It was either Jim Milroy, Tony's budget director, or Eva Hassett, Jim's boss, who came up with a novel idea. Why don't we take out an ad in "Variety" and tell action movie producers we had a building they could blow up in their next opus? We all got a big laugh out of that and then, reluctantly, turned our attention back to the financial issues.

I had occasion to leave and return to Buffalo via Central Terminal in 1977. I had been hired as a speechwriter in the NYS Assembly and I had to travel to Albany every week for the legislative session.

Flying was expensive. Driving was a drag. So, I tried the train. It left Buffalo at 5 a.m. and was supposed to get to Albany at noon. It arrived at 2:30 in the afternoon so I only used the rails that one time. But walking through the deserted, cavernous lobby at that early morning hour I could imagine the hustle and bustle of the place in days gone by.

I hope you will enjoy reading this book as much as I did writing it.

PROLOGUE

THE SKY WAS so blue I was searching for another word for it. The water shimmered and shined in the morning sun. Mornings were best at the cove where I carried out my morning ablutions at the altar of nature. The brisk swim across the bay washed off all the stink from a 90-minute *Muay Thai* workout and stale smells from last night: the second-hand smoke from the bar's patio clinging to my hair; the odor from the beer and booze that hung in the air; the sweat from whatever exertions the night called for. Those exertions ran the gamut from carrying a lot of Dos Equis, Tecate, and Corona out to slack the thirst of the hundred or so patrons who visited La Hacienda on an average night to throwing out the all too frequent drunks, druggies, and hustlers who made it past the door. I'm the bouncer/bartender/bar back/greeter at the biggest and best bar in Cabo San Jose, Mexico. How I got here is a long and sometimes unlikely story that I won't bore you with now. Suffice it to say I needed a break from a life in the States that had begun to throw me too many curve balls. I'm more of a fastball hitter.

I hadn't planned on a career change when I got here. I was looking more for a quick getaway than something steady. I spent a few days in the more populous, and rowdy, neighborhood of Cabo San Lucas and decided I needed something calmer. I found a place to stay and a place to enjoy a few cool ones every night at La Hacienda. One afternoon baking in the Mexican sun, I met the owner of the establishment, one Finn Bakker. He was under an umbrella constantly jabbering into the cell phone that seemed to be part of his ear. He had an interesting tattoo on a taut right bicep and he caught me staring at it.

"Like the ink?" he asked.

"Never seen anything like it," I said. "Is that a bull charging?"

"No vriend, it's a bison."

"No shit. I come from a city with the name of a bison."

"Is it in Wyoming?" he asked.

"No, in New York."

"Ah, Buffalo … Queen City of the Great Lakes."

I was stunned. How did this guy know about my hometown? Hell, half the people in Buffalo didn't know it was once the Queen City of the Great Lakes.

"And you knew that how?"

"I was thinking about repatriating to the States once. I read a lot of stuff about a lot of places."

"Well, San Jose is about as far from Buffalo as you can get," I said.

"Yeah. I spent some time in New York City. A little too dangerous for me."

"I know what you mean. Tell me more about that bison on your arm."

"It's a regimental crest, my regimental crest, the 43rd Mechanized."

"I served too … in Afghanistan."

"That explains the nasty looking caterpillar on your shoulder."

The look on my face must have told him I didn't know what the hell he was talking about.

"The scar, vriend. The scar on your shoulder."

Oh yeah, that, I thought. That caterpillar.

We talked for a long time that afternoon and into the evening. He talked of the journey that had taken him from the officer corps in the Dutch army to South Africa to Vancouver, Canada to this little corner of Mexico. Finn invited me to dine with him and his friend, a stunningly beautiful local woman with bronze skin, jet black hair and eyes I couldn't help staring at.

"How long are you going to be lolling around our fair metropolis?" he asked me.

I told him I had no plans to head back to the states nor any plans for anything else for that matter. That's when he offered me the job.

"I need someone around here to help me out. You interested?"

I was, and I am. At least I was until I saw young Xavier running down the beach waving his arms and shouting.

"Senor Coe... Senor Coe ... you have a phone call ... a call from the Estados Unidos!"

I broke from my leisurely drift across the water and paddled with a vengeance. There weren't many people who knew where I was and none of them were in a hurry to talk to me.

This was going to be interesting.

CHAPTER ONE

"WELL, COE, YOU screwed the pooch on this one!"

The shout coming from the phone was familiar in both sound and tone.

"Hey Lexi. Nice to hear from you too."

"Don't try to smother me in your bullshit, Coe Duffy! You have no idea what you've started back here."

Lexi ... Lexi Crane ... formally Patrol Officer Alexis Crane, Buffalo Police Department retired ... was right about that. I had no idea what she was talking about. In the interest of full disclosure, P.O. Crane and I had been an item a while back, before she had to arrest me. But that's another story.

"Lexi, I have no idea what you are talking about. Slow down and state the case, then accuse me."

I could hear her breathing so I knew she was still on the phone but she was silent for a few seconds.

"Do you remember that hare-brained idea you fed the mayor when you were still an American"

"I am still an American, Lexi; just residing outside the country right now. And which hare-brained idea?"

"Oh yes, I forgot you were constantly putting those kinds of ideas in the mayor's head. But I am referring to the one about the Central Terminal building!"

For those of you not familiar with my hometown, the Central Terminal was built to accommodate New York Central trains passing through Buffalo. It had the good fortune of opening in the heyday of rail travel but the misfortune of opening in 1929, just months before the Great Depression of the 1930s. But as with many other entities, the onset of our involvement in World War II gave a big boost to railroads that were moving lots of men and materiel around the country. Truth be told, though, the damn thing was horribly overbuilt, rising 271 feet above the street with seventeen floors comprising the structure. It went dark in the late '70s and was just a tall wart in the middle of a rundown neighborhood by the time my friend Shamus Culhane, became mayor of the city. The constant dilemma we faced was what to do with such a monstrous structure. Even demolition would put a strain on the city budget. Watching the sun set over Lake Erie one late afternoon, my colleague Ava Daley and I were musing about possible solutions to the Central Terminal problem.

"I bet there would be some interest among action movie directors to blow the big sonofabitch up," I joked.

"Yeah," Ava laughed, "maybe we should put an ad in Variety telling the industry we have a big-assed building they could demolish in their movie."

We looked at each other for a moment, struck with the idea. But we laughed and shook our heads that we couldn't do such a goofy thing. That didn't stop me from mentioning it at the next staff meeting in the mayor's office though. I did it as a joke but it raised hackles nonetheless.

"Christ, do you know what the preservationists would say?" the mayor said. "They'd skin me alive!"

"Hey, pal, I was just kidding. We haven't even asked for rate cards for Variety yet," I said. It didn't get the laugh I thought it might but it did elicit a sigh of relief from His Honor. I thought myself quite the innovative thinker and assumed that would be the end of it. But it had Lexi about ready to reach through the phone and choke me.

"Lexi, it was a joke. What's the big deal?"

"The big deal, Mr. Comedian, is that the new administration heard of the idea and is now going to act on it."

"It wasn't even an idea. It was a joke. Remember when you had a sense of humor? A joke."

"No one's laughing now, smart ass. They're getting ready to take out an ad in Variety."

I was still trying to figure out what all this had to do with me. Surely the statute of limitations on lame jokes had expired on this one.

"Can you jump to the punch line, Lexi?" I said. "Surely you aren't blaming me for this."

"No, I'm not blaming you. I'm giving you credit. Something big has come up and you have to get your expatriate ass home ASAP."

I wasn't expecting that. Lexi and I had a complicated relationship that ended when she slapped her handcuffs on me. We'd only spoken briefly since the cuffs came off. And get those dirty thoughts out of your mind. She cuffed me in the mayor's office.

"I had no idea you were that so preservation minded," I said.

"I'm not," she said, "but I am very money minded."

Money, I thought. Now there's something Lexi and I still have in common. I thought I'd push my luck a little.

"Pick me up at the airport?"

"Call Uber, asshole."

Still the same Lexi, I mused. She's never forgiven me for making her arrest me.

CHAPTER TWO

THERE ISN'T MUCH that would make me trade the soft ocean breezes of Cabo for the icy wind of Buffalo in March. Something that would was money. I had used most of my available cash kicking around the Baja Peninsula and the pittance that Finn gave me at La Hacienda just about paid my bar tab and rent. Lexi hadn't expounded on what money had to do with the demolition of the Central Terminal but I owed it to myself (and her?) to find out. Two steps into a Buffalo March made me wonder if this would be worth it. I called the former mayor and still friend Shamus and he told me me to come to his house on Nottingham Terrace to say hello and get some keys to a vacant apartment that had once been that of his recently deceased parents.

"Hey Shamus," I said as we hugged. "Sorry to hear about your mom and dad. They were aces."

"Thanks,'" he said. "They were great people. When my father died, I could see the life fade away from mom. They were that connected."

"Cancer?" I asked.

"No. My father's heart had been giving him trouble for a long time and it just finally got the best of him."

"Hard to believe," I said. "The last time I saw him he looked like he could still battle ten rounds with Rocky Balboa."

"The last time you saw him, he probably could. Where the hell have you been?"

"Just kicking around. I was in Mexico most recently."

"Still trying to get over Lexi, huh?"

"Hell no, man. I'm beyond that. We had a thing and it was good while it lasted."

Shamus went to refrigerator and got a couple of beers.

"So, what are you doing back here in March?"

I started to tell him about Lexi's phone call but thought better of that idea.

"I'm running a little low on resources and I thought tending bar and getting tips in pesos was not exactly a professional calling," I said. "I'm investigating some opportunities hereabouts."

Shamus laughed.

"You know I still have a pretty good bullshit detector and that sounds like bullshit to me. If you need a few bucks …"

"Shit, Shamus, I didn't come here for money. You know me better than that, Mr. Bullshit Detector.

"The use of your parents' old place is great. I have enough cash for a few months."

"Well, if I can help you just let me know. I owe you, Coe."

"Hey you don't owe me shit. Helping you help this city was all the thanks I'll ever need."

Truth was he did owe me. I worked my ass off getting him elected and worked even harder when he got elected. But I wasn't the Lone Ranger. Shamus worked just as hard and so did a lot of other folks.

"Hey did you hear about the demolition of the Central Terminal?" I asked him.

"Do you believe that shit?" he answered. "We made a joke years ago and they make it policy today. The Preservation Board is having fits."

"Well, nothing's been done to that building for fifty years. It's still just a big-assed eyesore."

"But people get attached to the old stuff, Coe. Even when the old stuff doesn't have a purpose anymore. The tower reminds people of when Buffalo was booming, when we were a city of a half million. Taking the building down erases some of the memory of the good old days."

"I guess. I'm going to get out of what little hair you have left and get settled in on Richmond Avenue. Thanks for letting me use the place. I'll treat it like it was my own."

"Hell no!" he shouted. "You always treated your stuff like shit. Treat it like it's mine."

Another ten-minute Uber ride and I was unlocking the door to a spacious, well-kept two bedroom flat with way more room than I'd ever need. The furniture was still in place, covered with old sheets, and the kitchen was fully stocked with Mama Culhane's pots and pans. She was Italian and met Dermot Culhane during the Second World War. When Papa Culhane came home, he brought Mama with him. She was in the habit of cooking for a big family in the old country and her house was always full of Shamus and his teammates from the football team at the University of Buffalo where Shamus was a star running back. In what the elder Culhanes must have used as a den were all the trophies, medals, pictures, framed jerseys, and stenciled footballs that marked the career of a damned fine athlete. I picked up one of the footballs and spun it idly in my hands. We'd played on the same team at UB for a year, until I got drilled in a game against Army and came out of the game with a broken nose and concussion. After that, I sought safer ways to exercise my athletic ability. I settled on baseball where I was a fair-to-middling catcher for the Bulls. But baseball didn't have the same cache as football in the hearts and minds of sports fans and coeds. I labored in relative obscurity while Shamus had his pictures slapped on the covers of magazines like Street & Smith and the Sporting News. When I graduated, I felt the need to escape Culhane's shadow and I enlisted in the Army. If I thought football was hazardous to my health, what I did in Afghanistan and who I did it for was no improvement. But that's another story.

I called Lexi after unpacking my rucksack and duffle bag. I needed to get something warmer than the flimsy jacket I traveled in. She answered on the first ring.

"Where are you?" she asked.

"Well, hello Lexi. I'm fine. The trip was OK and I did arrive safely."

"Stop being an ass. Where are you?"

"I met this hot chick on the plane and she told me I could stay with her as long as I kept her sexually satisfied."

I heard the phone click and figured I'd gone a little too far. I called her back. This time I didn't wait for her to talk.

"I'm at Culhane's parents' old place. He told me I could stay as long as I like."

"That's better. Just for future reference that flippant shit doesn't fly with me anymore. Save that glib stuff for the senoritas or whoever else you seduce."

"What do you mean 'anymore?'" I said. "It never flew with you ever."

"Good. You still have some semblance of a mind left if you have that much recall."

"Can you come and get me? I need to get something warmer for this climate than the Chihuahua baseball jacket and my UB sweatshirt."

"The house is on Richmond, right?"

"Yeah, it's …"

"Ten minutes. Be ready." Another click. Lexi was a woman of few words.

Nine minutes later she pulled into the driveway with a spiffy black Jeep Wrangler.

"Nice ride," I said, sliding into the front seat.

"You better have money. I'm not buying you anything."

"I'm good, at least for a little while. You mentioned something about money when you interrupted my professional tanning regimen."

"Where did you get that ugly-assed jacket?"

"I was a Dorado for twenty-five games, until the pitchers in the Mexican League figured out what American pitchers knew all along; I can't hit a curve ball."

"You were a pro?"

"In a manner of speaking. I got $300 US a game and $25 for every hit I got."

"So, $300 a game?"

Lexi was quite the comedian.

Then we drove in silence. Buffalo, like most cities, looks better in summer when the trees are bushy and green. Today, the bare branches stretched across the sky like veins. Not a lot had changed in my absence but then I hadn't expected it to. The big development was a thriving waterfront where once the land was used to pile snow from city streets. I got a glimpse as we drove passed.

"Hey Lexi, this looks really cool. Stop for a few minutes."

"Later," she said. "We've got shit to do." The same drive that made Lexi such a good cop made her a tad abrupt at times. A few minutes later we pulled up to a grungy looking building in the old warehouse district.

"What do you want me to do here," I asked, "roll a homeless guy?"

Her response was a solid punch to my arm, the arm that had the ugly caterpillar on top. I winced and she must have noticed.

"Did that hurt? she said.

"Hell yeah it hurt."

"Good. Get your ass out of the jeep and go into that army surplus store over there and get yourself a field jacket."

"Lexi, I promised myself I wouldn't wear any of that shit again."

"You lied. Get out."

I came back wearing my new purchases. A field jacket and liner and a bunch of warm shirts set me back less than $150. I wouldn't win any fashion shows but I'd be warm.

I got back into the jeep where the heater worked nicely.

"OK, I'm warm so what's the deal? Why am I here?"

She put the jeep in gear and sped through a nicely built-up area that had previously been weeds and broken asphalt.

"What's this place?"

"Larkinville. It's only open in the summer."

Seconds later we were heading north on Fillmore Avenue. Lexi made a right onto Memorial Drive and I knew we were headed to

Central Terminal. We came to a stop nearby. She put the jeep in park and turned to look at me.

God, she was still as beautiful as I remembered. She snapped me out of that brief reverie.

"Stop staring! We've got work to do and not much time to do it."

"What work? You keep insinuating shit without ever saying anything."

"Well, I already told you that your stupid suggestion to your boss is going to result in that big, beautiful building coming down, right?

In my former boss's defense, my tongue-in-cheek suggestion never got beyond the tongue in cheek phase. We all got good laugh at some of the ridiculous scenarios we came up with but that was the extent of it. The new mayor was not quite as good with the mental gymnastics as we were. To put it another way, he was so dumb he thought a Rhodes Scholarship was a job with the Streets Department.

"Well, they've already got a production company that wants to do the demolition. Said company is in town now and is looking over the layout of the building to see how they want to do it. We have about a month to do what we need to do; six weeks at the outside."

"So, tell me again, for the first goddamn time, what that work is?"

She popped me in the arm again.

"Don't interrupt! I got it on good authority that there is somewhere between two hundred and fifty thou and half-a-mill hidden somewhere in the terminal and we have to find it before the demolition buries it in seventeen stories of rubble."

CHAPTER THREE

"WHAT THE HELL are you talking about? Hundreds of thousands of dollars? You were a cop. I was deputy mayor. We both lived here all our lives and I've never heard a syllable about money hidden in the terminal," I said.

"But you haven't been around for what, three years now? Life went on while you were exiling yourself. Remember Cletus, the guy who shined shoes in the lobby of City Hall?"

"Sure, I remember him. I got my shoes shined in City Hall even when they didn't need it. How's the old guy doing?"

"The old guy is dead," she said. "He died a year ago. When he got too old to shine shoes, I used to go over to his house a few times a week and bring him roast beef sandwiches from Bailo's. The old guy loved those sandwiches.

"One afternoon, we're sitting at his kitchen table and he's enjoying the hell out of his lunch and out of the clear blue Clete says 'you get in that old railroad terminal and you get all the roast beef you want.'

"I asked him what he was talking about and he looked real dreamy staring out the window.

"'There's lots of money stuffed in dere,' he says. "'Lots of money.' So, I asked him again what he was talking about. He gives me that big smile with that mouthful of great teeth he had and told me.

"You remember when that wanna-be gangster held up City Hall?"

"Sure, I told him. I wasn't on the force yet but it was big news for a while."

"Clete said it was news but the biggest news wasn't the arrest of the guy who did the stick-up. He said the big news wasn't shared."

"And what news might that be?" I asked him.

"The money," he said. "That was the big news."

"Yeah," I said. "A couple hundred grand and the cops recovered all the dough.

"Cletus laughed and he said I was right about the money that was recovered but was wrong about it being all the dough."

About this time, I was going to take my chances and slap Lexi back into consciousness. I came back here because of the ravings of an octogenarian in marginal possession of reality? I couldn't believe it. This sounded like something James Patterson might have made up.

"What are you laughing at?" she asked.

"You," I said, "you and these cockamamie ramblings from an old guy who was only partially sane when I was here. Now you bring me back here on this bullshit?"

I tensed getting ready for another punch in the arm that never came.

"OK, go back to whatever Third World shithole you crawled out of," she said. "Be a beach bum or a bartender or a gigolo whatever you fancy yourself to be now. I don't need your ass. I just thought you might want to make something of your wasted life before it was too late."

Ouch. That stung. I knew Lexi and I didn't part on great terms but I didn't think she had such a low opinion of me. Besides, I had made something of myself. I was a big cheese in City Hall until she arrested me and I became an instant liability to my buddy Culhane. Some people have a nice, smooth, history. Mine was a bit more complicated.

"What makes you think this is real?" I asked her.

She pulled the jeep over on Fillmore near what used to be St. Rita's Church.

"I was just as skeptical as you," she said. "I put it all out of my mind and kept going over with sandwiches. I knew something was wrong when he ate only half a sandwich and asked me to wrap the other one up and put it in his refrigerator. I came back and sat with him. He took my hand and looked me in the eye and told me I didn't have much time. I asked him time for what and all he said was to find that money.

"A week later he was gone."

I still didn't understand why she would buy into this nonsense. Unlike me, Lexi had both feet on the ground. She was the last person in the world who would fall for something like this. There had to be more to it.

"And?"

"And what?" she said.

There is an 'and,' Lexi. There has to be. You would never bring me back here without an 'and.'"

She turned the engine off and proceeded to tell me the "and." She started researching old newspaper archives and talking to veteran detectives. The heist of City Hall was actually the robbery of the city treasury office. A wise guy, eager to get noticed by the made guys in the mob, pulled the job and got away with an estimated quarter of a million dollars. The mayor at the time had a loose arrangement with the mob. Don't do anything that embarrasses my administration and we'll leave you alone. This, obviously, embarrassed the mayor. He told the bosses they needed to give the money back, pronto. They didn't act on that demand fast enough and the mayor got the FBI involved and a lot of petty gangsters were pulled in for questioning. After a week or so of the dragnet the cops got the name they needed. They hauled his ass in and told the robber if the money was recovered it would go better for him in court. When two hundred grand was returned to the city, everyone figured that was the end of the case. Of course, the court didn't go easy on the robber and his ass was sentenced to about fifteen years. Lexi's sources had a lot of ancillary information about the mob in Western New York and who testified to what and when but none of it spoke to the existence of more money and the location of it.

"So, based on what old Cletus told you, you are convinced that a lot of money is hidden somewhere in the Central Terminal?"

"Yes," was all she said and that was good enough for me.

"What do we do if we happen to find said money?" I asked.

That's when I got the punch.

"We keep it, dumbass."

That was a relief. Knowing her, she might have wanted to give it to the Mercy nuns in South Buffalo.

Hell yeah, we keep it, I thought, if only we can find it.

CHAPTER FOUR

LEXI DROVE THE jeep up the long drive toward the front door. The building was massive. It towered atop a small rise in the ground, making it seem even taller. I stepped out of the vehicle and looked up at the clock face ten stories up. The art deco structure must have been something in its heyday but, in actuality, it never had a heyday. It was doomed to underutilization almost from the get-go. No one foresaw the looming economic catastrophe and fewer still, the popularization of the automobile. Now, it was to be blown to bits for a two-minute segment in a B action movie. The end of this building would be a lot more spectacular than any other aspect of it.

Lexi got out of the jeep and stood next to me.

"What do you think?" she asked.

"I think we're crazy. This is one big mother of a building. There are an awful lot of places to hide money."

"Well, genius, what's our next move?"

"I'm going to call my old man and see what he can tell me about this place. He's got to have made some contacts in and around here."

Lexi dropped me off at my temporary digs on Richmond Avenue. Chez Culhane was definitely better than a hotel room but there was still something about the place that made it feel sad. I'd had more than a few dinners here with Shamus and his family and laughter was served up like part of the meal. The stillness didn't go with the place. It was like the house was mourning just like the rest of the family. I looked out the window at my hometown. My dad had a friend from the Vietnam days who was seriously messed up emotionally from his time in combat. When he came home, the VA hospital got him involved in something they called art therapy. This guy would show up periodically in father's office with some crayon drawings of combat. The soldiers were stick people and the bullets sprayed from the crude helicopters he drew in dotted lines. He would sit and talk to my father and they would talk about the war and the shitty reception they got when they returned. My dad laughed at this guy's "art" but he couldn't laugh at what the war did to him. Somewhere along the way, the crayon drawings gave way to oil paintings in a style called "primitive naïve." My father used to laugh about the graduation.

"He got a new medium," dad would say, "but had the same kid-like approach."

The kid-like approach carried that guy a long way. Today, he hangs in some gallery in France and his paintings sell for a few grand apiece. This vet used to paint Buffalo scenes a lot and in them, the greens were brilliant green bubbles against gorgeous blue skies. As I looked out the window today, the bare branches scrawled against slate gray skies like pen and ink drawings instead of the brilliant colors of Jim Litz landscapes.

To break the melancholy, I called the old man. He lives in Florida these days where he says the heat helps him pick the shrapnel he brought home from Vietnam from his legs and back. We kind of lost touch after Lexi arrested me and I "left" the mayor's office.

"Hey Jericho!" the old man shouted. "Great to hear from you. Where are you these days?"

A little explanation here: my father, one Joshua Jeremiah Duffy, thought by naming me with a biblical reference similar to his own he could pay adequate homage to his mother, an intensely devout Catholic and more intense devotee of the Bible. He thought Jericho would be appropriate since Joshua, his namesake, scored a big victory over the Canaanites. For those not as biblically inclined as my grandma, the good book says that the Israelites marched around the walls of Jericho blowing their rams' horns and God crumbled the walls as the first step toward Josh's big win. My father never married and I was adopted at birth, so Joshua saw me as his Jericho, a big, unexpected win. See?

"I'm back in Buffalo for a while, dad. How you doing?"

"Good as can be expected for an old man, I guess," he said. "Kind of achy and sore most days but I still manage to work out three or four times a week.

"I thought you were taking called third strikes in Mexico."

"That was two years ago, Pop. I was in the restaurant business in Cabo most recently."

"Ah … you were a janitor," he laughed. "What's going on in Buffalo these days?"

"Not much. Lexi called me and wanted my help with something she's working on."

"You know, Jericho, I'll never forgive you for letting her get away. She is one great woman."

I hated this tangent in our conversations. I also hated the name Jericho, which is why from a very early age I insisted people call me "Coe." My old man was the last holdout.

"I didn't **let** her get away, dad. She left me."

"Yeah, well it had to be your fault. Besides, she was too smart to put up with your shit too long. So, what do you need me for?"

I casually mentioned the plan afoot to use the Terminal to sell movie tickets and he was outraged.

"Sounds like something those assholes would do," he said.

Having laid the groundwork, I knew he'd provide the foundation.

"I was wondering what you could tell me about Central Terminal and the mob history in Buffalo."

Ask my father about Buffalo or Vietnam and you had best have a comfortable chair, some salty snacks, and a few cold ones. He could, and often did, go on forever. As a certifiable war hero and a legend as a crime reporter, he had the bona fides to lecture.

For the next forty minutes, he gave me chapter and verse into the history of the Central Terminal, liberally spiced with his recollections of mobsters great and small. What he didn't give me was anything too far beyond what Lexi had already told me. There was one nugget though that grabbed my attention. It had to do with a novice gangster my father remembered as Patsy somebody. According to my father, this guy hung around the lobby of the terminal making a pest of himself with women and trying to strong arm the vendors who plied their trade there. Patsy made the mistake of trying to muscle a guy named Gabe Del Negro who ran the newsstand. Patsy wanted protection money from Del Negro. My father remembered Gabe as "a quality guy," which probably meant he gave my dad his newspapers for free. Anyway, Patsy tells Gabe he wants $25 a week to leave the newsstand alone. Gabe was probably taking home a hundred or so in his best weeks, so $25 was a pretty big reach. Gabe tells Patsy to show up on a certain Friday after business and meet him by Gabe's car in the employee section of the lot. Patsy shows up ready to make his score but he doesn't see Gabe; at least not until Gabe wants to be seen. He taps Patsy on the shoulder and when the thug turns around, he gets smacked in the puss with a straight right hand that breaks Patsy's nose and knocks him to ground. With the blood pulsing from Patsy's busted beak, Gabe proceeds to kick the shit out of him. It turns out Gabe was a denizen of Singer's Gym where all the good fighters in town trained. Del Negro was a Golden Gloves champ in his prime. He also knew most of the captains in the mob and told them what he wanted to do in response to the Patsy shakedown. When no one said no, Gabe took it as a yes and carried out his ambush. I got a kick out of the story of good triumphing over evil but it wasn't until my dad threw in an offhand remark that my ears perked up.

"I heard later on that this putz Patsy was somehow involved in the holdup of the city treasury."

I knew if I listened long enough, I'd get something I could use. Lexi said some of the take from the treasury was hidden in the Terminal. Now I had a link, if only a tenuous one, between the robbery and the Terminal. If this scumbag Patsy was involved, it might have been his idea where to stash the dough.

My father went on for another fifteen minutes before letting me say good bye. I told him I'd be in touch soon and started dreaming up scenarios. Things were getting interesting

I called Lexi and let her in on the new development.

"Can you see what you can dig up on this Patsy creep?" I asked.

"On it," she said and hung up on me.

Some things never change.

CHAPTER FIVE

I WAS THIRSTY after listening to my dad and getting my interest piqued. There was nothing suitable in the Culhane refrigerator so I saddled up in my new Buffalo climate clothes and headed up to Cole's to grab a beer. It was only six blocks to the watering hole but it only took two blocks for the cold and damp to sneak its icy fingers into the core of my being. How does anyone live here? I thought, ignoring the fact that I had for thirty years.

Once upon a time, I could walk into this Buffalo mainstay and know everyone in the place by first name. Today, I knew only the bartender.

"Hey Donnie Joe! What's shaking?"

"As I live and breathe, it's Coe Duffy! How the hell are you?" he asked.

We spent a half hour catching up on five years, who died, who married whom, who divorced whom, etc.

"So, what brings you back to town, Coe?"

"I heard the old railroad terminal is coming down and I wanted to get some pictures before the demolition.

"I do a lot of photography down south," I lied. "That building is a one of a kind."

"It sure as hell is," he said. "I wonder whose hairbrained idea it was to get it demo-ed?"

I let that one slide without response.

"Hey … you know who might have some shit you'd be interested in…" DJ said. "Sheila McCartan. She comes in here a lot and her office is in the Historical Society down the street. You can hop down to see her or you can wait for happy hour. She'll be here."

I weighed my options. The Historical Society was only a quarter mile or so from Cole's up Elmwood Avenue. It occupied the only building remaining from the 1901 Pan American Exposition held in Buffalo. The Expo was a world's fair kind of thing that was to put Buffalo on the map. It could have too, except for that nasty assassination. President McKinley was shot by some dickhead in 1906. The Expo was also a showcase for Thomas Edison's electric lights. Unfortunately, the lights were not yet installed in the operating room at the exhibition's medical center. Another invention that might have helped McKinley survive was also displayed here - the X-ray machine. It could have helped the docs locate the bullet that felled the prez but alas, no one knew what the new-fangled machine might do to the human body so it wasn't used. So much for the march of technology. In any event, the president died in eight days. The building, as I recalled, was a beautiful structure designed in the example of the Parthenon in Greece. I wondered when some asshat in City Hall might decide to let a movie company blow this building up in a film about ancient Greece. But as much as an aesthete as I am, my balls hadn't yet dropped from my jaunt from the Culhane house so I decided to wait for happy hour in the warmth of Cole's. It didn't take long for my phone to buzz.

"Hey Lexi. What's up?"

"What's that noise I hear?"

"I'm at Cole's, waiting to meet a contact from the Historical Society."

"You asshole! You aren't in town two days and you are back in your bad habits." Lexi always thought I spent too much time in bars. She always assumed that if I was in a bar, I would be drinking. She was intuitive that way.

Bad habits? I thought. Lexi was the only bad habit I had but I didn't think it the right time to mention it.

"I am assuming from your tone that you might have found something of interest from your friends in blue."

"That's right. Brett Joseph told me to go see a guy named Eddie Murray at a place called Shaughnessy's."

"Murray … I know that name, Lexi. If it's the same guy, he used to pal around with my dad. They were both in Vietnam at the same time."

By 'pal around,' I meant they often got shit-faced drunk together reminiscing about the war.

"I'll be there in ten. I'll beep. You come out," she said.

"What about my contact?"

"She can wait."

"I never said it was a she," I said.

"You're in Cole's so it's a she."

This girl would have been a great detective.

"OK, you beep, I come."

FIFTEEN minutes later, we were heading out to Buffalo's South End, the Irish enclave of the city. Where else would you find a pub called Shaughnessy's?

I called my father on the way.

"Sure, I know Murray," he said. "Good guy when we were drinking; great guy when he ain't. What do you want him for?"

"One of Lexi's cop buddies said Murray might have some intel about the old terminal."

"Shit! He's right. I should have thought about Mur-man. I think his dad was a ticket agent or something way back when."

"Is Lexi there with you? Tell her she's going to ruin her reputation hanging around with a shithead like you."

"She knows that already, dad. You're on speaker."

"Hello Josh," Lexi said. "You're still the smartest dad I know."

"OK, dad, you two have conspired enough for one day. I'll let you know what we find out."

"Tell Mur-man he's welcome down here in heaven's waiting room anytime he wants to get away and lose some golf balls."

"Will do. Talk to you later."

It started to rain during the drive, reminding me why I bailed on this town in the first place. But I looked over at Lexi's profile and I wondered why I bailed on this town in the first place.

We pulled into the parking lot of a place that looked like it was more than the usual dive you found in this part of the city. Murray must have done pretty well for himself, I thought. I had barely warmed up when we had to get out of the Jeep and walk twenty steps into the pub and twenty steps was all it took for me to start shivering again. Late winter in Buffalo is like mid-winter anywhere else. The only thing worse than mid-winter Buffalo snow was late-winter rain. When visitors complained about the weather when I lived here, I told them it was like being pregnant every year: we waited nine long months for those three glorious months of summer. Those ninety or so days were a great reminder of why we lived here, when I lived here.

We entered through a door marked "Bar" and encountered a stocky guy behind it polishing glasses. Other than him, the place was empty.

I introduced myself.

"My father wants to know when you might want to head south to lose some golf balls."

The guy looked up with a smirk on his face.

"You gotta be Josh's kid. He's the only one who would make an invitation like that."

"Guilty," I said, extending my hand. "Coe Duffy and this ravishing beauty is Lexi Crane."

That attempt at chivalry got me another punch in the arm.

"Hi, I'm Lexi and not happy to be traveling with this idiot but we have to make allowances."

"I like you already," Murray said. "I'm Ed, or Mur-man if you prefer. Can I get you something to drink?"

I was about to ask for a Bud but my conscience intercepted the request.

"Two Diet Pepsis would be great, Ed," she said. "Think my companion has had enough for one day."

"I had one beer at Cole's," I protested.

Ed chimed in on Lexi's side.

"Sometimes one's too many and a hundred's not enough," he said, repeating a mantra I heard the old man spout a few hundred times. My expression must have revealed my familiarity with the axiom. It earned another of Lexi's straight rights to the shoulder.

"Listen to the man! He knows whereof he speaks."

That drew a laugh for the Mur-man.

"I learned the hard way," he said, "me and your old man. But you kids didn't come all the way out here for diet pop. What can I do for you?"

Before I could say anything, Lexi gave the explanation, kind of.

"Coe heard about the impending demo of the Central Terminal and came all the way back from Mexico to take some last pictures of it. He's been doing a lot of photography lately."

I thought about a clever response to that, something like "I have?" but I was pretty sure I was already going to have a mark on my shoulder.

"My dad said that your father might have worked at the terminal and might have some insights into good camera angles, background information, interesting nooks and crannies that sort of thing."

"Well my dad did work at the terminal. He was head of baggage handling for the New York Central when it was a booming enterprise but his asthma is getting the best of him and he moved away about a year ago."

He glanced at Lexi.

"I haven't cleaned out his house yet," Murray said. "He left a ton of stuff. Give me a day or two to sort through it and see if there's any terminal stuff in the boxes."

"That would be great, Ed," I said. "Here's my cell number. If you think there's anything that might help, we'd appreciate the call."

"We'll even come back so Coe can buy me dinner," Lexi said. "thanks for the cold drinks."

Cold drinks, I thought. Everything in Buffalo in March was a 'cold drink.'

We got back in the Jeep with the rain turning to sleet.

"God, Lexi, how do you live here?"

"I wake up every morning thankful you aren't here anymore," she said. "That gives me strength to carry on."

I thought I detected a hint of a smile with her response but I didn't want to push my luck.

"Hey, wanna grab something to eat?" I asked.

"I have plans. Where do you want me to drop you?"

I told her and for the next half hour I was already feeling lonely.

CHAPTER SIX

I NEGOTIATED THE long uphill slant of the entrance to the Central Library on Lafayette Square like a speed skater, taking long strides to keep from falling on my ass on the freezing rain. I wasn't sure why I felt so blue knowing Lexi had "plans." I'd been gone a good long while and hadn't had much contact with her beyond the few calls during the first months of my self-imposed exile. There was no reason for her to wait and I hadn't ever mentioned it. But I still thought we might still have a chance.

What the hell? I thought, you've made worse mistakes … but none that hurt so bad.

Some detail about our girl might be in order here. Lexi Crane was one of the finest female athletes ever to grace the courts and fields of New York state. Actually, discard the "female" and you would still be pretty accurate. She was five foot nine, could run like a deer, jump like a kangaroo, and was stronger than most of the guys we played with. She was a terrific soccer player, a better basketball player, a great sprinter, and she dabbled in lacrosse. She could have earned a college scholarship in any of those sports or none of them. Her grades were that good. And she was a knockout: long slim legs, jet black hair, and eyes that seemed to change color with her moods. When I met her, they were a dazzling emerald color. When I left her, they flashed a brighter shade of green. She was the talk of the town when she competed in high school and stayed in the local limelight throughout her college exploits. There wasn't anything, it seemed, she couldn't do. She was applying to law schools when her life took a sudden turn. Her father owned a liquor store in North Buffalo that did land office business. One night, some punks decided to relieve him of the day's receipts. But Jackson Crane was not about to surrender his hard-earned cash without a fight. He emptied the register and told the thieves he had more cash under the counter. When he came up, he came up firing the .45 automatic pistol he'd brought home from the service. One of the thugs went down but the other one shot back and hit Jack in the throat. He got off another shot and wounded the thief before he bled out on the floor of the store he'd owned for twenty years. Lexi was four weeks from graduation when her dad went down but she left school to handle her father's affairs and never looked back. She became a Buffalo cop as soon as she could. She was just as successful on the force as she'd been in everything she tried. She was cited six times for valorous service. She rescued two women from a fire on Buffalo's West Side, breaking down a door and entering the house before the fire department got there. She was a special assistant to the commissioner in charge of establishing community policing in Buffalo. Everyone in or near the police department believed she'd be the first female commissioner.

I met her at one of the community meetings where she represented her boss and I rep-ed the mayor. I fell in love the minute I saw those eyes. Like every other sentient being in Western New York, I knew of Lexi Crane's triumphs and tragedy but I'd never met her until that night. I was dumbstruck watching her handle what started out as a hostile crowd and getting them to the point where she could have asked them for anything.

One particularly irate citizen got up in her grill complaining that the only time her neighborhood saw cops it was to arrest their sons and husbands. She was going at Lexi pretty good for about five minutes and Lexi stood there and took it. When the woman was all out of invectives, Lexi went over and took her hand.

"Ma'am, your anger is justified," she said calmly. "For too long, city administrations have looked at your community as a hotbed of crime. We turned our backs on good, decent citizens like you and focused instead on the crime here.

"We had precious little understanding that you are not criminals. You are victims, just like everyone else. I'm here to tell you and that handsome man over there from the mayor's office is here to tell you that ends today. From now on, you will see an officer walking the beat in this neighborhood. You are going to know that officer's name. You are going to know how to reach that officer when you need to. You are going to think of that officer as a member of this community because that's exactly what that officer is going to be – part of your neighborhood."

Lexi's incredible eyes never left those of the once angry, now docile woman.

She reached into her shirt pocket and took out a business card and handed it to the woman.

"If what I've just told you doesn't happen just as I said it would, call me and I'm going to come back here with the mayor's guy over there. I'll drag him by the neck if I have to. And when we get him here, we're all going to kick his ass till his nose bleeds."

Like everyone else in that room, I was transfixed by Lexi's calm voice and even tone and like everyone else I was eagerly awaiting the punchline, until I realized I was the punchline. The room erupted in laughter with a couple dozen fingers pointing at me and laughing their fool heads off. She looked over at me and winked. If she would have accepted, I would have married her that evening.

The woman was transfixed.

"Word, Miss Lexi, I see you gonna be mayor of this here city one day."

Lexi giggled and got them all laughing again when she smiled at them and shook her head.

"No ma'am," she said. "That's not the job for me. I couldn't take the cut in pay."

That started the house roaring with laughter again. I'd steal a movie line and say she had me at hello but she hadn't even said hello yet.

The meeting was breaking up and most of the elderly women who wanted to shook her hand and told her how impressed they were. When I got the chance, I sidled up next to her.

"Do you really think I'm handsome?" I said. "Do you have one of those cards for me?" I was already smitten.

At the library, I pushed through the heavy doors to get out of the rain. I was soaked and freezing and lonely. What better place to be than at the city library?

A nice clerk helped me find a lot of data on Central Terminal. It didn't tell me much I didn't already know so I tried my luck with the city treasury robbery. Again, not much new information. I don't really know what I was looking for except a little foothold from whence to begin our search. While I was looking at microfiche my phone rang. I was hoping it was Lexi but the calling number wasn't familiar. I drew a few disdainful looks so I stepped into the corridor.

"Yeah?"

"Coe, is that you?"

"Sure is. Who's this?"

"Eddie Murray from Shaughnessy's."

"Hey Ed, what's up?"

"Where are you right now?"

"I'm at the city library downtown."

"Is Lexi with you?"

"I wish."

"Good. I want to talk to you alone."

"Tomorrow OK?" I asked.

"No, tonight. You know where Brady's is, on Genesee Street?"

"Christ, is that place still going? Yeah. I know it."

"Meet me there in thirty minutes."

Before I could agree, he hung up. What was it with this town, I thought? No one says goodbye anymore.

Mercifully, the rain had stopped when I headed outside and walked up Washington Street the four or so blocks to Brady's. By then, of course, the freezing weather punched my balls up into my belly and I wondered if I'd ever see them again. I also wondered if I'd ever need them again.

Brady's was one of those great neighborhood saloons in the midst of downtown. It was dark and smelled of stale beer. It had a wood stove burning hot in one corner and I snuck over to try to grab some of its warmth.

The bartender gave me a funny look.

"Hey man, you cold? This is about as close to spring as we get these days."

"Really," I said. "I never want to be here for winter then." I didn't tell him I'd spent twenty or so winters there already.

"What'll you have?"

What I wanted was hot coffee poured straight down my pants but I didn't think the barkeep would understand.

"Can I have a Bud?"

"Whoa, a real Bud? Not one of those UltraLight, Light Platinum, or double light panther piss that's all the rage these days?"

Apparently, I'd touched a nerve.

"Just Bud, the way God intended it be made."

"Well, hot shit, my man. This one's on me. You always drink Bud?"

"I guess," I said. "I wasn't very choosy until my old man told me Gussie Busch donated about a million dollars' worth of beer to the troops in Vietnam. After that, I was a Bud man for life."

The bartender opened one for himself and we clinked bottles.

"Here's to the poor fuckers who fought that shitty war."

"Hoo-hah," I said.

"Hey man, you served?"

"Yeah, I did. Spent some time in Sand Land near the 10th Mountain."

"Welcome home, bro," he said tapping my bottle again.

We shot the shit for a bit until Mur-man showed up. He motioned me to a table near the stove.

"You want a drink, Ed?" I asked.

"Sure,"

I got the drink and sat down at the table. I wasn't quite ready for the conversation that followed.

"What the hell were you and that broad doing in my place this afternoon?"

"We told you. We're going to take some pictures of the old Terminal before it's the climax of some shitty action movie."

"Bullshit. I called your old man after you left and told him you were looking for shit on the old terminal but he didn't know what was going on. If you want me to help, tell me what the hell brought you back from Mexico."

Perceptive sonofabitch, this Mur-man, I thought. Now what should I tell him?

CHAPTER SEVEN

SHE WAS IN ecstasy, or at least as close to it as she'd been in a while. Lexi's sweat ran down her face in rivers as she twisted and shoved and writhed and pushed. She was not normally very vocal but tonight her grunts and groans became primal shouts and screams. Despite her exertion, she could still see flashes of the pained look on Coe's face when she told him she'd already had plans for the night.

He thinks he can waltz back into my life and I'm going to pretend I've been in suspended animation waiting for him, she thought. He screwed with me. Now I can screw back.

Her body was on fire. Each long, lithe muscle was firing full blast and she was getting maximum pleasure from the effort. She thought of Coe again and whipped out a straight left jab followed by a swift, short right upper cut. When she connected with each punch, she felt that tension run the length of her arm and give her that pulsing feeling in her shoulder that comes from getting maximum power out of the effort.

Kevin, her trainer, was driven back two steps as he tried to steady the heavy bag against her onslaught.

"Hey girl, take it easy on an old man, will ya?"

For the first time in ten minutes, Lexi stopped.

"Sorry Kevin, I just wanted to close with a flourish," she said with the proof of her exertion shining on her face and arms.

"Flourish, my ass, Lexi, you closed like a hungry dog just thrown a bone," he said. "That was some workout tonight."

She smiled at the compliment but knew she had special incentive tonight. She had to keep Coe off balance, just like her Krav Maga training taught her. She added her own credo to the training: hit his soft parts with your hard parts. Lexi knew Coe's soft spot. She knew he never stopped caring for her and that was one of the reasons he ran away. But if wants me back, she thought, he's going to have to work his ass off.

Lexi trained twice a week religiously, and worked out on her own two more days. After the attack that turned her life upside down, she vowed that she would never be vulnerable again. With her heart rate slowing toward normal she thought of that fateful night again, just as she did whenever she worked out this hard.

Two punks snatched an old lady's purse on William Street. Lexi and her partner rolled up on the scene with the lady on the sidewalk and her purse running down toward Jefferson Avenue.

"Stay with her!" Lexi yelled to her partner and took off after the purse snatchers. They probably thought no donut downing cop could catch them as they ran away but they hadn't counted on a cop like Lexi. She started the pursuit two blocks behind and caught the punk holding the purse as they crossed the fourth block. She grabbed the kid by the collar and yanked him down. The purse hit the sidewalk before he did.

The kid looked up her with the knees torn out of his jeans and sweat running down his face.

"Shit, lady, you fast," he grinned. "But is you tough?"

She thought about the second kid just as he swung a bat at her. She turned to face him and got a hand up to block the bat but took a solid shot on her fingers. The pain shot up her arm, just as the first kid kicked at the back of her knee. Her leg buckled and she went down. She fought her way back to one knee but took another shot to the right shoulder from the bat. A punch landed on the left side of her face and sent a bolt of pain through her jaw. She tried to wend off another blow from the bat but she managed only to deflect what might have driven her nose into her forehead. The lights in her brain started to dim but she had the presence of mind to reach her pistol. But by the time she got it out the punks were turning the corner a block away onto Jefferson Avenue. Then things got fuzzy and she felt the sidewalk smack again her face.

When she woke up at Erie County Medical Center, every bone in her body ached. She tried to sit up but felt herself restrained.

"Easy Sleeping Beauty," a nurse said as she loosened the straps on Lexi's wrists. "These are just a precaution to make sure you don't fall out of the bed."

The nurse turned to a cluster of white coats.

"Doctor, Officer Crane is awake," she said.

Officer Crane might be awake, Lexi thought, but she sure as hell doesn't know what's going on. She tried lifting her head but even the slightest movement started her head throbbing.

"Hey, relax Officer. You've had a rough go this evening. Just lay back and let me look at you."

Lexi laid back and the doctor shined a light in each eye then told her to follow his finger with just her eyes.

Holy shit, Lexi thought, even moving my eyes hurt!

The doctor was scribbling some notes when he turned to the nurse.

"She looks like she's in some real discomfort. Give her a shot of dilaudid and we can talk to her later."

When Lexi woke up the second time, she got the inventory of her injuries:

Two broken fingers on her right hand, sixteen stitches in her mouth to close some cuts from the punches and the bat, a broken collarbone, and a Class 4 concussion. She spent a week in the hospital and another four weeks off duty. When she did report back, the Commissioner gave her a plum assignment to ease back into policing. She would occupy the desk in the mayor's office where the most exertion she'd get was walking back forth to the ladies' room. That's where she got to know Coe Duffy.

He was charming, smart, and acceptably good looking. He had deep blue eyes she caught herself repeatedly staring at. But most of all, he had this infectious smile. When Coe Duffy smiled, you just had to smile back. She liked the way Coe was deferential to Mayor Culhane when the public was around but talked straight truth to him when they were out of earshot. She was on the verge of asking him out when he spared her the embarrassment by asking her first. Lexi enjoyed every minute of his company. He knew when to talk and more importantly, when to listen. He held her hand softly when she related the night she'd been beaten almost to death. Coe didn't try to inject any stupid platitudes into the moment. He just sat silently until she stopped talking. Then he brought her hand to his lips and kissed it gently.

"I can't imagine going through that," he said, just about a whisper. "You are some tough lady."

Lexi found that she was looking forward to going to a job she thought she'd hate. She couldn't wait to see him in action every day, interacting with citizens and pumping up the other staff. He frequently stopped at Mazurek's Bakery on the way into work and brought all kinds of diabolically delicious treats for the office. He never forgot to get enough for the maintenance staff in the bowels of City Hall.

There has to be something about this guy I don't like, she told herself. Nobody's this good all the time.

They'd been going out for about three weeks when she decided. They just finished a quiet dinner in the elegance of Oliver's Restaurant. As they got in Coe's car, she made a request.

"Hey, stop at CVS, will you? I need a few things."

He drove a few blocks and pulled into the almost empty parking lot. He started to get out of the car to go in with her.

"Stay here," she said. "I won't be a minute."

True to her word, she was back in a flash with a small bag.

"I guess you really did only need a few things," Coe said. "May I ask what's in the bag?"

"You may," she said, flashing a big smile.

She pulled a toothbrush, small can of shaving gel and a razor out of the bag.

"I hope you use a medium brush."

When they entered her flat, she wanted to rip his clothes off but he took his time.

"Are you sure?" he asked.

"I'm sure that if you don't hurry up and get me out of this dress, I'm going to scream!"

Lexi knew she wasn't the most experienced woman when it came to sex but she also knew that this is the way she'd want to make love for the rest of her life. Coe was a master kisser and that she already knew. What she learned that night was that he kissed everywhere with the same alternating patience and intensity that drove her crazy. She moaned and yelled and he clawed and caressed and when he finally entered her she was ready to explode. All she could do was gasp and shudder as the waves of pleasures swept over her. His mouth, his hands, everything worked in synchronization. She was in sync too: her breasts, her neck, her lips … everything was washing over with pleasure. Lexi wanted to do something in response but she was powerless in the wake of Coe's unending attention. When he finally rolled off of her, they were both covered in sweat. She spoke when she caught her breath.

"Dear God, do you practice that?" she gasped.

He leaned in close to her ear and whispered.

"You can't practice something like that, sweetie. That's spontaneous … you know … when you feel for someone."

"Right answer," she said and mounted him for round two.

Coe was in the bathroom using his new toothbrush when Lexi saw the scar across the back of his left shoulder. She came up and hugged him from behind making sure he felt the hardening of her nipples. She traced the scar lightly with her finger.

"What happened here, Coe?"

He spit into the sink.

"I got shot."

"Where?"

"Right there, in the shoulder, dummy."

That earned the first of a thousand or so punches to come.

"Where were you when it happened, wise ass? In Buffalo?"

"Nope," he said, turning to kiss her. "I was in Afghanistan."

His tongue started a mating dance in her mouth but she wasn't having it. She broke away.

"You were a soldier?"

"Not exactly"

"What does that mean? Not exactly?"

"I was in a combat zone, doing soldierly things but I wasn't a soldier. That's what it means."

His hands tried grabbing her ass but she twisted away.

"You were a spook?"

"Let's just say I was employed by my country and leave it at that."

"Hell no, we ain't leaving it at that. Why didn't you tell me?"

"What's to tell? I was in, then I was out ... end of story. "Sides, it's need to know and you don't need to know."

"I'm going to need to know, my dear ... that and a lot of other things about you."

Then she kissed him.

"I forgot to get you some new underwear," she said as they dressed.

"No sweat. I have some in the office"

"Who keeps clean underwear in the office?"

"Guys who occasionally have to sleep there" he said.

"Really, you sleep in the office?"

"Not often. But when I'm on the phone all day, I don't get a chance to write so I have to do it late. Then, there's little point in going home. I have a couple shirts there too."

"You are a wonder, Coe Duffy, a goddamn wonder."

Lexi rode into work that morning with a burning in her loins and a big smile on her face. Two weeks later, the smile would be gone.

Shamus Culhane was a lot like Duffy. He was smart. He was good to people. He always remembered from whence he'd come and he was generous to a fault. One of those faults was trying to help out old teammates down on their luck. Most of the time, it worked out well. Given another chance, most of the guys who came to the Mayor's office seeking a favor showed their appreciation by being good employees. The operative word there was "most." Every once in a while, a guy just couldn't be helped; booze, drugs, whatever it was just wouldn't let the guy alone and he was too stupid to leave well enough alone.

Albert Davis was one of those guys. The mayor would put him to work and two weeks later, when no one had seen him for those two weeks, he'd be out. He'd wait a month and come crawling back begging for another chance and Culhane just didn't have the heart to turn him away. This had happened a couple of times before Duffy had enough. As he was passing the receptionist's desk, he heard her talking on the phone and assumed it was Davis.

"I'm sorry, Mr. Davis, but the mayor isn't in the office right now. I'm not sure when he'll be back but I'll make sure he gets your message. Of course, I have Mr. Davis. I've given him all the messages you've left. Please don't use that language with me, Mr. Davis. I'm a God-fearing woman … "

That was enough for Duffy. He motioned to get the phone and the receptionist was more than happy to give it to him. She mouthed "I think he's drunk" to Coe.

"Hey Al, this is Coe. What's going on?"

Al was shouting on the other end of the phone and he sounded drunk.

"I know you need a job, Al, but you wouldn't need one if you had showed up to work in any of the other three jobs Shamus gave you. Yeah, yeah, yeah, Al, I'm Shamus's flunky but at least I have job, pal. Whoa, you kiss your mother with that mouth? Do yourself a favor and stay the hell away from this office."

Lexi's desk was ten feet from the receptionist.

"If he calls back, you give me the call," Duffy said. "The mayor doesn't need any more shit from Davis. Sorry about my language."

The receptionist laughed.

"Oh Mr. Duffy, you don't never need apologize to me for your language. Mine is worse than yours. I just use that God-fearing stuff to calm down the crazies."

Coe smiled and went back to his office. Thirty minutes later, he heard a loud voice at reception -- Davis. Now is as good a time as any to end this shit once and for all, he thought. He went out to reception and saw Davis weaving around and ranting like the drunk he was. Lexi wasn't at her post.

"Knock it off, Davis. We've heard enough of your crap for one term. If Culhane gets re-elected, come back and see us then."

"Motherfuck you, Duffy, I ain't here to see no flunky. I'm here to see my friend."

"I just checked, and you are fresh out of friends here. Now grab your ass and get the hell out of here."

The two men were face-to-face now with just an ornamental railing separating them. Davis was bigger than he remembered, Duffy thought.

"I ain't going nowhere till I see the mayor," Davis slurred. Then he grabbed Duffy by the tie. After that it was reflex. Duffy shot out a straight right that landed on Al's mouth. Blood and spittle shot out one side as Lexi pushed open the office door, just in time to see Davis collapse as though he'd been shot.

"What the hell?" Lexi yelled. "Coe, what's going on?"

She hurried over to try to help Davis to his feet.

"You saw that, right, officer? You saw that sumbitch punch me for no reason, right?"

"I don't know what the hell I saw." She said.

Coe had blood on his knuckles and Davis had blood all over his mouth.

"I want him arrested!" Davis shouted. "You saw what he did."

The mayor walked in at that point.

"What's all the yelling about? He said.

"Your goddamned flunky knocked one of my teeth out," Davis yelled. "I want his ass in jail!"

"Coe, what the hell?" the mayor said. "Did you really punch him?"

"Well, yeah. I guess I did. He grabbed my tie and …"

"I didn't grab shit, mayor. He just sucker punched me."

The mayor turned to Lexi.

"Did you see what happened?"

"When I came back from the rest room, Davis was on the floor. I didn't see what precipitated it, Mayor."

"There wasn't no goddamned precipitating. This motherfucker done punched me."

"Davis, shut your mouth!" the mayor said. "Are you drunk?"

"Well, I had a few but I ain't drunk."

The mayor looked at the receptionist.

"Did you see Davis touch Duffy in any way?" he asked.

"No sir," she said. "I knew Davis was going to be trouble when he walked through that door and Mr. Duffy said he'd be handling Mr. Davis so I wasn't looking."

"You lying bitch," Davis said but never got to finish the sentence.

Coe hit him again. This time it was Davis' nose impacted. He went down again.

"Don't be talking to her like that, asshole."

'Shit Coe, you leave me no choice," Lexi said, taking her cuffs off her belt. "Turn around and put your hands behind your back."

Duffy complied and felt the cuffs snap around his wrist as Lexi read him his rights.

This isn't going to end well, Duffy thought. Not well at all.

THE scene played out in her head while the shower splashed around her. She replayed it a dozen times a day and it ended the way it always ended, with her sobbing.

CHAPTER EIGHT

I WAS JUGGLING two thoughts in my mind in front of that hot stove in Brady's. One was Lexi having "other plans" for the night and the other was what to tell Eddie Murray sitting silently in front of me.

"Ed, you know Lexi was a cop, right?"

"Yeah, I know that."

"Well, she and one of her partners had a case a while back that didn't go the way she wanted. Remember when the two punks jumped her and knocked her out?"

"Yeah. That was some sorry shit, man."

"Well, one of those dudes didn't fare so well in a drug deal a few years later and it was rumored he got whacked. No one ever found a body though, so for Lexi it's unfinished business. She got a tip a couple weeks ago that her mook's body got stashed at Central Terminal, so she asked me to help try to find the remains and get some closure. I'm sorry we weren't truthful when we came to see you but this is Lexi's show and I didn't want to muck it up for her."

Murray stared at me for a minute then laughed.

"I knew you were bullshitting me about that photography bit. Thanks for coming clean."

"Well, now that you know what we're trying to do can you help us out?"

"I think so, Duff. My dad is out in Arizona living large in the sunshine and dry heat. Probably scoring with those old blue haired widows too. I'll give him a call tomorrow and see what he can tell me. Why don't you come by the restaurant around two o'clock? The lunch crowd will be gone and we can talk."

"That's great, Ed. I really appreciate it. See you tomorrow."

With that, Murray rose, shook my hand, turned up his collar and was out the door. I leaned back in the chair and soaked up the glorious heat from the stove knowing I'd dodged a bullet. I didn't need to piss off one of my dad's closest friends. I was weighing my desire for another beer with the time it might take me to walk all the way back to Richmond Avenue when my phone rang. I was surprised to see Lexi's name on the caller ID. Before I could say hello, she spoke.

"Want to grab something to eat?"

Her date must have sucked, I reasoned.

"Sure. Where are you?"

"I'm just leaving my gym. Where are you?"

"Brady's on Genesee and Ellicott."

She laughed and not a funny, ha-ha laugh.

"I should have known you'd be in a bar. Be there in ten."

Click. She was gone.

Damn, I thought, if she'd called a little earlier, I could have impressed her by telling her to pick me up at the main library. I was kind of relieved that her "date" was at the gym and not with some Jim.

Ten minutes later I saw her jeep pull up in front. I thought it would be pretty cool to make her come in but then I realized she might have just left me there with an hour to walk in the frigid air. I waved goodbye to the bartender and jumped in the jeep. Five minutes later we were in the comfortably warm Bijou Grille on Main Street. The owner came over and gave Lexi a big hug.

"It is great to see you, Lexi," she said. "Where have you been?"

Only then did she look at me and her jaw dropped.

"Dio mio! Is that you. Coe? I'd almost given up on seeing you ever again," she said.

I stood and gave her a big hug.

"It's great to see you, Bea. But you know you can never count me out."

"It's almost like old times," Bea said, hugging Lexi.

"Yeah," Lexi said quickly, "almost."

The Bijou was "our spot." It didn't matter how crowded it was, whenever we showed up, Bea always found us a table. If she couldn't find one, she brought out a new one.

"Sit down. I'm going to bring you something special," she said.

I pulled out Lexi's chair and she sat without a word. The place, the face, the fact we were together … all had a familiar and comfortable feel. I liked it.

A waiter hurried to the table and set down two glasses of red wine.

"Chianti," Bea yelled from the kitchen. "I just got a case from Italy. Smell the bouquet of those Sangiovese grapes. Magnifico!"

Bea wasn't lying. The fragrance was surpassed only by the taste. I sipped and savored. Sometimes you don't know what you've got until you don't have it anymore. The joy of familiarity was one of those things. Another was sitting across from me.

A few minutes later, Bea emerged from the kitchen with a tray of steaming soup. I don't know how long it had been since Lexi was here but Bea remembered that Lexi liked her soup almost too hot for human consumption. If there weren't flames coming off the bowl, it wasn't hot enough for Lexi. Bea placed the bowls in front of us.

"Pasta fagioli," she said. "My own recipe. I was making it tonight to take home but such a special occasion deserves special food."

"Special" hardly described the soup that looked more like a stew, overflowing with cannellini beans, ground beef, and an odd piece or two of sausage. Bea kissed us both on top of the head and set out for the kitchen.

We sipped and slurped for a few minutes without a word. Then Lexi took a break from her meal.

"So, what did you do tonight, besides swill beer?"

"Well, I started out at the main library …"

Lexi feigned spitting out her wine.

"Give me a break," she said.

"No, seriously. I went to the library to see what I could dig up on the terminal and the robbery."

"Did you find anything useful?"

"Not really; mostly stuff we already knew but I got interrupted before I was finished."

"Interrupted by what?"

"It was a who, not a what. Eddie Murray called me and asked me to meet him at Brady's."

"What would Murray have wanted?"

"He wanted to know why we were bullshitting him about the reason for our visit."

"Really? He didn't think you looked like photographer? What did you tell him? You didn't tell him the real reason, did you?" She looked alarmed.

"No, Lexi, I didn't tell him he real reason" and I proceeded to tell her the rest of the Murray saga.

We ate silently for a few minutes then she spoke again.

"That was actually pretty smart," she said. This time I feigned spitting out my wine, earning myself another whack on the arm.

"Now we have an excuse for poking around in all the nooks and crannies without him being more suspicious," she said. "That should work out. I knew I brought you along for a reason." This time she was smiling and no matter how cold it was outside; my heart was getting warm. We finished the rest of the dinner quietly. I didn't want to say anything to ruin the mood. I went to the kitchen to pay.

Bea was busy putting her creation in jars for the journey home.

"Bea, you outdid yourself tonight. What do I owe you?"

"Don't wait so long in between visits," she said. "That's all you owe me. Now get out of here with that gorgeous girl." I kissed her on the cheek and hugged her.

"We'll be back soon," I said, hoping I wasn't lying.

Back at the table, I helped Lexi on with her coat and got a good whiff of her aroma. She smelled of soap and shampoo, no perfume. She smelled clean and sweet and pure, just like I remembered. She hooked her arm in mine as we walked to the jeep and for a brief, fleeting moment, it felt as though I'd never left town.

We rode in silence, except for a huge burp Lexi spewed. We laughed and she smiled at me again. She pulled up on Richmond and I blew the mood.

"Want to come in," I asked.

"Hell no, Romeo, I don't want to come in. I'll see you tomorrow."

I was mentally kicking myself in the ass for trying to rush things with Lexi.

I should have known better. She was still dealing with the incident in the mayor's office and had a lot of residual anger. You might be thinking why she was pissed off about that? After all, I was the one who was arrested, charged and booked. I was the one who had to come up with twenty-five large to pay for medical expenses for the "victim." I was the one facing an actual jail sentence for aggravated assault. But I wasn't the only loser. Lexi lost something too. She lost the career she loved. Rather than testify against me in court, Lexi took her medical retirement and left the police force. She was nowhere to be found when the court tried to serve a subpoena to get her to testify. Before she left though, she hit me a lot harder than I hit Davis.

She came by my apartment to return the stuff I'd left at her place. She dropped the box outside my door and refused to even enter the apartment.

"That's all of it, asshole," she said, "the last remnants of you in my life."

"Hey, we don't have to make such decisions now …" I said, but she stopped me.

"I don't care what kind of decision you make, Coe. I've already made mine."

She turned to leave but stopped and turned around.

"Nice going asshole. With one punch you ruined two careers."

I didn't know what she meant by that until my court date when my lawyer told me things were "looking good" with Lexi gone. One of the court cops told me what had happened and no matter what the court did, it couldn't hurt me anymore than my stupid decision had. With Davis' word against mine and no other witnesses to the first punch, the judge took into account my payment of Al's doctor bills and fined me another ten grand but gave me no jail time. None of it mattered though. I had already cooked my own goose with Culhane. As much as we liked each other, I knew I was a huge distraction for him and what he wanted to do for the city. The reporters at the Buffalo News were having a field day, wondering in print if I would be cold-cocking everyone who disagreed with the mayor. The news director at one of the television stations sent over a pair of boxing gloves with a note that read "Next time don't hurt your hand." I resigned the next day, heartsick about ruining my career and heartbroken about Lexi.

I started a computer search about the Central Terminal mulling over something my father used to say.

"Actions have consequences, Jericho. Never forget that."

I ditched the search and got in bed. I thought long and hard about the pot of gold at the end of this supposed rainbow. I wondered if it really could be mine after all the angst and the self-imposed exile, after all the hurt and the regret, after the relentless hoping and dreaming; could I really be getting close to the treasure? I fell asleep dreaming about it and the treasure I was dreaming about had just driven off in her jeep.

CHAPTER NINE

I GOT UP the next morning and risked exploding my lungs by going for a run in the frigid air. I went up Richmond to Forest Avenue and went into Delaware Park. I found the old path the high schools used to use for their cross country meets and took a hard lap around Hoyt Lake, driving hard up the hill behind the art gallery before stopping in front of the rose garden. I stopped long enough to catch my breath before jogging back to Chez Culhane.

My phone was ringing as I walked in the door. I saw the caller ID and picked it up.

"Hi babe …"

"Hi babe my ass! Where have you been? I've been calling for an hour."

"Cool your jets, Miss Crane," I said. "I wasn't aware it was my day to report to you. I went for a run in this freezing shit you call air. What's the problem?"

"No problem yet, asshole. When I can't reach you, I wonder if you bailed to some third world shithole again."

Touché, I thought, and when did my name change to asshole?

"Are we still on for Shaughnessy's," Lexi asked.

"Yeah, Eddie said to come by about two when the lunch rush

slowed down."

"I'll pick you up at quarter to."

Click. The call ended. She really needed to work on her good-byes.

I heard the horn at precisely fifteen minutes to two. I ran to the car, motivated by her quasi-religious attention to punctuality and to get into a warm car. I adjusted a vent to direct some of that soothing warmth my way and got a punch in the arm.

"Don't mess with shit in my car."

"Damn, Lexi, I'm just trying to keep warm in this terrible climate. And stop hitting me!"

She pulled the jeep to the curb.

She faced me from the driver's seat.

"Let's get two things straight: one, I brought you in on this because I think I can trust you; no other reason, and two, don't raise your voice to me again."

This time she hit me square in the chest. I tried not to show it but she just about knocked all the air out of my lungs. Damn, I thought, she is working out.

Twenty minutes later, Eddie greeted us at the door.

"Hey you two, come on in. Sit anywhere you want. I'm just finishing up."

We watched him clear and wipe down two tables before he sat down with us and put two beers on the table.

"Thanks, Mur," I said. "You got anything for us?"

I started to take a swig from but caught a stern look from Lexi out of the corner of my eye. I stopped and she sent me the tiniest hint of a smile before she drank from hers.

I didn't know whether I was amused or pissed off that she could still manipulate me like that. I decided amused was better.

While we drank, Murray went into a long monologue about the conversation he'd had with his father. I wanted to urge him to get to the point but I thought courtesy was a better option. Finally, he got to the heart of the matter.

"The old man said if he had to stash anything at the terminal, he'd use one of two places. First was the baggage building behind the main terminal building."

"The baggage building was a big, long four-story building running behind the tower of the terminal.," Eddie explained. "Pa said there were enough rooms in that building that you could search for a month and still have rooms you hadn't hit yet."

"The second place was the old mail building on the grounds. He said there was a big open area but a bunch of smaller, under-utilized rooms and corridors that led off in all directions. He said that place would be a nightmare to search."

"What about the upper floors in the tower?" I said. "There were fifteen stories, right?"

"They were never used to any great extent," Murray said. "I asked my father and he said not to waste time there."

Lexi looked into Eddie's eyes.

"You didn't tell your father what we were looking for, did you Ed?"

"Well, I had to tell him something so I told him you two were looking for some evidence that might help with a cold case."

She gave him a harsh look before changing it to a marginal smile.

"That's more than I'd like him to know but I guess it's okay, Mur."

He gave her a nod in response. She'd set the hook in deeper, making Murray think he was borderline spilling the beans. We had another beer and Mur-man told us some war stories about him and my dad. I could have listened to them all afternoon but Lexi rose, signaling an end to our reminiscence.

I wanted to pay for the beers but Eddie wouldn't hear of it. Lexi gave him a peck on the cheek.

"Thanks for everything, Ed. You've been a Godsend."

Murray smiled at her and I think he was blushing when we left.

"Okay, what now? I said, sliding into the jeep. "I have no clue about anything Eddie was talking about."

"I have something that might help us clear things up," she said.

"I hope it's a magic wand because this shit is getting about as clear as mud for me: baggage building … mail stations … fifteen floors in the terminal."

Lexi said nothing but I did get that little sliver of a smile that made me think she had things under control.

And she did.

We pulled up to my abode and she surprised the hell out of me by getting out of the jeep. She went around to the back of it and opened the back window. She pulled out one of those long cardboard tubes used for mailing and storing artwork and big documents.

"What have we here?" I asked.

"We don't have anything. I have the blueprints to the Central Terminal."

"Holy crap, where did you get those?"

"I, unlike you, still have some friends in City Hall."

We entered the house and she went straight to the dining room table.

"Move some of this stuff so I can spread these out," she said.

When I'd cleared the table, she laid out several blueprint pages. She dropped a couple to the floor.

"Those are plans for the tower," she said. "I don't think we need them right now. Murray talked about two other buildings: the baggage and the mail buildings."

She smoothed out the plans for the baggage house first. The building was like a medium-sized office building with four floors of corridors and dozens of doors to offices opening to either side. It would take a long time and a lot more people to search all those offices on those floors.

"Shit, Lexi, we'll need a small army to clear all those rooms," I said.

"See? There's the difference between you and me. You think like a bureaucrat and I think like a cop. I don't think we need to search every room. Most of them are just empty space surrounded by four walls. No one would hide anything in plain sight like that, especially cash. What we are looking for are out-of-the-way places; places no one would easily see or think about looking for anything valuable.

"We need to think like criminals."

We poured over the blueprints for the next two hours. Lexi had a magnifying glass enlarging some of the small print. I found a flashlight that I used to illuminate the places she pointed out. When we were done, my eyes were blurry and I had a massive headache. Lexi had circled four places on the blueprint in pencil.

"Okay, now we look over the mail building," she said.

"Whoa. Hold on a sec. I need a break."

"A break from what? All you've been doing is holding a flashlight. I'm doing all the work."

"That's because it's easier for you to think like a criminal than it is for me."

I knew that would draw a response. She punched me hard on the arm. Damn, that might actually leave a mark, I thought. Her working out is being a big pain in the ass for me.

She gave me a wry smile.

"Let's not forget who between us has a criminal record," she said.

"Duly noted," I said and moved the light to the next drawing.

We studied this one for more than an hour. Lexi's pencil was a lot busier on this plan than it had been on the baggage house.

I felt like Stevie Wonder when she finally looked up.

"I may never see correctly again," I said.

"Stop whining, you wuss. I'm still doing all the work and doing all the work has made me hungry. Get us something to eat."

No one had talked to me like this in a long time. Even my boss in Cabo had more finesse. I liked it but I couldn't tell Lexi that.

Thirty minutes later, Just Pizza was at the door with a cheese and pepperoni for me and a white pizza for Lexi. There wasn't any wine in the Culhane house but there was some beer. We sat at the table stuffing our faces while Lexi did double duty scribbling down some notes. She was in the middle of her third slice when she gave me the plan.

"I think we start with the baggage building," she said. "The possibilities there are fewer than in the mail building. If we can clear the potential hiding places in the baggage house, we can focus on the other."

"When might our quest begin?" I asked.

"Tomorrow. It's not like you have anything else to do. We can drive over there in the afternoon while there is still light and check the place out."

I started to say something when Lexi's right hand started toward my face. I jerked back reflexively.

"Be still, asshole. I was trying to wipe the sauce off your face."

Her hand felt good. Who would have thought the chin an erogenous zone?

"What are you going to do tomorrow morning?" she asked.

"I still have to get over to the Historical Society and meet with that McCartan chick. She might have something we can use."

"All right. I'll be here at one."

"Why don't you pick me up at Cole's? That way I won't have to walk all the way back here."

She gave me the stare that used to make me fear for my safety, then just nodded her assent as she was walking out the door. The door had just closed when she opened it again. She marched into the dining room and grabbed the box with two remaining slices of white pizza.

"You don't need this," she said and left for good this time.

I sat in the living room with the rest of my beer and wondered what the hell I was doing here. So far, all I'd accomplished was dredging up these old longings for Lexi, reminding me what I'd lost in that fleeting minute of anger, and gotten frozen to the core of my being. This notion of buried treasure sounded like something Robert Louis Stevenson had concocted. Even if there was money in that decrepit old building, we were never going to find it. It was too big and there was too much to search. But if that's what it took to get close to Lexi, that's what I was going to do. I looked out the window at the light snow falling and wondered if I'd ever see La Hacienda again. I hoped not.

CHAPTER TEN

IT WAS ABOUT 9:30 when I walked into the beautiful Historical Society building and asked if I could see Sheila McCartan. The elderly woman sitting behind the desk looked up at me over the top of her bifocals and made a sour face. If there was a standard look for historical society employees, this woman would have been the poster child. Her gray-steaked hair was balled up in a bun and her glasses l were thick enough to stop hockey pucks.

"Is she expecting you?" she said.

"Nope, she was referred to me by Donnie Joe from Cole's."

"Figures," the crone said before hitting a button on her phone. Someone must have answered.

"Miss McCartan, there is a gentleman here to see you. He doesn't have an appointment but was referred by your friend Mr. Don at Cole's."

She put down the phone and pointed to a staircase heading down.

If the crone at the front desk was the illustrated dictionary depiction of the historical society type, the woman I encountered at the bottom of the stairs was the antithesis. In a word, she was stunning. She had perfectly coiffed hair that touched her shoulders with soft, blonde curls and wore a simple white silk blouse and black pencil skirt. She was elegantly sexy. Her black heels clicked across the marble floor as she came to meet me. Her smile was a tribute to good dentistry, great genes, or both.

"Mr. Duffy?" she asked.

"Yeah … but how did …"

"Donnie Joe from Cole's told me you might be stopping by," she said. "How can I help you?"

"I'm not sure you can," I said "I'm interested in the old Central Terminal and DJ, Donnie Joe, thought you might know of where and how I might get more information."

"Funny, isn't it? No one gave a hoot about the building for most of half a century but now that its destruction is imminent, there is all this renewed interest."

I was surprised by "renewed interest."

"You've had other recent inquiries?"

Before she answered, she glanced up the stairs. I turned to see the nosy hag busying herself while glancing down at us.

Ms. McCartan touched my elbow an sent a little jolt of electricity up my arm.

"Let's go into my office where we can talk."

She led me to modest office where I saw the name plate designating her as Director of Research and Interpretation. Two chairs faced a desk with a high-backed leather chair behind it. She sat next to me, not behind her desk. She crossed her legs and made me wish I had a pencil to drop.

"You were saying, Mr. Duffy?"

"Please call me Coe. I'll forget who you're talking to if you continue to call me Mr. Duffy."

"And I'm Sheila," she said, smiling that gorgeous smile again.

"You mentioned renewed interest in the old building."

"Oh yes. I haven't had a lot of inquiries but more than usual. One was rather odd. An acquaintance of one of my mother's former paramours was in just last week. He was seeking blueprints for the terminal."

"That's a pretty specific request," I said. "Did you have them?"

"Oh no. Things like that would be in City Hall, not here in the Society. I thought he might be working with a film company. You've heard of the pending plan to demolish the building?"

"Yes, I have. I have been away from Buffalo for some time but I have been told of the new plans."

"It's been what? Four years since the incident that caused you to leave former Mayor Culhane?"

Wow, she's good, I thought.

"Well, yeah, it's been about that," I said. "But how …"

"Coe, our business here is history. Your story was part of that history."

That smile again. She made me want to jump her right there in her chair. But I needed to know more about this other guy looking for blueprints.

"I wonder why someone would want blueprints to a building that is going to be demo-ed?"

"I wondered the same thing," she said, "since the inquisitor didn't seem to have any scholarly interest in the history of the terminal. He just wanted to know how the building was constructed."

Shit! We had competition, I reasoned. This isn't good.

"And what might your interest in the old building be, Coe?"

She threw that smile around like she knew what it was doing to me.

"Some friends of my father used to work in the terminal and I thought it might be nice to do a little compilation for them, so I'm just looking into the traffic the terminal handled and things like that."

"Well, you know Buffalo had another rather large terminal right in downtown. Do you have any interest in that building?"

She didn't wait for my answer and pulled a volume off a credenza behind her. She opened the book to reveal a large multi-columned building.

"This was the old Lehigh Valley Terminal. It has an octastyle colonnade in the old Greek style while Central Terminal was art deco."

Her voice was as mesmerizing as her smile and I was content to let her prattle on about the design differences in the two terminals. She continued for a few minutes and then showed me those teeth again.

"I'm sorry," she said. "I'm afraid I'm boring you to death with my incessant chatter. I'll have Dorothy upstairs make some copies of materials on Central Terminal. They will be ready in a few minutes. In the meantime, feel free to roam around and look at some of the exhibits."

She stood and took my hand convincing me that if I should ever merit Heaven her hand would be what a cloud would feel like.

"Do come again, Coe," she said. "It was a pleasure meeting you."

She held my hand a little too long to be a handshake and not long enough for it to be suggestive. Damn, she was good.

"Thank you, Sheila, for everything." I put a little too much emphasis on 'everything' and I was certain she caught it.

"Not at all, Coe. Any time."

Fifteen minutes later, I was walking down Elmwood to Cole's with a thick manila envelope under my arm. I was certain it didn't have any information that would be helpful to my quest but when I sat down at the bar and opened the packet, I found I was wrong. Sheila's card was clipped to the first page.

Oh Lord, give me strength, I thought.

DJ came down with my Budweiser.

"You met Sheila I see," he said, grinning.

"Why didn't you tell me she was an absolute babe?" I said.

He just laughed.

"Somethings are best found out on your own."

"What's her story? She is drop-dead gorgeous."

"Not really sure, other than she's supposed to be as smart as she is beautiful. When she's here, guys are all over her like white on rice. She's always friendly but I've never seen her leave with anyone."

"She married?"

"Not that I'm aware of. Like I said, she's always pleasant with me and leaves a healthy tip. I heard her mother was quite the looker in her day. She used to pal around with the boys in the mob. She got pretty tight with one of the Pisans."

I was half listening and half lusting in my heart until I heard the word 'Pisan.'

"What did you just say, Donnie Joe?"

"What? About the mob?"

"Yeah, about the mob … and Sheila's mother."

"Well, word is she liked the action around the boys and she got really chummy with one of them. That's all I know."

I combined Donnie Joe's comments with Sheila's comments and the result was trouble for us. I called Lexi but it went to voicemail. I left her a message, took a swallow from my beer and waved goodbye to Don. I needed to figure this stuff out.

The walk back to the Culhane house chilled me to the bone. I put the packet from the Historical Society on the dining room table and did a few jumping jacks to get some blood flow back in my limbs. I just hit twenty when my phone rang.

"What's up?" Lexi said.

"We need to talk," I said. "We may have competition."

CHAPTER ELEVEN

L<small>EXI WAS HAVING</small> beers and chatting up some old-time cops at a place called DiTondo's when I called. Her visit with her cop buddies was part social but mostly informational. She was going at their collective knowledge of the terminal and the City Hall heist to see if she could make some more connections between the two. One guy nearing retirement was pounding draft beers and reminiscing.

"My old man was a cabbie and used to tell me stories about going out to the terminal to pick up wounded GIs coming home on the train," the cop said. "His eyes were full of tears when he'd tell me about the guys missing limbs or blinded or hobbling on crutches. That shit tore him up. Every once in a while, he'd get a GI whose wife took up with someone else while he was gone or a girlfriend who married another guy. Same shit I saw in 'Nam. But my father told me he got half a dozen diamond rings and other kinds of jewelry from jilted GIs. They just gave him the stuff because they figured they had no use for it anymore.

"He got to calling it Nightmare Terminal."

The cop paused just long enough to take a long draught from his beer.

"I got really familiar with the place on the beat," he said, wiping his mouth. "We'd get called out there just about every other night. Mostly kids drinking and starting fires in the place or a stolen car set on fire in the old parking lot. It got worse when the East Side gangs started using the building as a meeting place."

Another cop weighed in.

"Hey Tony, remember the night we caught that wanna-be in the building?"

"What's a wanna-be?" Lexi asked.

"That's a guy who wants to be in the mob but ain't in it yet or, in most cases, ain't ever going to be in it," Tony said. "you usually find them around bars and restaurants frequented by 'the boys,' you know?

"But one night we pull up quiet, no light or sirens. We got a tip there was a big drug deal going down. We leave the cars on Curtiss Street and we walk up to the building. Surer than shit, we walk in on about ten guys with a couple bags of coke and lots of cash.

"All of the guys are members of some street gang over there except for one dude who is sticking out like a snowflake in a coal bin… Some lowlife named Petrelli or some shit like that."

Tony says they get all the gang bangers cuffed and the evidence marked and photographed then they pull Petrelli aside, cuff and Mirandize him.

"What the fuck you doing over here?" I asked the kid. "He says it ain't what it looks like. He ain't got no part of the dope deal.

"So I says what the hell are you doing over here then? You ain't got no business here unless it's drugs. But he gives me this cock and bull story about his cousin or his uncle or some other asshole relation said to hang out there back in the day. He says he's here, at 11 p.m. to find out some shit about his relative."

"Did you lock him up?" Lexi said.

"Yeah, we got him on a gun possession charge or something but I think he got out pretty quick."

"Did you buy his story?" she asked.

"Hell no, we didn't buy his story. Who goes to Central Terminal at 11 PM to research his family tree?"

"How long ago was that, Tony?" Lexi asked.

"Three or four years maybe. I can't remember exactly."

Maybe Tony couldn't remember exactly but she knew who could.

The table conversation took off in different tangents as Lexi punched a number on her phone.

"Hey Brett. It's Lexi. Can you look up an arrest for a guy named Petrelli from a few years back? He would have been busted on a weapons charge at Central Terminal."

"A guy with that name was a little out of his element at the Central Terminal, wasn't he?" Brett said.

"Yeah, that's what caught my eye."

"I'll call you back."

She took a look at her phone and stepped away from the table. She saw that Coe had called. She called him back and got his cryptic message. Things were changing rapidly, and not for the better.

WHEN Lexi got to Richmond Avenue, she had the two staples I needed: food and information. She brought spaghetti Parmesan from DiTondo's and some information from the Buffalo PD.

"This Petrelli guy was some low-level soldier in the mob and he got picked up during a drug bust. My contact says he wasn't involved in the drug deal but was at a wrong place at the wrong time thing," Lexi said.

"It would have been better if he'd been part of the deal," I said.

"How so?" she asked.

"Then he'd have a reason to be over there. As it stands, though, he was there for something that had nothing to do with drugs. Maybe something to do with what we're looking into."

Lexi ate her pasta for a minute then said:

"It's nice to see you still have some of that analytical mind left. I was thinking the same thing but didn't want to seem paranoid."

"Well, let me lay this one on you just to pique that paranoia. Someone was poking around at the Historical Society, looking for blueprints of Central Terminal."

Lexi stopped eating.

"Are you kidding?"

"Nope and to make matters worse, my contact at the Society said the guy doing the poking was a friend of a friend of her mother's. Donnie Joe at Cole's told me the mother used to pal around with some mob guys."

"The plot thickens," she said. "These mob guys must be thinking the same thing we're thinking."

"See? It's not just your paranoia. We better get moving on this."

The pasta was heavenly, something I hadn't tasted in too long. I wanted to savor it but I had this churning in my stomach that wouldn't let me. What started out as a long shot was getting more complicated. We just didn't have a big, honking building to search, we might have to beat competition to do it. And that competition was not noted for playing by the rules, if there were any rules to begin with. We were going to have to get started on a plan pretty damned quick and get over to the terminal soon. Lexi must have been reading my mind.

"Okay, ace, we better start plotting a strategy."

I told her I agreed and would be able to devote all my attention to the task as soon as I finished with this delicious pasta. That earned me another arm punch but I didn't care.

"I knew I should have waited to feed you until after we talked about a plan."

I hoped she took my silence as my agreement. I didn't want to talk with my mouth full. She was too busy unfolding the blueprints to notice though. I wiped the marinara from my mouth.

"What, when, where, and how. That's how we learned to plan in Sand Land."

She looked up from the plans and wiped the corner of my mouth with her finger. That familiar electricity jolted me.

"You had some spaghetti sauce on your face."

"You can touch me any place, anytime, anywhere," I said. This time I got a smile instead of a punch.

"What do you think?" she said. "How do we proceed?"

"We know where. We know what. We need to figure out when and how. If we're right about competition, we need to get started clearing buildings pretty quick."

"How quick?"

"No more than a day or two. The sooner the better. But we'll need some gear. Your army surplus store probably has what we need."

She nodded in agreement.

"Do you carry?"

She turned around and hiked her shirt. She was carrying.

"Do you carry?" she asked me.

"Not for a long time."

"Guns can be helpful at times," she said.

"Not for me. I'd be more likely to shoot myself."

Ten minutes later, the kitchen was clean and we were on our way to Larkinville and the surplus store.

An hour and $150 later, we had some of the gear we'd need to explore the terminal. I say "some" because we didn't get the night vision goggles.

"What the hell do we need with night vision goggles?" she said.

"To see in the goddamned dark! What the hell do you think they're for?"

"Holy shit! Did you see how much they cost?"

"That's because they let you see in the dark." That one earned me a whack.

"Too much", she said, "for one operation. What would I do with them when we were finished?"

She did have a point there. I still maxed out my Visa card and bought a single lens see-in-the-dark scope.

"If you want to waste your money on that shit, be my guest," she said.

"It won't be wasting it if it helps find what we're looking for, will it?" I steeled myself for another whack but it never came. We loaded up the stuff in the jeep, except for one of my buys. I picked out a nine-inch boot knife and a belt knife. That's the kind with the small blade hidden in the big buckle. You never know when you're going to need a good knife.

I suggested we take a ride around the terminal to check out activity. I would have said suspicious activity but at this hour any activity would be suspicious. It didn't take long before we hit Memorial Drive and the hulking tower of the terminal.

"Drive up to the main door and see if we attract any attention," I said.

Lexi rolled up the drive to the battered marquee. Nothing moved. We drove around to Curtiss Street and cruised past the old mail building. Still nothing.

"Stop here," I said. When she did, I left the jeep. I moved along the side of the building in the shadows, careful not to crunch any of the glass that littered the place. I went about a hundred feet, listening as much as moving. I caught some movement to my right but it was either a rat or a cat in search of one. I headed back to the jeep.

"Okay, let's head out," I said.

We drove back to Memorial Drive and back to the West Side.

"What were you expecting back there?" Lexi said.

"Anything, nothing, I don't know. But if we're going to be exploring, I want to know if there are other life forms about. I thought on a cold-assed night like this, there might be some neighborhood activity or some homeless dudes," I said. "But we saw no fires, no lights, no signs of life."

"And?"

"No and," I said. "I just like to reconnoiter a little before I go into an area."

"Whatever," she said and we drove the rest of the way in silence.

When we pulled up to the Culhane house I didn't bother to ask Lexi in. I didn't want another snarky rejection for one and I knew I was going to be haunted for another. Since I returned from Afghanistan, I was prone to some pretty horrific memories elbowing their way into my psyche. Creeping along the wall back at the terminal, I could feel the tingle and felt the heat on the back of my neck that was all too familiar. This would not be a comfortable night. I left Lexi at the curb and went into the house. I didn't turn on any lights and watched her through the window. She sat there for a few minutes, looking at the house then peeled out in a screech of spinning tires.

I went to the Culhane's liquor cabinet and found what I was looking for. After every home game that Shamus played, we'd head over to the senior Culhane's for a recap of the game and a couple of sips of Tullamore Dew. We drank it straight as Pa Culhane insisted it be drunk.

"It's too fine a whiskey to be cheapened with anything but the human tongue," he said.

And he was right.

I poured gently at first, not wanting to deplete the Culhane stock but realized there was only me to drink it. I stopped at three fingers and settled back in the dark living room to replay the highlights of my semi-successful SW Asian tour. The VA shrinks called these "intrusive thoughts." I called them waking nightmares. I closed my eyes and heard the cacophony and felt the chaos and smelled the stink of gun powder. I felt the heat creep into my skin. I saw all those faces flashing in front of me, faces hidden by the shemaghs or framed by the keffiyehs I saw them flit across the dusty streets before they fell when I shot. Some exploded when hit with armor-piercing shells. Buildings blew up. Bodies came apart. I stepped in the blood-soaked mud in the streets as I moved house-to-house, wondering if the doorway in front of me might hide the haji who might end my life or if I'd missed something behind me. I was never so terrified, never so excited in my life. I prayed now as I had then.

God, please make it stop … make it stop.

But now, as then, it didn't stop.

The next thing I knew it was 3 a.m. and I was soaked in sweat. I took my first sip of the Irish whiskey and flopped onto the bed, not bothering to take my clothes off or get under the covers.

CHAPTER TWELVE

My CELL PHONE woke me up. It was Lexi.

"Hey …"

"You awake?"

Why does everyone ask that stupid question when they call in the morning? If you heard my voice, you must have deduced I'm awake.

"Yeah, I'm awake. What time is it?"

"It's ten o'clock. I thought we could start clearing some of the rooms in the baggage house."

"Can we do it this afternoon? I want to run down a lead."

"What kind of lead?" she said.

"Something that stuck with me after I left the Historical Society yesterday. I just want to check something out. It'll take me about an hour."

"So, I pick you up about one?"

"That's good. See you then."

She clicked off in usual Lexi fashion: no good-bye.

I hunted through the packet I got yesterday at the Historical Society and found Sheila McCartan's card.

She picked up on the second ring.

"Sheila McCartan speaking."

"Hello again Sheila. It's Coe Duffy. Do you have a few minutes this morning? Something you said yesterday stuck in my mind and I wanted to see if I could flesh it out."

"For you, Coe, I'd make time. When can you get here?"

"About eleven?"

"That's good for me. I have a lunch date."

I jumped in the shower and headed up to Elmwood Avenue. I don't know if I was wishing it were warmer or if it actually was getting warmer but whatever it was, it felt good. I made it to the Historical Society five minutes before the appointed hour. When I entered the lobby, the gray lady just pointed to the stairs.

"She's expecting you," she said.

I made it down the stairs and saw Sheila standing in her doorway looking like someone who should have been on the cover of Vogue. Today's ensemble was a navy suit with a very form fitting skirt and a one button jacket. Beneath the jacket she wore a white silk blouse with a scoop neckline that revealed only the slight hint of cleavage.

How could a woman dressed so professionally look so damned sexy, I wondered?

"Coe, how nice to see you again. Come on in."

She was standing in front of her desk as I came in. I reached for her hand but she gave me her cheek, which I was only too glad to kiss gently. She smelled of something that was making me light-headed in a good sort of way.

"What is that scent? "I asked.

"Beautiful."

"Why yes, it is but what's it called?"

She gave a playful punch. I must look like a punching bag to beautiful women.

"No silly. That's the name – Beautiful. But you didn't come here to inquire about perfume, did you?"

"No, Sheila, I didn't. I wanted to ask you about the guy who came looking for the blueprints."

"I figured as much," she said. "So much interest swirling around the old terminal these days. It would have been nice if some of that interest were present before the notion to tear it down."

"I can see that from your vantage point, Sheila. Some things deserve to be preserved as testament to our past."

She looked at me and smiled that gorgeous, seductive smile.

"Why Mr. Duffy," she said, "spoken like a true preservationist. If I didn't know better, I might have mistaken your interest in the building as being sincere."

"Why Ms. McCartan, I'm sure I don't know what exactly you mean?"

"Cut the shit, Duffy. You might think I'm some little cupcake you can bullshit into giving you information but I can assure you I am anything but."

Her words surprised me but not as much as her tone. Gone was the beautiful ingenue with the gorgeous smile. A snarling Cruella de Vil took her place. I was glad I didn't have a puppy with me.

"You waltz back into town after three years of God knows where just as plans are in the works for the demo of the terminal asking for information on a building you didn't give a shit about even when you were in a position to do something about it."

She leaned in closer.

"You tell me what the fuck is going on right now or I'll kick your ass out of here and tell security you aren't allowed back in the building – EVER."

Beautiful and perceptive, I thought, what a dangerous combination. I thought for a second or two but I already had a cover story handy.

"All right, here's the real deal. Remember the police officer who arrested me in the mayor's office after I punched that asshole?"

"Yeah, I remember," Sheila said. "She quit rather than testify against you, right?"

"Right. She got the gig in Culhane's office because she'd been beaten pretty badly while a beat cop. She's never given up trying to find the two assholes who did that. She recently got info that one of the dudes was killed in some gang shit and his body was stuffed somewhere in the terminal, so I want to do her a favor and see if we can get her some closure."

I hate both the word and the notion of closure but it looked like she was buying it. Sheila sat back on the front of her desk.

"Then you tell me about some mobbed-up guy looking for blueprints and I start thinking that maybe the killing of this punk was a mob hit and if it was the guy who came to see you might be able to close the books for us."

The smile came back to her beautiful face.

"See? That wasn't hard now, was it?" she said.

"We're still talking about what I said, right?"

"Hmm … handsome clever, and quick … I like that," she said, standing and kissing me on the cheek.

The kiss was great but I needed more information.

"So, where do we go from here?" I said.

"We don't go anywhere. I go see my mother and see what she can tell me about the Terminal. If we go, she won't tell us squat."

LEXI picked me up promptly at one o'clock and I filled her in on the developments with Sheila McCartan.

"You're losing your touch," Lexi said.

"What do you mean?"

"You used to be able to bullshit your way in and out of anything," she said. "Seems like this broad is onto you."

"That's it! Stop the fucking car! Stop!" I was yelling now. It must have made an impression as she pulled over.

"I put up with your shit as long as I'm going to," I said. "I never bullshitted you, about anything! So, knock it off. This is your gig, remember? If you think you can get more out of this source than I can, have at it. In the meantime, knock off the cutesy bullshit about me. You asked me to help and I'm helping. Got it?"

She looked at me as though her eyes could shoot killer rays but she stayed silent and drove on in silence until we reached the terminal. I put on the watch cap I'd bought at the surplus store and pulled the headlamp over it. She did the same.

She finally spoke.

"What now, commander?"

"Still with the bullshit, huh?

She gave me that wry smile that meant "don't push your luck." I did anyway.

"Here's what's now. I am going to scout out the baggage house and you are going to either stay here or check around the outside of the building for any secondary doors."

"Like hell. If you're going in, so am I. I'm not standing out here like your chauffeur."

"Lexi, I want to check out stairwells and doorways to make sure we can get out once we get in."

"Good deal. We both check things out. That way, we cut the work in half."

"You win. Did you bring your pry bar?"

She slid hers out of her belt. I insisted we'd need these things when we were getting outfitted at the surplus store. It was only five inches long but made of titanium.

"I noticed the windows and doors had plywood sheets covering them when we cruised past the other night. We'll need these to get in."

She gave me a mock salute. I was either going to throw her down on the ground and make mad, passionate love to her or give her a bloody lip. Of course, I did neither.

"I'll take the far end and you start here. It looks like a building this long will have four stairwells. Just note the ones we can get up and down easily."

She was already on her way to a window. I didn't like doing recon in daylight but I thought it would be better than poking around in the dark, at least until we got an idea of where we were going. I started jogging down to the far end of the building, avoiding a couple hundred beer bottles, cement blocks and broken bricks. It looked like someone had already started demolition. I got to the far end and saw that someone else had my idea. The plywood sheet was just propped up against the door. I moved it and saw the door had been kicked in, saving me the trouble. I didn't like that someone had been here before me but wasn't surprised. In all these years of dormancy the neighborhood kids must have made this a hideout. I squeezed behind the plywood, switched on my headlamp, and entered the building.

The first thing that hit me was the smell. I'd been in latrines in Sand Land that smelled better than this. I supposed it made sense. If someone was squatting in the building, this would be the living room and the bathroom. I saw a couple of old steel trash cans that had been used for warming fires and hundreds of bottles, some broken, most intact. Ahead of me was a couple hundred yards of corridor. As we'd expected, rooms branched off the hallway every ten feet or so. It would take a lot more time than we had to go through every room. I went into a couple to see what we had. There was no furniture, just the horrendous odor and shit, some figurative and some literal, was strewn everywhere. The first two I entered didn't have any likely place to hide anything. That, of course, is the definition of a hiding place but unless someone had taken the time to pry up the floor and stash the cash beneath the floor, there really wasn't any place that wasn't out in the open and if the money was stashed under the floor, we'd never find it. There was just too much space to check.

I went back into the hall and was expecting to see Lexi's light shining back at me. I didn't see it and wondered if there was a wall separating the building in the middle. I didn't like not knowing so I moved faster down the hall, skipping the rooms on either side. I traveled about fifty yards and still no light.

"Lexi! Lexi, can you hear me?"

No response. I moved faster. I figured I was about halfway through the length of the building.

"Lexi! Lexi, are you there?"

Still no answer. Goddamn it. I thought, this is what I was afraid of, getting separated.

"Lexi!"

Her beam shone down the hall.

"What the fuck are you yelling about?"

You got to love this girl.

"Just checking," I said. "I didn't see the bright, shining light you are and I wanted to make sure I still had a ride home."

"These rooms would take forever to clear," she said.

"Yeah, and there aren't many places to hide anything in these offices. Maybe we should knock this off and check the mail building."

"I agree. I can feel the stench from this place crawling into my clothes."

We started out the door Lexi entered through and we found a reception committee. Two dudes with do-rags and a third with the ubiquitous baseball cap on backward were standing about five feet from the doorway, blocking the easiest path back to the jeep.

'What the fuck you two doing here?" the baseball cap said.

Lexi squared around to face him directly.

"Any-fucking-thing we want," she said.

"You got some mouth on you, bit ..."

I know what he was going to say and so did Lexi but she didn't let him finish. She finished him instead. Her right leg shot out with a side kick and smashed into the guy's balls with an impact that left him stunned for a second before he dropped to his knees. Her other leg was coming around in a round house kick but she saw it was overkill. Her foot stopped an inch from the dude's head. The do-rags backed up. I didn't even have time to reach for my boot knife.

She spoke to the two guys still capable of comprehension.

"Get your friend and get the hell out of here. If I see you around here again, I'll make sure none of you will ever be able to have kids and that's before I run your ass in."

The two guys grabbed their still gasping friend by the shoulder and hoisted him to his feet, half dragging, half walking him away without a word. I was impressed. In addition to rendering the loud mouth leader incapacitated, she also planted the hint she might be a cop.

"Nice going," I said, "but next time, leave something for me."

"Not a chance. You snooze, you lose. I like instantaneous response to aggression.

"And no one calls me a bitch." With that she winked at me.

"I'm just giving you a heads-up in case you want to start lecturing me again."

"Let's call it a day before these cowboys come back with reinforcements."

She didn't say anything but started walking back towards the jeep. When we turned onto Curtiss Street we saw an old man with a shopping cart full of cans standing near our ride. Lexi started tensing up again. I put a hand on her shoulder to reassure her. We stopped and I spoke to him.

"Hey my man, how you doing?"

He was hunched over and was wearing two coats that still wouldn't be warm enough for the Buffalo climate. He wore an old Dodger baseball hat that looked like it came from the rubble of old Ebbets Field. He had on a pair of crusty Converse sneakers of indiscriminate color the crud having dyed them some shade of gray. He held on to a couple of empty beer cans like they were prized possessions.

"I'm doing jes' fine," he said. "Cold out here, but I'm used to it.

"I peeked my head around this corner and saw your lady do some fine work on that punk jes' now." He said that with a big smile on a tired face.

I was going to say Lexi was no lady but she's already warmed up and I didn't want her kicking my ass.

"She does know how to greet some folks, doesn't she?" I said. I thought he could probably give us some important intel about the neighborhood, if not the Terminal itself.

"I'm Jericho … Coe for short." I extended my hand. Lexi still looked tense.

"Jericho," he said. "That's a right fine Bible name. I'm from the Bible too. My name is Moses." He took my hand. He was as cold as ice. Then he looked at Lexi.

"I don't know you ma'am but I did see you at the funeral for my brother a ways back."

Lexi looked puzzled.

"Who's your brother?" she said.

"Cletus, ma'am. Cletus Mosbee. He shined shoes in this here building."

Lexi reached out for his hand.

"Cletus was a fine man," she said. "I'm Lexi."

"He was that, ma'am, and he told me all about you."

CHAPTER THIRTEEN

"Clete, he loved those sandwiches you brought him, Miss Lexi. He always said you was very kind to him."

"Your brother was a dear friend, Moses. I'm sorry he's gone."

"Me too, ma'am. Now I'm all alone."

Moses looked down at his ratty sneakers and I knew he was really missing his brother.

"Did you live with Clete, Moses?"

"No, I live right here."

"In this neighborhood?"

"No, I live right here in these buildings. See these kids come 'round here at night and they up to all sorts of no good. So, I keep out of the way until they go home and then I find a building to hang out in."

Damn, I thought. What a shitty way to live

"When do the cowboys come back around, Moses?" I said.

"Oh no, they ain't no cowboys. I seen cowboys in the movies when I was a boy and they was good. These boys ain't no good. No good at all."

I stood corrected.

"When it gets dark, they be back," he said.

Lexi was still holding Moses' hand.

"Did your brother tell you we might be coming here to the terminal someday?" she said softly.

"No ma'am, he didn't. He did tell me that he told you some secrets about these parts but I don't know what they may be."

"Have you seen anyone else around here who looks like us, Moses?" I asked.

"No, I ain't seen nobody like you here. They was some trouble here a ways back but I ain't seen nobody since then."

"What kind of trouble, Moses?" I said. "How long ago?"

Lexi stopped me.

"Hey Coe, no more questions for now, okay? Moses here looks kind of cold and he could probably like something to eat, right Moses?"

His eyes lit up and he broke into a big smile.

"I could eat some," he said.

"Come on, Moses. Take a ride with us. Can you leave your cart here?"

"It'll be fine till them wild boys come back at dark."

I helped him into the back seat of the jeep. Moses looked a little cramped but he didn't seem to mind. Lexi cranked up the heat and he looked peaceful back there. We happened by a Kentucky Fried Chicken store several blocks from the terminal.

"I do like me some fried chicken," Moses said and that settled that.

"What kind of chicken, Moses?

"When Cletus and I was small, momma would fry up some chicken. I did love them breasts."

"A man after my own heart," I said and that earned me a pretty hard punch.

Ten minutes later I was out with a hot bucket stuffed with breasts and legs. The smell was enough to put a big smile on Moses' face. I felt warmer, thinking how good it felt to make someone smile.

"That will tide you over for a while, huh, Moses?" I said.

He grinned while taking a bite out of a large breast.

Lexi was more practical than I.

"Do you have some place you can keep the chicken you don't eat tonight, Moses?"

"I surely do. I know where to put it so's the rats won't get into it."

Oh God, I thought, what an awful way to live.

"Would you like to sleep in a bed tonight, Moses?" I asked.

"No. I'll be fine at my place. I went to a shelter one time and when I woke up all my stuff was gone. Thank goodness that shelter had me these sneakers."

"How long ago was that, Moses?"

"A long time, Miss Lexi, long time ago."

Looking at his sneakers, I knew he wasn't lying. It had to be a long time ago.

Lexi had the jeep heading back in the direction of the terminal.

"Moses, can you do us a favor?" she asked.

"If I can, Miss Lexi, but I ain't got no money."

Lexi smiled.

"Moses, we just need your friendship, like I needed Clete's friendship. Will you be our friend?"

"Sho' Miss Lexi. I be yo' friend."

"Well, when we come back in a few days, will you tell us if anyone has been snooping around?"

"Uh huh," he said, smiling.

"Thanks, Moses," I said and held out my hand. He took it and found the ten-dollar bill I had in it. He started to say something but I winked at him and he smiled. We dropped him off and drove in silence for several blocks. I think the enormity of the task ahead of us was sinking in.

"What do you think?" Lexi said, finally.

"Seriously? I think we got way out in front of this thing thinking about the payday without being real about the work we have to do to get there. Looking at blueprints is one thing. Being in the building and seeing the enormity of just that one building is something else. We'd need a platoon and a month to do a thorough search of just the baggage house."

"We haven't got a platoon or a month," she said.

"I know. What we need, then, is better intel. We need to be able to narrow the search parameters. We can't be wandering through that maze aimlessly."

"Any suggestions?"

"I have to check back with that McCartan woman and see if she learned anything from her mother. Other than that, it's just you, me, and half senile old homeless guy."

Lexi was quiet. I knew this wasn't the answer she wanted but it was the one she needed to hear. From my vantage point, we were on the verge of ending this quest. I told her to drop me off at Cole's. I could check in with Sheila from there. She must have really been bummed. She dropped me off without a word.

"I'll call you," I started to say, but she sped off before I could finish. I found a stool at the end of the bar near the door. Donnie Joe waved to me. He broke off a conversation with another customer and brought me a Bud.

"Where the hell have you been, all dressed up like a cat burglar," he said. "And what's that fucking smell? You stink like shit."

I forgot I still had my creepy crawler duds on.

"You OK, Coe? You look like you just struck out with the bases loaded."

"Almost DJ. I got a little piece of a curve and fouled it off. I got one strike left."

I pulled out my phone and Donnie Joe nodded and walked off. I called Sheila's number but got voicemail.

"Hey Sheila, it's Coe. Give me a call when you can. We need to talk."

I saw her before I heard from her. She walked past the window and came into the bar. I couldn't figure out how she did it. It was windy and raw but she looked like she just came from her stylist. This lady must have some designer genes, I thought. She came over to me, kissed me on the cheek and sat down next to me.

"Buy a lady a drink?" she said.

I was going to motion to Donnie Joe but he was already on his way with a cosmopolitan for Sheila.

"Come here often?" I said, smiling.

"First time." She smiled back, but it didn't last long.

"I talked to my mother," she said, "for a long time. She thinks it best if she speaks directly to you and I agree."

"Did she have any information worth sharing?" I asked.

"Yes, in fact, she did."

"When can I meet her?"

"I told her we'd be there in ten minutes. She lives over on West

Ferry."

That sounded great until I remembered how I was dressed.

"I can't meet your mother looking like this."

"It's a one-time offer, Coe. Mom doesn't talk to too many people about what she's got to say to you."

"Shit. Do you think she'll mind if I show up like this?"

"If she does, she'll let you know. She's pretty direct."

I wanted to hold out for a shower and a change of clothes but I could see from Sheila's face she wasn't kidding about the one-time offer.

"Okay, let's go," I said and we walked out the door on to Elmwood Avenue. The wind was howling and I hoped it might blow some of the stink off me.

"Where have you been, Coe?" she said as we walked. "You really do stink."

So much for the wind.

"I did a little recon over at the terminal. It's not a locale known for its hygiene." I did a few twirls hoping the wind would chase away some of the smell. Her car was nearby and I slid into the front seat of a BMW X6. Sheila got in the driver's side and looked at me as though she preferred that I just run alongside the car.

"I needed to get it detailed soon anyway."

Five minutes later we were pulling into the underground garage of a luxury residential tower, one of the few in Buffalo that still had a doorman. I knew it by location and reputation. I never knew anyone who lived there. Mercifully, the elevator went right from the garage to the tenth-floor condo occupied by Marsha McCartan. I lived in Buffalo most of my adult life but this was the first time I'd ever been in this building. It was beyond impressive. When we got off the elevator, Marsha's door was open. I followed Sheila inside, walking on parquet hardwood and trying to avoid traipsing my dusty boots on the luxurious oriental rugs that were placed strategically around the living area. Ms. McCartan was standing in front of French doors that looked out at the dismal sky. Some dark clouds punctuated the sky like strands of dirty cotton. The elder McCartan woman wore a long cashmere sweater that couldn't hide the line of her ample bust. She had on tight jeans that were curved where they should have been and straight everywhere else. She wore Etienne Aigner loafers. Her hair was so perfectly coiffed, I thought it might have been made of plastic. Sheila was gorgeous in a "holy shit" kind of way. Her mother was more understated but no less beautiful.

"What a beautiful home you have, Ms. McCartan. I wish I could have dressed for the occasion," I said.

"Thank you, Mr. Duffy. I was terrible at marriage but wonderful at divorce."

She gave me one of those smiles Sheila used to make me forget why I'd left Buffalo.

"Sheila indicated you might have some information that might help my friend and I in our quest."

"Well, since neither Sheila nor I know fully what that quest is and since you've been less than forthcoming about the specific nature of it, I'm not sure whether I do or not."

She motioned to a chair across from a settee where she settled in. Sheila sat next to her mother. I could have argued the point but I saw no point. I wasn't going to be able to bullshit her any more than I'd been able to fool her daughter.

"After a couple of decades around some of the more, shall we say, colorful characters, in Buffalo one does gain insights into some peculiar details of local history."

"That's a rather elegant way of saying it, Ms. McCartan," I said, with a smile.

"Please, Mr. Duffy, call me Marsha."

"Of course, and I am Coe. And allow me to say that you and your daughter are strikingly beautiful."

That got smiles from both of them.

"Flattery is a wonderful icebreaker, Coe, but I am afraid that we will have to dispense with the niceties – for the time being anyway – and get right to what brings you here this afternoon. What I am about to reveal to you might be a bit disconcerting to you. You may find some of what I have to say will stun you.

"Are you sure you are ready for it?"

That preamble left me speechless. Disconcerting? Stunning? What the hell?

"I think so. Go ahead."

"How much do you know about your father?"

CHAPTER FOURTEEN

For the next thirty or so minutes, Marsha took me on a rollercoaster ride that had me alternately smiling and on the verge of tears. As it was, disconcerting and stunning were not strong enough words to convey what was happening to me.

"Your understanding of his heroism is true and correct and all a part of his pre-history, so to speak," she said. "I got to know him after Vietnam.

"The war left him with wounds no one else could see and no one else could treat. He drank a lot, way too much. He became an adrenalin junkie, always pushing the bounds to see how far he could go into his own darkness. He was a pretty scary guy, Coe."

A guy I'd never seen, I thought. To me, my father was the modicum of stability. He was a force but a force for good. He taught me to question everything, to study, to research, and arrive at my own conclusions. He told me the biggest sin anyone can commit is to let someone else do the thinking for him. This guy Marsha was describing was a stranger to me.

"I met your dad shortly after he was discharged," she said. "He was going to school, night school I think, at UB. He was a pretty nice guy … until …"

She stopped and looked into my eyes.

"Until what?" I said.

"Until he started drinking," she said. "Then Dr. Jekyll turned into Mr. Hyde and very few people wanted to be around him. He had a sidekick back then; someone who never left him; a guy named Eddie Murray."

"Murray who now owns Shaughnessy's?"

"Yeah, that's him. He and Josh served with or near each other in Vietnam and the two were inseparable.

What the hell, I wondered. I never knew any of this and I wanted to get mad at Murray for not cluing me in until I realized I'd never asked him about any of it. I was focused on Central Terminal. Marsha broke me from my thoughts.

"Your father and I were an item for a while. I could read him pretty well and see when the demons were going to pop up. Then I'd stay away and let him and Murray, your dad called him Murman, go off and get into trouble on their own."

"What happened," I asked her, "between you and my father?"

"A couple of things, actually. First, he dumped me and then I started hanging with Tony Calvaneso and the crew."

"Wait … What? He dumped **you**?" I was incredulous. The math told me this woman was in her seventies and she still looked terrific.

She laughed and continued.

"I assume that's a compliment, Mr. Duffy, and I thank you. But I wanted to save your father and he told me one night he didn't want to be saved. He told me I deserved someone who was worth the effort I was spending on him; someone worth saving."

"And you thought hanging with the mob was going to be better than saving my dad?" I said.

"No, I thought hanging with the mob was what I deserved for

not being able to convince your father he was worth saving. So, I went along where the action was. I was being wined and dined and pampered and primped. It was supposed to be an exciting life but I saw it shallow and contrived and empty. I liked the nice things I got for being one of their show ponies but I knew they were using me and I don't think they knew I was using them. I got less attractive to the boys after I got pregnant.

"It was nice while it lasted but I knew it wouldn't last long."

"You got pregnant," I said, "with my dad?"

"If you are thinking I might be your mom, Coe, be assured I'm not."

"Well, what happened to my dad after you were gone?"

"He was on a downward spiral that no one could stop," she said. "I was convinced he was taking a slow walk to suicide."

"How so?" I asked.

"His drinking was out of control. Half the bars in Buffalo wouldn't serve him and the other half he shouldn't have been in. He stepped in it pretty deep, though, with his gambling.

"Josh was working as a stevedore on the docks during the day and still trying to get his degree at night. He was making decent money but he wasn't making enough to cover what he was losing and he was owing it to the guys I was hanging with."

Marsha continued to tell me about a conversation she overheard at Calvaneso's bar.

"They were talking about some Mick asshole who was into them for a grand and couldn't pay," she said. "I knew it had to be your father. I asked about what the next step in collecting the debt was and Tony told me they were going to send Eric the Red to convince this asshole he had to pay up."

"Eric the Red?" I said with a laugh. "The Viking?"

"You're close," she said, seriously. "Eric was about six foot six and weighed well over three hundred pounds. He was a vile, disgusting, nasty man. Every time he saw me, he'd paw my breast like some greedy kid reaching for candy. I told Tony about it once and he said Eric was just having some fun and to 'roll with it.'"

"God, these guys let someone do that to their woman?" I said.

"I was a possession, Coe, hardly different from a nice car or a new suit."

She went on to tell me about her call to my father, warning him of what was coming down the pike.

"What did he say?" I said.

"He just said thanks and we'll be happy to make his acquaintance."

"We?"

"I assume he was referring to Eddie Murray. All I know is that after meeting with your father, no one ever saw or heard from Eric the Red again."

I was dumbfounded. For all my life, my dad was the mild-mannered newspaper guy working in Buffalo for a wire service. I knew little of his past, other than his distinguished combat record.

Marsha went quiet but I was still wanting more.

"Then what?" I said.

She stood up and walked over to the French doors. She looked out the window for a minute, then turned back to me.

"Come over here, Coe. From these windows you can look out east all the way to that big building in the distance."

I looked and saw the hulking mass of Central Terminal.

"That building casts a dark shadow over everything," she said.

"You'll have to get the rest from your father but make sure you are equipped to deal with what he has to tell you."

I shook her hand and said thank you. She leaned in and kissed my cheek.

"They say the truth shall set you free," Marsha said. "I'm not so sure."

Sheila rose and offered me a ride home. I told her I needed time to mull over what I'd just learned so I'd walk. She walked me to the elevator. As the door opened, she took my face in her hands and spoke in barely a whisper:

"Please be careful."

CHAPTER FIFTEEN

As soon as I got home, I called my father, detailing much of what I'd learned from Marsha. He must have known what was coming.

"Did she mention a guy named Eric?" he said.

"She did."

"What did she tell you?"

"Only that he was a big, vile, disgusting pig who couldn't keep his hands off her tits. Have anything to add?"

"Not over the phone, Coe. I'm going to hang up and call Dan Crawford, my travel guy. Give him half an hour then call him. He'll have flight information for you to get down here."

"How about Lexi? Should she come with me?"

"Sure. Bring her. It will be good to see her again. Besides, she's not a cop anymore."

That sounded ominous.

I hung up and called Lexi. She was resistant to the idea of traveling down to Florida until I gave her some of the details about the revelations from Marsha McCartan. When I'd finished, she asked how long we'd be gone.

"I can't see staying more than a day or so," I said. "Unless something my father tells me pisses me off. Then we could be out of there faster."

I called the Crawford Travel Agency and spoke to Dan. He said he'd spoken with my father and had booked Lexi and me on a morning flight to Ft. Myers the next day. He said the tickets would be at the Southwest desk at the airport. I called Lexi back and gave her the details. She said she'd pick me up in the morning at eight and clicked off. That left me with a full twelve hours to speculate on what my father had to tell me and wonder if anything he would say had anything to do with our quest. I thought a shower might help me relax but I was wrong. It just made me clean and tense.

I went over the known facts in my head. Eddie Murray was my dad's bestie. My dad let a fox like Marsha McCartan slip through his fingers. My dad was engaging in a lot of self-destructive behavior. My father was into the mob for a pretty fair sum of money. The mob was sending muscle to collect the money. The muscle was never seen nor heard from again.

I fell asleep with a couple of recurring thoughts bouncing around in my head.

What the fuck did you do, dad? Who the hell are you?

Lexi was there promptly at eight. I threw my rucksack into the back and slid into the front seat. She looked at me for full minute.

"You worried?"

"More confused," I said.

"Me too."

For the first time since I'd been back in Buffalo, she looked empathetic. I took that as a bad sign.

The plane took off at ten fifteen with the two of us sitting comfortably in first class. The flight attendant offered Bloody Marys but we both asked for coffee. I wanted a clear head for whatever it was my father might reveal.

"Do you think your father might have any information about what we're looking for at the terminal?" Lexi said.

"I'm not sure what he might offer. Something is going on though. I thought it was kind of odd that Murray would want to meet the other night in Brady's and that he was so pissed about us misleading him. So, they know something about the terminal we haven't discovered yet. I don't know if it has anything to do with stashed money, though."

She went quiet and stared out the window. I hadn't been home a full week and so much had already happened. I needed to put things in perspective, to give them context, and map out where we'd started from, where we'd gone and how we ended up here. Even the most complex problems can be simplified by context and perspective, I hoped. If they couldn't, it might just rain on Lexi's parade. Somewhere over North Carolina it hit me.

"Hey," I said. "I think I got it."

"Got what?" she said.

"I'm not sure what the 'it' is yet but I know we got played."

"How?" By whom?"

For the next thirty minutes, I walked her through the where, what, and how.

She looked at me then frowned.

"Sonofabitch," she said. "Sonofoabitch."

"Don't say anything," I said. "We keep this to ourselves and use it to our favor."

She looked at me and nodded her assent.

We deplaned and walked up a long hallway that led into the main concourse at RSW airport. I wasn't sure whom to expect waiting for us but it sure wasn't Eddie Murray. He saw us and waved.

"Hiya kid," he said, as we approached. "Hi Lexi."

"Well, well, well, Eddie, you're everywhere. When did you get here?"

"I thought I'd take your old man up on his invite. That Buffalo weather is a bear, you know?"

"Yeah, I do know. It's kicking my ass." I had a half smile, half smirk on my face. Lexi had a fixed scowl.

"What's the matter, Lexi? You don't like the sun?" Eddie asked.

She just scowled. We followed him into the parking garage where he pointed out a silver Lexus.

"Nice wheels," I said.

"Josh has got good taste," Eddie said. Lexi hurried to the car to line up by a rear door, leaving me to get in front with Murray. I might have said she did it to hide her feelings but she'd already used her silence and scowl to let Murray know where she stood.

"Good flight?" Murray said.

"Yeah, Eddie," I said. "It was fine. It gave us a lot of time to think things over."

We drove the rest of the way to my father's house in silence.

This is about to get interesting, I thought.

We pulled into my dad's driveway and he was standing on the porch. We all got out of the car and met him on the porch.

"You didn't tell me this was going to be a group hug," I said, looking at Eddie. He stared back.

"Come on in," my father said, holding the door. "We've got a lot to talk about."

"I suppose we do," I said, getting a little anxious because Lexi still hadn't said a word.

My eyes adjusted to the dim light inside the house, and I was impressed. I knew my father was comfortable in his retirement but I didn't know he was this comfortable. The spacious living room had a large leather sofa, two recliners and another small sofa. A 60-inch TV was wall mounted. My father touched my shoulder and guided me into a nice kitchen with a center island and granite counter tops. I reached for Lexi's hand but she didn't let me take it. She did follow me on the tour through Casa Duffy though. A good-sized dining room was attached to the kitchen on the other side of a high counter. The lanai to the left looked big enough to play half-court basketball in. On the right was his office with a computer, printer and another wall-mounted TV.

"There are two bedrooms in the back," he said, "and one off the office but you get the idea."

"I do get it, dad," I said, "but I had no idea a reporter's retirement would pay for such a great house."

Murray piped up.

"Prudent investment, Coe," he said, smiling.

I didn't get the joke so I didn't return the smile. From the look on Lexi's face, I thought she was going to go for Eddie's jugular. I grabbed her hand, not letting it escape this time.

"Let's sit in the living room," my father said. "We've got a lot to talk about."

Eddie went to the refrigerator and took out a couple beers.

"You want one, Coe? Lexi?"

We both said no and sat.

"You want me to start?" I said, and my father indicated he did. I ran through a Reader's Digest version of her revelations.

"That about sum it up?" I said.

"Pretty much," he said, "but you kind of buried the lede."

"How's that?" I said.

"The key part was near the end of your recap," he said. "Why do you think I would let a woman like Marsha go? It was because I was too fucked up to let her stay."

My father looked at Lexi.

"Sorry for the language, Honey."

"No sweat," she said. "We're all adults. Carry on."

He smiled at that and went on.

"My mental state should be at the beginning, not the end of the story. I was a mess but I didn't realize how much of a mess until Marsha was around to show me. My only good moments were when I was with her. When I was alone, the emptiness was overwhelming. I can't tell you how many times I thought about ending it."

"Well then, why didn't you let her pull you out of the darkness?" I said. "If she was the savior, why push her away?"

"Because I didn't want to drag her into my sickness," he said. "She was too good, too pure, too loving for me to make her go through all that with me. It was bad enough I was dealing with all that shit. It would have been worse if I inflicted it on her."

"So why didn't you get some help? Why didn't you go to the VA and get counseling?"

"The VA?" he said. "I didn't even like driving by the fucking place much less think about going inside. That was the image of the government that sent us into that shithole, into that madness. I saw them as part of the problem, not the solution."

"What changed?" I said. "I only knew you as a caring, considerate, stable father. You obviously made some adjustment for the better."

In that instant, he aged before my eyes. Sitting in that chair, holding his beer, he stared out the window and looked old and tired. I wondered if this wasn't a big mistake. Sometimes a little knowledge is, indeed, a dangerous thing.

Murray took up the story.

"Your old man and I became friends," Eddie said. "We were hanging around a place on the southside called Smitty's. We both hadn't been home from the war too long but your dad was working and I was just drinking. One day he asked me if I wanted a job. I told him I did and we started work on the docks together. We got close.

"There weren't a lot of people you could share your experiences with back then and even when you found somebody who'd listen, they didn't get it. It was different back then."

"Are we ever going to get to the part of the story with Eric the Red?" I said.

"Just wait a minute, kid!" Murray barked. "I'm getting there."

"Let me take it, Ed," my father said and he leaned forward on his chair.

"Marsha told you I was into the mob for some money I didn't have," he said. "One night my phone rings and some asshole on the other end tells me he's going to come to my place to collect the money or else. I'd had a couple beers …

"And a few shots," Murray chimed in.

"And a few shots," my father said. "So, I tell the guy to go fuck himself, or something articulate like that." My father was smiling again.

"He tells me what pleasure it's going to be, knee-capping me, and

I didn't take that too well. I tell him this is all a big misunderstanding and he can meet me the next night at the casino in Cazenovia Park and I'll settle up. He agrees and hangs up."

"That's when your father called me," Murray said, "and we came up with a plan."

Eddie took over the narrative at that point. The Caz Park casino wasn't a casino in the gambling sense of the word. It was more a community meeting room. In front of it was a small circular drive. My father would sit in Murray's pick-up on the road and Murray would hide behind one of the dozens of trees that dotted the area. When the muscle showed up, my father would face him while Murry creeped up behind him. The two of them would then proceed to beat the shit out of him.

"What the hell did you think that would accomplish?" Lexi said. "You would just piss the boys off and they would send someone else to collect! You didn't really think you could scare the mob off, did you?"

"We weren't thinking at all," my father said. "We were pissed off because this goon threatened me and no one was going to get away with that."

"Okay," I said, "you've got a shitty plan so what happened when the guy showed up?"

"He pulled up in this '69 Caddy that was longer than Mur-man's truck," my father said. "When he got out of the car, I could see why he needed a car that big."

"The guy was ee-fucking-normous," Eddie said, laughing. "I could see we were going to need a better plan. Your old man didn't know it but I had a 33-inch Louisville Slugger stuck in the back of my belt. I knew this was going to go sideways fast."

"You and that fucking bat," my dad said laughing. "I get out of the truck and I face him. That's a bad analogy though because I was looking at the buttons on his shirt, not his face. He says 'you got my money?' with this shit-eating-grin that told me he planned on kicking my ass whether I had the money or not.

"I said yeah, I got your money here in the back of the truck and I started to reach into the truck bed for a tire iron I knew was back there but this was apparently not Eric's first rodeo. As soon as I turned my back, he grabbed me by the neck. His hand went almost all the way around it."

Eddie and my father had been smiling up until now but started laughing hysterically as they recounted the battle.

Eric had my father by the neck and turned him around to punch him in the face. When he did, my father came up with nothing from the truck to defend himself. Eric threw a punch at my father's face but dad ducked and the goon slammed his fist into the top of dad's head.

"I thought I got hit with an axe handle," my father said. "His punch drove me into the bed of the pick-up and knocked the wind out of me. I had a sap in my pocket … "

"Sap?" I said.

"Lead weight encased in leather," Lexis said. "Cops are the only ones who can have them legally."

"Anyway, I have this sap," my father said, "but I'm too hurt to reach it. I tried to think of something to do but his punch scrambled my brain. I'm pretty much helpless when Eric takes me by the hair and slams my head against the side of the truck. I figured one more of those and my lights were definitely going to go out."

"That's when I come out from behind my tree," Eddie said. "I run up behind this asshole and I tap him on the back with my bat."

"Why didn't you just coldcock him?" Lexi said. "Why alert him?"

"It would have been cowardly to hit him from behind."

I was waiting for laughter from Eddie and my father but it never came. These dudes had a strange sense of honor, I thought.

"So, the goon turns around, kind of surprised to see me," Murman said. "He was even more surprised when I brought the bat up from the street and whacked him in the balls … "

"Saving my life, I might add," my father said.

I was stunned. The scene playing out in my head was more Goodfellas than my father and his buddy. In relating it, the two men seemed more than a little casual. I could hardly wait to see where it was going.

"Eric stands there for a second or two with this awful look on his face," Murry said. "Then he grabs his balls with both hands and I get a good swing of the bat to the side of his head. He goes down to his knees but the fucker is still conscious. I couldn't believe that … "

My father jumps in.

"I'm still trying to shake the cobwebs out of my head when I hear the smack of the bat on the side of Eric's head. I used the side of the truck to stand up and I see two of Mur-man walking over to me. He helps me up just about the time Eric stands up and grabs Eddie around the neck with those two meat hooks he had for hands. I figure Murray's dead unless I do something so I grabbed the bat from Eddie and I give Eric a smack on the head. But I must have been too dazed to have much power because this asshole continues to choke the life out of Eddie."

"He sure as hell was," Murray said, rubbing his neck.

"What the fuck?" I said. "You guys were like the Keystone Cops. What the hell were you thinking?"

Lexi had the answer.

"Booze is a terrible thing," she said.

My father was undeterred.

"I'm thinking I had a fractured skull and Mur-man is about to be choked to death but I still have the bat. Eric is so intent on strangling Eddie he isn't aware of me lining him up for a swing to his face. When he sees me getting ready to swing, he lifts his head and instead of whacking him in the forehead, I catch him right smack in the throat. He lets go of Murray and grabs his neck while he's going down to his knees."

"Then blood starts shooting of his mouth like a fountain," Murray said. "He's coughing and spitting and bleeding and making some hideous noises and then he falls flat on his face and the noise stops. I roll him over and see his open eyes staring into space. The blood is bubbling around his lips"

"What did you do? Did you try to save him?" I asked.

"Save him for what? To come after me again?" my father said. "Fuck no, we didn't try to save him."

"We got a bag of peat moss from Eddie's truck and we smothered him with it," Murray said

"Holy shit," I mumbled now realizing why my father had made the comment about Lexi not being a cop anymore.

"Then what?" Lexi asked.

"Then we took a while to clear our heads and struggled for about an hour getting the body into the bed of the pick-up," my father said.

"What did you do with the body?" I asked.

"We dumped it at Central Terminal."

"And the car?" Lexi said.

"Funny thing about the car," my father said. "I called another Vietnam vet I knew whose old man had a junkyard. I asked him to pick up the Caddy and crush it."

"Did he?" I said.

"Of course, he did," my father said, "and he called me the next day to tell me I could pick up two hundred dollars at the junk yard."

"What the fuck," I mumbled.

"I took that money, the money we took off Eric's body and got a loan from the credit union and made an appointment to see Tony Calvaneso."

"Jesus!" I said, "after you killed his goon?"

"I had to pay the debt," he said, way too calmly. "Otherwise, as Lexi already pointed out, they would keep coming to collect."

"What happened at the meeting?" Lexi said.

"I gave Tony his money and I said that in the future he would respect me enough not to send hired muscle to collect because I would always respect him and pay my debts."

"He didn't ask about Eric?" I said.

"He did," my father said, "and I told him that I would be coming to meet with Mr. Calvaneso myself - that there was no need for him as a middle man."

"He accepted that?" I said.

"He had no choice, I guess. I was there with his money. That's all they really cared about."

"Holy shit," I said. I looked at my father and said "who are you?"

He took a long drink from his beer and looked at me.

"You mean who was I?"

We were all quiet for a few seconds then Eddie spoke.

"You want to tell them the punch line, Josh, or should I?"

My father nodded to Murray, so Eddie went on.

"A week or so later, Tony C. calls your old man and asks him to be the new debt collector. Me and your old man were collecting debts for the mob."

I almost gagged. This was an awful lot to take in during a ten-minute conversation. None of it fit with the longstanding image I had of my father. In fact, none of it fit with anyone I knew in my entire life.

"So, you murdered a guy and got his job?" I asked.

"Killed, not murdered," my father said. "I killed a lot more guys wearing the uniform and my country said that made me a hero."

"You were in a war, dad … a fucking war! Don't tell me that whacking a mob guy is the same."

My father's eyes closed to slits and I saw a look on his face I'd never seen before.

"Listen to me. That guy was mob muscle, not the same as a mob guy, and he was going to kill me. We killed him first. It was self-defense so don't go getting all self-righteous on me. You've probably done the same thing in Afghanistan. You're no one to judge me."

I was stunned. He and his pal killed a guy and rationalized it. Now, my father was mad at me! Lexi spoke up and I was hoping she'd defend my proposition. She didn't.

"How much did you get paid?" she asked.

Murray answered.

"Some weeks were better than others," he said. "Normal week, we'd get a grand apiece. Good week, we'd get twice that."

"Did you have to do any more killing?" she said.

Murray and my father both laughed.

"That was the beauty of it," my father said. "Most of these losers had been shaken down by Eric the Red. When they saw us instead of him they usually asked where he was. When we told them we took care of the big piece of shit, they were more afraid of us than they had been of Eric. We never had much trouble."

Muddled as my mind was from all these new revelations, it could still do the math of Eddie's disclosure. They were clearing somewhere between fifty and sixty grand a year. That explained a lot about the life style we lived in those days. It also explained why we were sitting in such great house here in Florida.

"So, you asked me what changed in my life, Coe. It was you. When you came along you saved my life."

"Eddie, I think I'll have that beer now," I said. He smiled and headed to the kitchen with Lexi not far behind.

"Marsha told me she cared a lot about you," I said.

"She was the best thing that ever happened to me and the worst mistake I ever made," he said. "The best because she never stopped caring; the worst because by the time I was ready for a relationship, she'd moved on. I would see her every week when I went to see Tony Calvaneso. Each time was like a dagger in my heart."

"Why didn't you start up with her again? She obviously liked you."

"She was smart enough not to do something like that," my father explained. "If she did, there is a better than average chance we'd both be dead now. The mob was funny like that."

Eddie and Lexi returned from the kitchen. She handed me a

Budweiser and I took a big swallow.

"Now that we've come clean, Coe, it's time you did too," Eddie said. "What are you two doing snooping around Central Terminal?"

Before we could answer, the phone rang and my father picked it up.

"Well hello to you too, Marsha. Yes, it has been a long time."

CHAPTER SIXTEEN

WHILE MY DAD made happy talk with his once and former romantic interest, Lexi took a call on her cellphone. I knew it couldn't have been anything good because her mood went from bad to worse the longer she stayed on the call. She ended the call without ever saying a word. I didn't like the look on her face at all.

"We have to get back," she said.

"What's going on?" I asked.

"Moses" she said. "Someone beat him near to death."

I was already on my feet.

"Eddie, can you get us back to the airport?"

"Sure, kid, let's go."

My father paused his call and put his hand over the mouthpiece.

"Your flight isn't for another couple hours," he said. "Don't you want to stay?"

"We got to go, Dad. A friend of ours is in trouble. I'll call you in a day or two."

He told Marsha to hang on, stood and gave me a hug.

"I love you, you know," he said.

"I know, dad, and I love you too. We'll talk soon."

WE didn't speak much on the trip to the airport. What I had to say to Lexi could wait until Eddie was out of earshot. When we entered the airport, I asked her for an update on Moses.

"My buddy Brett at BPD told me another homeless guy found Moses laying on the ground in a pretty bad way," she said. "He waved down a taxi and had the driver call for an ambulance. Moses is at the Erie County Medical Center and still unconscious."

"Motherfucker," I whispered. "Somebody's going to pay for this." She took my arm on the way to our gate.

"Are we going to ignore the information Murray fed us about the terminal?" she said.

"Not really. Now that we know he's trying to steer us in the wrong direction, we go the opposite way. We stop thinking about the baggage house and the mail building and we focus on the tower."

But I didn't want to dwell on that right now. I had something more important on my mind. If I was shocked by what my father had told me about his past life, it might be his turn to be shocked to know what I was capable of.

The only good thing about the three-hour plane ride happened about halfway through when Lexi put her head on my shoulder and dozed off.

It was after midnight when we landed, too late to head to the hospital. As we headed toward Lexi's jeep, I asked her to swing by the terminal.

"Why?"

"I want to see what goes on over there this time of night."

"Don't you just want to go to bed?" she said.

"Is that an offer?"

She hit me really hard but she did drive over to the terminal. In front of the hulking building, all was quiet, but when she took a no-lights, slow turn behind it, we got a different picture. There were about dozen guys and half that many girls. They were gathered around a trash can fire boozing out of bottles wrapped in paper bags. One of the girls was getting rammed from behind by a particularly energetic stud. No one else was paying any attention to them. Lexi eased the jeep back out their line of sight.

"The next generation of our leadership," I said.

"Hardly worse than the current leaders," she noted.

"I guess. At least those two were screwing each other in public."

That actually got grin out of Lexi. I was making progress.

We got back on Memorial Drive and headed west toward the Niagara River. We traveled a few blocks before Lexi spoke.

"What was the purpose in that?" she said.

"I'm interested in the mating rituals of young Americans," I said. "Actually, I wanted to see how many of these assholes I'd have to take out on Moses' behalf."

She went silent for a while then dropped the bomb.

"I'm exhausted," she said. "I'm too tired to drive home so I'm crashing at your place."

I was making more progress than I'd thought.

"But don't get any stupid ideas just because you saw those delinquents," she added quickly. "We're just sleeping."

"I've got it, just sleeping," I said, thinking baby steps. Just take baby steps.

Twenty minutes later, we'd stopped at a Rite Aid and got Lexi a tooth brush and pair of flannel pajama pants resplendent with pink unicorns. I didn't realize how tired I was until I felt the comfort of the bed. Lexi climbed in on the other side. She stayed a foot or so away from me, for a minute or so.

"It's cold in here," she said. "Didn't you turn up the heat?"

"When would I have done that?"

"Well, it's cold. Come over here and snuggle. No bullshit. Just snuggle."

I complied and put my arms demurely around her waist, spooning against the soft contour of her back and butt. I thought I heard a contented sigh before we both fell asleep.

"I loved this part of us," she said, "just snuggling. I think I liked it better than sex."

I had a snappy retort but this hardly seemed the time. I fell asleep wondering what's wrong with this woman?

AT some point during the night, we switched positions. I could tell because I felt the soft swell of her breast against my back and the warmth of her hips on my butt. I thought I might make my move when I awoke but when I opened my eyes, I was alone in the bed.

Hell, did I just dream her spooning against my back? I'll never know, I guess.

I got up, showered, dressed and waited for her to call. Thirty minutes went by and I had all the waiting I could stand for one morning. I called an Uber and took a ride to the terminal to check things out solo. We were going to need some serious sleuthing or, better yet, a tip to get us started in the right direction. Without either or both, Lexi's quest was going nowhere. Even assuming the information we got from Eddie Murray was misdirection, we still had way too much building to search and far too few searchers to do it.

When the driver pulled up at the main entrance, he gave me a concerned look.

"This is some shitty neighborhood," he said. "You sure you want me to leave you here?"

"Well, now that you mention it, how about you come back here in an hour? I'll be done by then."

"Man, you might be done for in less than that but you're the boss. See you in an hour, I hope."

I walked around to the back, armed with my pry bar and lots of good intentions.

Lexi was already at the hospital. She was giving the nurses the third degree about Moses' condition. Moses was still out and the nurses thought he might be out for a while. The docs had put him in a medically induced coma because of the trauma his head had suffered. Keeping him under, they reasoned, might help reduce the swelling.

"Do you have any idea what might have caused his head injuries?" Lexi asked.

"There was a heel print from a boot," the nurse said. "We took a picture of it and gave it to the cops who came in behind the ambulance."

"That's great," Lexi said. "Did you ever see Moses in here before?"

"We didn't," the nurse said, "but some of the nurses in the addiction unit have seen Moses before. He's one of their favorites. They all talked about how polite he is and how apologetic about showing up again."

"Thanks for all you are doing for him," Lexi said, handing the nurse her card. "Could you give me a call when he wakes up or if there is any change in his condition?"

The nurse nodded. Lexi waited until she was in the lobby to call Det. Brett Joseph. She filled him in on the boot heel print the nurses photographed and he assured her he'd track the picture down.

"What's the deal, Lexi?" he asked. "Why the interest in this guy?"

"His brother Cletus was a friend of mine. I met Moses a few days ago and he was a real nice guy. But it wouldn't matter if he was a complete stranger. No one deserves to be beaten to a pulp. Speaking of which, do you have any notion of who might have done this?"

"I have a call in to the guy running the gang unit. I'll let you know what I find out."

"Thanks, my friend. I appreciate your help."

Lexi got in the jeep and called Coe. Her call went to voice mail. She thought that strange. Where could he have gone? she wondered.

GETTING into my back door in Cabo was harder than getting into the terminal. After I pried the plywood sheet back, I did my best to lean it back to cover the opening. I pulled my headlamp over my forehead and switched it on. The beam caught the dust floating in the cavernous building and cut a swath through the blackness. I didn't know what I was looking for and had less of an idea of where I was going so I just meandered through. It was clear that the narrow beam from my headlamp wasn't going to be enough so I switched on my tactical flashlight. It cast a wide beam that gave me a better idea of the enormity of the room I was in. It had a vaulted ceiling at least a hundred feet high. There were a lot of arched windows but they were boarded up. I got a much better idea of what a grand structure this must have been in 1929. I threw the light over the marble floor and saw the intricate designs inlaid to the floor. I saw a number of entryways labeled "To Station," "To Office," and behind me "To Buses and Taxis." All along the far wall, I saw a bunch of cubicles with the legend "Tickets" over each. I turned the beam to my left and saw a booth with "The Union News Company" across the top. This was where my dad's friend Gabe Del Negro sold newspapers. I could only imagine the hustle and bustle of thousands of people moving through here every week. I moved a little farther into the lobby and saw a sign over one corridor that said "To Trains." I walked through the archway and moved ahead. There was no light except from my flashlight, no sound except that from my footfalls. I was thinking what a spooky damned place this was when a scream shattered the silence and a bright light flashed into the room. I turned in the direction of the light and the noise but a little too late to stop the board swinging toward my head. I turned just enough to catch it on the side of my head instead of square in the face. I swung my flashlight at the light that was blinding me and felt it connect with a cracking sound. I then switched my beam to its full power and heard another scream. I brought my free hand forward to ward off any other blows but there were none coming. I reduced the beam and focused it on a bundle of rags bending low in front of me. I was about to throw a front kick that I could see now wasn't necessary. The bundle of rags started moaning and pleading.

"Don't kill me, man. I'm an old man. Please don't hurt me no more."

"Stand up, old man!" I said, in my command voice. "What the fuck's the matter with you? Why'd you hit me?"

I could feel the blood oozing down the side of my face but I didn't take my eyes off the old man.

"Come on," I said. "Stand up!"

The old man got off his knees and stood up - well, mostly stood up. He was bent over at a painful looking angle.

"You okay?" I said. "I didn't mean to hurt you but you scared the shit out of me."

"I'm sorry, mister, I truly am. I thought you was one of them wild boys who beat up my friend Moses."

I shone the light on his head where I thought I might have smacked him with the flashlight. I didn't see any marks. But the blood on the side of my face told me he was a better aim than I.

"You know Moses?" I asked him.

"Moses is my friend," he said. "But them wild boys done kilt him last night." The old man started to cry.

"No, they didn't kill him, old timer. They almost killed him but Moses is tough. I think my friend might be at the hospital now checking up on him. What's your name?"

"I am Louis," he said. "Like Joe Louis."

"Well, Louis, my name is Coe. Let's go somewhere where there's light so we can look at each other and talk."

"Well, I be damned," he said, "you Coe the chicken man."

We started walking toward the lobby.

"Chicken man?"

"Yessir, you the chicken man," Louis said, laughing. "Ole Moses tole me about a man and a woman who bought him the chicken we ate last night, just before them boys set on him."

I should have known Moses would share his bounty.

"Yes, Louis, I'm the chicken man. So, you know I mean you no harm. Any friend of Moses is a friend of mine."

We reached the spot where I entered the terminal.

"Let's go outside. I need you to take a look at where you hit me. I think I'm going to need stitches."

"Sorry 'bout that, sir. I truly am. I thought you was one of them wild boys coming back to get me."

It wasn't sunny outside but the daylight still took some getting used to. Now I could see Louis clearly. He had some white hair on his head and face, a face that had seen better days. His eyes were rheumy and yellowed where they should have been white. He looked at my head wound.

"I am truly sorry for doing that."

I wanted to reassure him it was OK but my phone buzzed. I answered it.

"Where the hell are you?" Lexi said.

"Where the hell are **you**," I returned. "I woke up this morning and no Lexi, no note, no nothing, so don't give me shit about where I am. Just pick me up at ECMC."

"I just came from there. Moses is in a medically induced coma. No need to go there."

"I ain't going to see Moses," I said. "Just pick me up there in an hour."

"What ... ," she started.

"No questions now. Just be there." Then it was my turn to hang up abruptly.

That felt pretty good, I told myself. But she might kick my ass for feeling that good.

I glanced at my watch and saw it was almost time for my Uber guy to be back, I reached in my pocket and pulled out a five-dollar bill.

"Louis, you take this," I said. "I'm going to be back here with my friend in day or two. Don't hit me again." I smiled and he took the bill.

"Thank you, Coe. Moses tole me you a nice man. He was right."

He reached in his pocket and handed me a dirty handkerchief.

"Put that on your cut," he said.

I could only imagine the germs thriving on that piece of dirty cloth but I took it anyway. I didn't want to insult Louis when he was trying to be gracious.

"I'll be seeing you later, Louis," I said as the car pulled up. Louis waved in response.

I got into the car and the Uber driver took one look at me and shook his head.

"I told you this was a bad idea," he said. "Where to now?"

I laughed and asked him if he had some paper towels.

"ECMC," I told him. "I think I need a seamstress."

CHAPTER SEVENTEEN

I waited about an hour in the emergency room. When I finally got ushered into a treatment room, a kindly nurse looked at my wound.

"It's right along the hairline," she said. "The scar won't show much but if you want, I could call for a plastic surgeon to sew you up."

"How long would that take?"

"Another hour, at least."

"Let's sew it up now," I said.

Forty-five minutes later, I walked out of the hospital with the blood wiped from my head and eleven neatly placed stitches in my hairline. Lexi was standing outside the jeep. I waved and approached.

"Okay, asshole, what happened now?" she said.

I filled her in on my encounter with Louis and she laughed.

"So, you let an old homeless guy beat the shit out of you?"

"I'd hardly call it beating the shit out of me," I said. "He came out of the dark before I had a chance to see him. He thought I had evil intent."

"He had great perception then," she said, still laughing.

Then her right hand shot out like a cobra, smacking me on the shoulder. She could really punch.

"What the hell?" I said. "What was that for? Can't you see I'm in a weakened state?"

"How about I give you a whack for not telling me where you were going this morning?"

"If you try, no one will ever even know where you're buried."

I sort of believed her.

We got in the jeep and Lexi questioned me about my impromptu look around the interior of the terminal.

"That must have been some beautiful building in its heyday," I said, filling her in on the marble, the vaulted ceiling, and the other fine details. She laughed.

"When did you go to work for Architectural Digest?" she said. "What I meant was did you see anything that might help us find the money?"

I allowed that I hadn't but I did relate one additional asset I'd discovered.

"Louis is my new buddy," I told her.

"Louis?" she said, "the guy who smacked you upside the head? That Louis?"

"Hell yeah, **that** Louis," I said. "He's my new bestie."

I could see she wasn't quite picking up on what I was implying.

"Lexi, who knows that building better than guys like Louis and Moses? We could wander around in there for weeks and not see anything but Buffalo's history. I think we can get Louis to help us at least get some direction."

She was mulling that over when I asked her what she learned about Moses and his condition. She filled me in but didn't look too hopeful when she said he would probably be okay. That just made me all the more convinced someone had to pay for what they did to our friend.

Whatever they'd used to numb me during the stitching was wearing off and my head was starting to throb again but when Lexi suggested the Bijou for dinner, I couldn't say no. I had no idea when she might start off on her own to investigate shit and I liked the time I spent with her, so the Bijou it was.

We got our usual welcome from Bea but when she hugged me, I winced and she got a look at my stitches. I gave her a brief, and totally phony, explanation of what happened as we sat down.

She brought back some of that extraordinary wine from our previous visit before setting our dinners on the table: veal parm for me and eggplant parm for Lexi. The plates were piled so high it appeared we might be having guests join us, guests like the Buffalo Bills or the 82nd Airborne. The wine took a little of the edge off my gathering pain. I didn't want to spoil the mood cast by great wine and good food but it was time.

"Have you contemplated the possibility that we might not be able to narrow the search down?" I asked.

"You want to quit already?" she said. "It only took one whack to that thick skull of yours to do you in?"

"My thick skull has nothing to do with it, Lexi. The size of that building and the endless possibilities of where someone might stash that much cash has everything to do with it. Even eliminating the building Murray told us about leaves us with track beds and seventeen floors to search. That's a lot of searching, honey."

"I'm not your 'honey,' so knock that shit off right now and if you are telling me you want to quit, just say so and I'll go it alone."

"How the hell are you going to go it alone? You've got that big-ass building, the lurking gang of no-goods in the area, and no real plan of attack."

"I should have anticipated this from you," she said. "You are noted for walking away when things get tough. If you want to walk away again, I'll take you to the airport and be done with you."

I wished I had a snappy retort to lighten the mood but Lexi was right. When the shit hit the fan after the Albert Davis affair, I couldn't stomach the embarrassment stemming from my lack of control. The media coverage was relentless, making me even more convinced that I needed to bail. I had spent a professional lifetime cultivating relationships in Buffalo and they all seemed to disappear in the heat of controversy. The worse feeling, though, came from knowing what my two minutes of stupidity had done to Lexi's career.

I put down my knife and fork and took her hand, even as she tried to pull it away.

"If you are telling me you are going to go to the wire with this thing, I'm going with you," I said. "But we really need to stop for a few minutes and plot out a strategy. We can't just wander around the terminal hoping to trip over a stash of cash. We seem to be tripping over everything but cash."

She stopped trying to wiggle her hand from mine. Her eyes were welling up with tears.

"I know this was a long shot," she said, "but I thought the two of us could figure it out. You might have figured this out but since I gave up my badge, I've been kind of lost. I need something to put some drive back in my life and I thought this could be it.

"But you're telling me we can't do it and I hate to surrender like that. If that building comes down and we don't have anything to show for it, that's one thing. To walk away before then just makes me a quitter. I can't be a quitter, Coe."

I leaned over and kissed her on the forehead.

"Eat up," said. "We've got a lot of studying to do."

Once the dishes were cleared and our copious leftovers boxed, we settled up and gave Bea a hug. Fifteen minutes later, we were back at the Culhane house with blueprints spread over the dining room table.

"Want a beer?" I said.

"You planning on getting me drunk and taking advantage of me?"

"Hardly. I just need one to calm the drum that's beating in my head."

"Shit," she said, with a laugh. "I completely forgot you were wounded."

I got the beer from the kitchen and we started examining the plans.

"We need a timeline," I said. "When did the robbery occur? When did the FBI start in on the mob? When did the edict from the mob go out that the money had to be returned? When did the low life get picked up and when did he go to jail?

"If we can line up all those elements, we can figure out when the dough might have been stashed. If we know when, we might be able to figure out what parts of the building were being used and which weren't. That might help us narrow down the possibilities."

Lexi put down her beer.

"We know the heist was at the end of December," she said. "Can you ask the Historical Society chick when trains stopped running?

I'll look into the investigation part."

My head was killing me at this point but I saw the hint of a smile on her face.

"Good," I said, "at least we have a strategy."

In the back of my mind, I was thinking about how I was going to inflict some payback on the punks who almost killed Moses. Some things, you just can't let slide.

"I need to take a break," I said. "My head hurts."

"That's from all the thinking you just did," Lexi said. "Your head isn't used to it."

I wanted to laugh but it hurt too much, so I closed my eyes. When I opened them, I was lying in the bed with all my clothes on and I was alone.

CHAPTER EIGHTEEN

Lexi called me from the hospital.

"You okay?" she asked.

"Yeah, I'm doing fine. Where are you?"

"ECMC. I came to check on Moses."

"Any good news?"

"He's still under," she said. "The nurses are telling me it's normal but I'm kind of worried."

"Are you going to stay there?" I asked.

"No. I'm going to have breakfast with an old contact from the FBI. I'll call you when I'm done."

"An old contact huh? Well, just limit the new contact, make good choices, and leave enough room between you two for the Holy Spirit."

"You're an ass," she said. Before she hung up, I detected a note of a giggle from her. That was a good sign.

I called Sheila McCartan. She was exceptionally cheerful and that was also a good sign. I wasn't sure how she was going to treat me after my meeting with her mother.

"How did the meeting with your father go?" she asked.

"Honestly, it was kind of surreal," I said. "There was a side to him I never knew and now still find it hard to believe."

"I get it," she said. "I keep getting trickles of information from my mom that make me incredulous about her past."

"Sheila, when we first met you mentioned that someone else, one of your mom's old friends, I think you said, was looking for blueprints to Central Terminal," I said. "What do you know about him?"

"Why do you ask?"

"There's something strange going on out there and the more I find out the more it leads back to some old mob stuff. What can you tell me about the guy who came here?"

"Not much, I'm afraid," she said, "other than he was an unctuous, awful excuse for a man."

"Why do you say that?"

"Because when he came into my office, the first thing he did was undress me with his eyes. He made no attempt to hide that fact. Then he said I must have inherited my fine tits from my mother. Then he had the nerve to ask me for a favor."

"Wow, so he was an asshole," I said, knowing that guys like him thought social grace was a prayer before meals. "What did he want?"

"He wanted to know all that we had about the City Hall robbery that took place a long time ago."

The asshole read my mind, I thought.

"Do you have much information about that?"

"Of course not," she said. "Lurid items like that are in the newspaper archives, not in historical records. I told him that and he left but not before he told me I would look better with a couple of buttons on my blouse undone."

She was right. The guy was an awful excuse for a man.

"But now you are on the phone asking for similar information and it gets me to wondering."

"Wondering what exactly?" I said.

"Just what the hell is going on that is generating such interest?"

I was wrestling with just how much I should tell her. She was a pretty good source but could I trust her without giving our entire mission away?

"I can tell you what the real nature of my interest is, Sheila, and I assume I'm not the only one with such interest but I'd rather not do it on the phone or in your office. Are you free for lunch?"

"I'm afraid not, Coe, but I could be enticed with one of DJ's cosmos. Say around four at Cole's?"

"I'll see you then, and Sheila, one other thing. You can keep the buttons buttoned for me."

"Aren't you sweet?" she said. "For you, I might just undo one."

That's what I am afraid of, I thought. I called Lexi to chase those thoughts away.

"How's Moses?" I asked her.

"No change," she said. "They didn't say as much but I could tell the docs and nurses are worried."

I was worried too. I'd seen way too many brain injuries in Afghanistan that got guys sent home with a lifetime of problems and many of them didn't even lose consciousness. Head trauma was nothing to fool around with.

"What's next?" I asked her.

"I'm going to meet with my FBI buddy to see what intel I can glean."

"Just remember about the Holy Spirit," I said. "I'm going to head back to the library and do a deeper dive into the robbery in case I've missed anything. I have an appointment with Ms. McCartan at four.

Something she told me before needs some fleshing out."

"I'll pick you up at Cole's about six."

"How do you know that's where I'll be?" I said.

"Really?" was all she said before hanging up.

THIRTY minutes later I was at the information desk at the Central Library. I'd posed my questions and requests to a different but equally helpful librarian named Jennifer who helped me load the microfiche into the machine and left me to study the archived articles. Buffalo had two newspapers back then so I had twice as many articles to read. A Courier-Express reporter named Marshall Brown did a lot of reporting on the City Hall heist. He honed in on the story so I poured over his articles. He did three articles on consecutive days, questioning the city's tabulations of the take in the robbery. In the first one, he pressed the city treasurer for the total but was told the count was being taken. The second day, the treasurer told him "the estimate is between two and three hundred thousand. Brown's story said "it is inconceivable that city wouldn't know how much public money was stolen down to the penny" and indicated he would stay on the matter of the stolen cash. The third installment included a simple "no comment" from the treasurer who noted that he provided all the information he was going to. Brown tracked down other city officials but didn't get any more specific information. Then the articles stopped and didn't pick up again until the FBI came on the scene two weeks later. Neither Brown nor any other reporter from either paper made mention of the amount of money actually stolen. There was one other interesting piece about Marshall Brown in the archives – his obituary.

If I couldn't talk to Brown was there anyone else around who might have information? I wondered. All this thinking was making my head start to throb again. I was about to give up when I remembered one of my journalism professors at UB once worked for the Courier-Express. I called the university and learned that he'd retired a few years ago but still lived in the area. I started digging through the phone book and found a likely prospect living not far from the school. I called the number and was instantly impressed with my sleuthing ability when the voice on the other end was familiar.

"Is this the Lee Coppola who taught in the J-school at UB a few years back?" I said.

"Well, it's been more than a few years but yes, I taught there. Who is this?"

"Mr. Coppola, it's Coe Duffy. I don't know if you remember me but I was in your Communications Law course a while ago."

"I can't say I remember you from class, Mr. Duffy, but I do recall you from the mayor's office. What can I do for you?"

"I was hoping I could talk to you about a crime reporter you might have worked with at the Courier …"

"Marshall Brown," he interrupted.

"Exactly," I said, "Marshall Brown. Would it be possible to pick your brain a bit about Mr. Brown?"

It took about thirty minutes but I finally turned our conversation to the City Hall robbery story.

"That was Marsh's *pièce de résistance*," Coppola remembered. "He beat the snot out of those guys from the News. Marsh was a digger. He was relentless."

"I got that impression from the articles I read in the archives at the library," I said. "He was particularly relentless about the sum that was stolen. Do you recall that?"

"Of course. That was the one aspect of the story he couldn't tie down. He knew the treasurer was giving him the run-around. How could the guy not know how much money was taken? Brown tried a few end runs around the guy but all he could get were winks and nods from other people in City Hall. Apparently, Carlyle … I think that was his name … apparently Carlyle kept a pretty tight lid on information and tighter lid on the city's money."

"Until the robbery," I said.

"That's right," Coppola said, "until the robbery. Then, the best he could do was a guess that it could have been anywhere from couple hundred thousand to who-knows-how-much?"

"I noticed that Brown's pursuit of the amount stopped right around the time the feds came on the scene. What do you make of that?"

"Well, that became the story," Coppola said. "The FBI was hauling in every nickel-and-dime crook in the city trying to get one of them to flip but nothing worked until they started bringing in the mob guys. The wise guys didn't like being rousted and I think they knew it was a matter of time before someone dropped a dime on some of their activities."

"You think the wise guys themselves ratted the guy out?"

"Not me. Marsh Brown. He was the one who developed the theory."

I almost dropped the phone.

"How the hell did he figure that?" I said. "I don't know much about the mob but I do know they aren't big on squealing."

"You're right, Coe. They aren't. It's called 'omerta,' the code of silence. But the robbery of City Hall, Brown figured, was a violation of a hear-no, see-no, do-no arrangement between the mob and Buffalo's mayor."

"You lost me," I said, and for the next twenty minutes, Coppola gave me chapter and verse about the mob and its strange relationship with the mayor.

The mayor, while a good, decent, upstanding man of impeccable character, traced his ancestry to the same eastern Sicilian village that spawned one Lucca Bagarelli who was the boss of organized crime in Western New York. The two men couldn't be farther apart in terms of their character. The mayor earned his reputation for decency as first an assistant, then district attorney who was relentless in his prosecution of bad guys. Bagarelli was the opposite. Together, they were the yin and yang of Buffalo. Brown had long theorized that there was an unspoken agreement between City Hall and the mob not to embarrass each other. But the robbery of the city treasury broke that arrangement. The city was mightily embarrassed by the robbery and again by the inability to attach a price tag to it.

"The mayor thought the robbery was the breaking of an unspoken but very real truce," Coppola said. "That's why he called in the feds. His thinking was if the mob was going to muck things up for him, he would do the same to them."

Coppola went on.

"The feds smelled blood in the water and they became sharks," he said. "They were hauling in punks at every level and sweating them for hours. The doo-doo hit the fan, though, when Bagarelli himself was brought in. It wasn't long after that the name of the robber came out and an arrest was made.

"Brown just put two and two together and came up with four."

Christ, I thought, I've lived in this city most of my life, served it in the highest levels of government and I never knew any of this shit. I wondered how much more there was about Buffalo I didn't know.

"So, the FBI makes an arrest," I said, "and the thief is caught and the money gets returned. Case closed."

"Not exactly, at least not according to Marsh Brown," the professor said. "Remember how Brown kept trying to nail down the amount stolen? He wasn't just being a good reporter; he was trying to figure out how much needed to be recovered."

"Let me guess," I said, "and he never did."

"He never did. But even after the story faded from the public's attention Marshall kept poking around."

"Did he learn anything from that poking?" I asked.

"Not much," Coppola said, "but he did find out that the city treasurer retired twelve months after the robbery to a big-assed house in Ft. Lauderdale."

As Alice once said in Wonderland, it gets curiouser and curiouser.

"Professor, you've provided a wealth of information and I thank you," I said.

"Anytime, Duffy. You take care now."

LEXI was pissed. After agreeing to meet with her, her FBI contact just used the occasion to hit on her.

"Just dinner," he said, "nothing more."

"Screw dinner. You said you had some information about the city treasury heist!"

"Oh yeah, that." he said. "The guy who pulled the job, Lou Petrelli I think his name was … well, he's dead. Got shanked at Attica about ten years ago."

Shame on me, Lexi thought, for believing I'd get anything out of a fed. She stood up to leave.

"Hey, wait, Lexi. You haven't finished your drink."

"Yes, I have," she said and she dumped what was left of it in his lap.

CHAPTER NINETEEN

I GOT TO Cole's in time to have a beer before Sheila got there. Donnie Joe was in exceptionally good spirits, so much so he bought me the beer.

"What happened, DJ?" I asked. "Your ship come in?"

"Sort of," he said, "Bonaventure won and covered. I had them with the points and on the money line."

"Nice score," I said. I'd forgotten how much Donnie Joe liked to bet on sports.

But I was too intent on digesting what Professor Coppola had told me to be much interested in Donnie Joe's wagers. Some of the pieces were fitting together but the picture of this puzzling quest was still unclear. I had no doubt that not all of the money that was turned in from the robbery was really all of the money taken in the robbery. Any doubt I did have was dispelled by the interest of a wise guy in Central Terminal and my certainty that the city treasurer had been bought off with a bribe – a bribe big enough to buy a big house in Florida. Yet, only the word of a now deceased old man put the money in the terminal.

I was still mulling things over when I was alerted to Sheila's arrival by all the male heads in the place turning to watch her come in. She smiled and kissed me on the cheek as she took the stool next to me. Sheila didn't have to voice her order. Donnie Joe was already mixing it. And she had all her blouse buttons buttoned, thank goodness.

"You were very dramatic on the phone, Coe. You said you wanted to tell me something."

"I do have something to tell you, Sheila, but I'm hoping what I have to say can be held in strict confidence."

DJ placed the cosmo in front of her. She took a sip and smiled at him.

"Perfect, Donald, as always."

Then she turned to me.

"We haven't known each other long, Coe, but I think we know each other fairly well. Unless there is something that puts me or my mother in danger, I assure you I can keep a secret."

Convinced I could trust her, I spent the next ten minutes telling her the tale of terminal treasure.

"Now you tell me some wise guy shows up at your office wanting information on the terminal and that makes me think that not only are we onto something but that someone else might be looking for the same thing."

Sheila gave me that fill-your-loins-with-lust stare and sipped her drink again.

"Thank you for being up front with me, Coe," she said. "I spoke to my mother after you called to see if she had any thoughts on the sudden interest in an abandoned building no cared too much about in the past.

"She related a tale quite similar to that which you just spoke of - of missing cash, stashed away in a dark corner of the city. But she assured me that she **was** in a position to know about such things and that it was all a fantasy created by an over-zealous newspaper man."

"Marshall Brown," I said.

"Yes, that was the name she mentioned. She did tell me how angry the upper echelons of her associates were when they learned of the robbery. They knew that a crime so bold could damage the delicate balance between them and the city administration. For a time, they considered eliminating the robber but dismissed the idea when the FBI came to town."

"So, it's all a fantasy and I've been running around the city on a wild goose chase then?" I said.

"It would appear so, Coe. I'm sorry."

"I appreciate your input, Sheila," I said. "You and your mother have been a valuable resource." I knew there was no benefit and perhaps a liability, in suggesting her mother might be wrong.

She kissed my cheek again and we made small talk for an hour. She finished her drink and refused the refill I offered. She rose, turning heads again.

"I'm afraid I have to go. I'm having dinner with mother. I could call her if you'd care to join us."

"Thanks, but no. I am meeting someone in a bit. Please tell her how much I appreciate all that she shared with me"

"I shall, Coe, and I'm sorry to be the bearer of such bad news."

"No sweat, Sheila. You've been great."

She almost reached the door when a thought hit me.

"Sheila, did your mother know that name of the dirt ball that came to your office?"

"She knew in an instant," Sheila said. "She said he was a, and I quote – despicable piece of shit, a hanger-on, a nobody named Petrelli. She told me to let her know if he caused me any trouble.

"But I'm meeting mother for dinner and must be going."

She hugged me and was out the door.

Lexi pulled up promptly at six. I slid into the jeep and she just put it in gear and sped away from the curb. We were heading south on Elmwood a little faster than the speed limit, about twenty miles per hour faster.

"I'm assuming you are having a bad day," I said as we jerked to a stop at a light.

"Fucking Feebies," she said. "I should have known better than to think they'd give anything up."

"Well, if you don't kill us in the next ten minutes, I might have something of interest."

She made a hard right on to Lafayette and pulled up to curb.

"Spill."

I gave her details of my conversation with Professor Coppola and her eyes started to widen.

"I think we can reasonably assume that there is money around here somewhere," I said. I got a very hard punch on the arm for that.

"What the hell?"

"It took a conversation with a teacher to convince you of what I told you right at the beginning," she said.

"It put things in context," I said. "You stated a hunch. He gave me the background to support that hunch. Stop punching me, will you?"

Lexi let a hint of a grin sneak on to her mouth.

"Did you get anything from your FBI dude?" I said.

"Nothing except the name of the perp who pulled the heist and the fact that prison was extremely hazardous to his health."

"And the name?" I said.

"Petrelli. He got knifed at Attica a while back and is no longer of this world."

Petrelli, I thought. The pieces of the puzzle were fitting together and although I still couldn't see the picture but things were getting more interesting. I tried to lighten Lexi's mood a bit before springing this new connection on her.

"Let's go over to the hospital and check on Moses," I said.

She made a quick U-turn and we headed east. I wondered if Lexi might be in training for a road race. We made it to the hospital in something close to a land speed record. We needn't have bothered. We spoke to the charge nurse in ICU and she didn't have good news.

"He should have been coming out the coma by now," she said. "If he doesn't awaken soon, the damage might be irreversible. The swelling should have resolved itself by now but we'll give it a few more days and see what develops."

We thanked her and started to leave but she stopped us.

"I have a favor to ask," she said. "We still have his clothes here and they could use a good cleaning. Could I ask you to take them?"

"Sure," I said. "Glad to."

The nurse ducked into a room and saw the patient's belongings bag. On the floor next to the bag was a piece of paper and an odd looking key. She figured it must have fallen out of the bag so she put them in with the dirty clothes.

She brought the bag out to us and even wrapped in the plastic bag, I could understand why she was anxious to be rid of it. They weren't just ripe, they were rotting.

The nurse thanked us thanked us and we went back to the jeep. We passed a dumpster on the way.

"I'm going to toss these," I said. "They stink."

"Don't," Lexi said. "I'll take them home and wash them. They're all Moses has."

"Hell, we could buy him new duds, some that don't make your eyes water."

"We could do that too," she said, "but I'll take care of these."

When we were in the jeep, I gave her the news about the Petrelli connection.

"This guy comes in to see Ms. McCartan," I said, "and starts ogling her before he tells her she inherited her mother's tits."

"What?" Lexi said. "He actually said that?"

"I am quoting from Ms. McCartan's description."

"And?"

"And what?"

"And did she inherit her mother's tits?"

"What kind of question is that?" I asked.

"The kind that's going to get you a punch if you don't answer."

"Where are you going with this?"

"Look Romeo. I was out in front of Cole's to see who you were going to meet. I expected some schoolmarm-looking chick with thick glasses and a bun. Instead, I see what appears to be a runway model coming out. Now I know you met her mother and I know you've seen her more than twice and I know you fancy yourself to be a connoisseur of women's breasts. So, I ask again, did she get them from her mother?"

I sensed a punch coming regardless of my answer.

"Yep, she sure did."

Lexi wound up but didn't punch me.

"Honesty is your best policy, Coe."

"But you've distracted from what I was going to tell you. What do you think this mook's name was?"

"Guido?"

"Petrelli," I said. "His name was Petrelli."

Then she punched me.

"No way!"

"Way," I said. "So now we know all the money wasn't recovered. We know the guy who stole the money is gone but someone with the same last name is snooping around and we know that the city treasurer was probably involved."

"Damn, Coe, you're a sleuthing genius. What's next?"

"I want to call my old man down in Florida and then I think it's time we settled some scores for our pal Moses."

That brought another hint of a grin to her face.

CHAPTER TWENTY

"Yeah, dad. The guy's name is Lenny Carlyle. He lives over in the Lauderdale area."

I filled my father in on what I was looking for and where he could find it. Eddie Murray was still down there with him so I figured between the two of them they could do a pretty fair job of convincing Mr. Carlyle to tell them what they wanted to know.

"Just let him know no one is interested in prosecuting him. I just want to know how much money is roaming around. If he knows where it is, that would be a big plus."

I could sense my father's excitement piquing on the other end of the phone.

"Sure," I told him before we hung up. "You can break something of his if you want to." That got a laugh out of my old man.

"Have you got a plan for tonight or are we just going to wing it?" Lexi asked.

"I've got something in mind," I said, "but I'm wondering if you have any equipment left over from your cop days?"

"Hell yeah, I do. But I'm not down with shooting anyone."

"No," I said, "no shooting. I was thinking more of the billy club kind of equipment."

"I think I have a few things that might interest you."

"Can we stop by the army surplus store?" I said. "I need to get some make-up."

She looked at me with a funny look but twenty minutes later we were pulling off the Thruway at the Hamburg Street exit. It was another minute to the store. We got there just as the manager was getting ready to close.

"Just so you know," he said, "you don't have a lot of time to browse. I'm getting ready to lock up so if you know what you want I'll take care of it."

"Yep," I said, "I just want some camouflage face stick."

The guy pointed to a rack near the register and we were back in the jeep as the he was turning off the lights.

"What's next?" Lexi asked.

"I need a truncheon."

"You mean a billy?" she said, smiling.

"Yeah, but I wanted to dazzle you with my command of the language."

"Your days of dazzling me are over, smart ass." But she was still smiling.

We pulled up to her building on Ellicott Street. It had once been a warehouse but had been developed by a friend of mine into some pretty cool apartments. I started to exit the jeep but she stopped me before my foot hit the pavement.

"Wait here."

She went into the building and was out in five minutes. It looked like she was empty handed.

"Your stock diminished?" I asked.

"Hardly," was all she said as she told me to get out of the jeep. She had an object in her hand about the size of a flashlight.

"Darlin'," I said, "you do know I intend to visit mayhem on someone tonight, not check their ID, right?"

Lexi flicked her wrist and the object extended almost to the sidewalk.

"Whoa," I said, "what the hell is that?"

"It's called an expandable baton. It's made out of stainless steel and aluminum. The steel is for strength and the aluminum makes it lighter. I guarantee it will visit all the mayhem you wish to bring."

Lexi put the tip against the sidewalk and pushed it back to flashlight size.

"As you can see, it's easily concealable and will break bones if used properly."

She handed it to me and after a couple of tries, I mastered the wrist flick to extend the baton. This would do very nicely, I thought.

We got back in the jeep but she hesitated.

"Wait a minute," she said. "I've got to get rid of these foul-smelling clothes."

"Not just yet," I told her. "Let's head over to Richmond Avenue."

"Then open your window," she said. "I'll never get the smell out of this vehicle as it is."

The drive didn't take long, they rarely did with Lexi driving, but I froze my ass off nonetheless with the windows open. We pulled up in front of the Culhane house and she started to get out of the jeep.

"No. Wait here."

"Oh, you are going to punish me for not letting you come up to my place?"

"No, Lexi, I'm not punishing you," I said, walking around to the back of the jeep. "I'm saving you. I'm going to put these clothes on in the back yard."

"You are going to wear those nasty things?" she said.

"Yep. I'm going fishing tonight and I need the right bait."

I think she caught on.

"Well, you sit in the back seat if you are wearing those clothes. It's bad enough I have to smell them at all but I'm not going to have them sitting next to me."

I gave her a bow, took the bag, and headed down the driveway. The clothes weren't a perfect fit but then they weren't a perfect fit for Moses either. I went back to the jeep and had Lexi throw me the camo stick. I applied it to my face and hands to hide my whiteness. I stepped back and had Lexi look me over.

"There some white showing below the pant legs," she noticed. After coloring my legs, she gave me another look and then a thumbs up.

"Are you sure you can't just run alongside the jeep?" she said, wrinkling her nose. "You smell terrible."

I climbed in the back of the jeep, the way back of the jeep.

"This is the best I can do," I told her. "Remember, I've got to be in fighting trim when I we get there."

As we drove to the terminal, I wondered how Moses could make it through a Buffalo winter dressed like this. Spring wasn't too far off and it was still in the upper thirties. The air coming through the windows chilled me to the bone.

When we got to Memorial Drive, Lexi pulled to the curb.

"Okay, what's the play?"

"Let's go around the back on Curtiss Street. No lights. I'll take a little stroll and see if I can generate some interest."

"When do I get to play?" she asked.

"You should be able to hear a ruckus if I make contact. Then you ride in to rescue me."

"Again?" She wasn't smiling this time.

As we drove up Memorial to Newton Street, I noticed a dark car parked under the terminal marque.

"Looks like someone else is here," I said.

"Want to abort?"

"No, let's take a look first. I'll decide after we see who's here."

Lexi turned off her lights and made the right on to Newton. We passed alongside the tower and stopped at Curtiss, near the baggage house. I listened for a few minutes. I heard some voices and smelled wood burning so I knew there were fish in the pond. I didn't yet know how many. After making sure the baton was secure in the belt behind my back, I pulled the Dodger hat down low over my eyes and I started a slow shuffle imitating Moses as close as I could. As I came around the building, I saw about a dozen people standing around a fire in a steel barrel. Off to one side I saw a guy in a topcoat talking to a couple of guys who looked like they might have played for the Buffalo Bills. I decided they were my targets. I kept on with my slow shuffle with my head down drifting over toward the group of three. A thought struck me as I headed toward them. What if someone had a gun? We hadn't seen one in our first foray at the terminal so I hadn't prepared for one but the well-dressed guy now present was a wild card. I closed in to within about twenty yards before anyone paid attention to me.

"What the fuck?" one of the big guys said. "I thought we took care of ya' tired old ass."

The guy in the topcoat looked spooked but he kept doling out some cash to the other big guy. I veered off to the right to make it appear I was trying to avoid the trio and the guy with the mouth took the bait. He left the other two and came at me.

"I told you, old man, not to bring that tired ass around here no more. This here is our turf now."

With that, he closed on me quickly expecting to beat the shit out of a tired old man. But I had my hand behind my back gripping the baton. I pulled it out and snapped my wrist, extending the wand to its full length. I swiped it at the outside of his left knee and he stumbled, momentarily stunned. Before he could react, I gave him a straight kick to the balls and doubled him over. I brought my knee up hoping to break his jaw but he moved slightly and I got him flush on the nose. His head snapped back and I gave him another straight kick that put him on his back. That got the attention of the other two guys. The topcoat guy took off like a shot, dropping a wad of cash on the ground. The other big guy made the mistake of looking at all that money, giving me a chance to poke the steel rod into his stomach before slamming it down across his collarbone. When I was a ballplayer I could always tell when I connected because I could feel the impact all way up to my shoulders. I can't say I had that feeling this time, but I did get some satisfaction out of the cracking sound of the steel on bone. But the guy kept coming. I have to give him credit for balls, if not brains. He stopped though when the rod made contact with his kneecap. He screamed and went to the ground, not too far from his buddy. I got between them and bent down so they could hear me.

"The next time I hear of anyone fucking with my friend Moses or anyone else in this area, I'm coming back here but I won't be bringing this rod. I'll be bringing a Glock and someone is going home in a bag. You two assholes hear me?"

The first guy was trying to talk through the blood pouring from his nose and pooling in his mouth. He said something that sounded like "fuck you." He obviously had not learned so I gave him another lesson. I gave him a smack with the billy just below his knee. If I didn't break his tibia, I damaged it enough that he would need help getting home that night.

I looked at the other guy, writhing on the ground.

"I hope you learn faster than you friend here."

He waved his hands in surrender. While he laid there, I took out my cell phone and took a picture of the soles of his Timberland boots. The other mooks by the fire hadn't moved. I didn't know what their collective story was but as long as they didn't look or act threatening, I paid little attention to them. I set about picking up all the cash that was on the ground and saw a lot of hundred dollar bills. This would be a nice score but I wondered what the top coat guy was trying to buy. I picked about twenty bills and started back toward Curtiss Street, wondering all the while what happened to my back up. When I got around the building, the jeep was gone.

CHAPTER TWENTY–ONE

I PANICKED. I had stuffed the cash into every available pocket and ran around the building to the main entrance. There was the jeep in front of the other car I'd seen but no Lexi.

"Lexi! Where are you Lexi?"

She stepped around from behind the jeep, waving and smiling.

What the hell? I thought.

I ran up to the jeep and saw the reason for the smile. Topcoat guy was on his knees next to the door of the car. He was bleeding profusely from the mouth and his wallet and its contents were spread out on the ground.

"I thought you were going to backstop me," I said.

"You had the situation under control," she said, "but I saw this asshole bolting so I couldn't let you have all the fun. Meet Max Petrelli, the guy who still doesn't know how to speak to women."

"What happened?"

"I told him to identify himself and he called me a bitch."

I looked at the guy and shook my head. Lexi had either punched him or hit him with something. Whatever it was, his teeth were cracked and his lips split.

"You've probably come to the conclusion that was a mistake, right Max?"

He looked up at me and snarled something unintelligible.

"What is it with these assholes, Lexi? The guy back there gave me the same attitude." As I was talking, I swung the baton down on his shoulder and heard the collarbone crack. Max went down on his side.

"If I hear you ever say a fucking word to Sheila McCartan again… any word at all and I'll be back and we'll chat again."

"You're pretty good with that thing," Lexi said. "But don't get any ideas. You can't keep it."

We got into the jeep and drove casually down the driveway to Memorial. But casually only lasts so long after the adrenalin rush of combat. Heading west toward downtown, we couldn't stop talking about what we'd just done.

"I forgot how much I like this shit," Lexi said. "Damn, I missed the rush."

"You're going to like it a lot more when I count all this," I said, taking the money out of my pockets.

"Where the hell did you get that?" she said.

"That Petrelli asshole was giving it to the dudes I took down. When the shit hit the fan, so did the cash. It didn't seem right to leave it there, tempting all those people to do bad things with it."

Lexi waited until we got to Washington Street and pulled over in front St. Michael's Church. I continued to count.

"Twenty-seven hundred in big bills and about two hundred and forty in the small bills," I said.

"Good," she said. "Now get out of those smelly clothes. You're going to have to pay to get my car detailed after stinking it up."

"You're just trying to get me naked, aren't you?" I smiled.

"If I wanted you naked, all I need to do is ask and you'd be falling all over yourself to strip."

"Touché."

"Should we just throw these nasty duds out?" I said. "We can buy Moses something more suitable with the cash."

"No, we'll wash them," she said. "They belong to Moses and we shouldn't get rid of them without his say-so."

"Gotcha. There's a washer and dryer at the Culhane place. I'll throw them in tonight. But now, I want a beer. You up for one?"

"I could use a cold one but seriously, you need to get out of those clothes."

We stopped at a 7-Eleven on Elmwood and got a six pack before heading up to Richmond Avenue.

"You want to take your three beers home or would you like to come in while I shower?" I said.

"I'll come in for a while but I'm not showering with you," she smiled.

"I can live with that."

We pulled up in front of the house and I let her in. Then I went around back to retrieve my own clothes from the back hall. Fifteen minutes and a whole lot of scrubbing later, I felt and smelled human again. I was still toweling off my hair when I walked into the living room thinking lusty thoughts. There was the object of my affection, lying back on the couch, her legs splayed wide open and… snoring to beat the band. Half a beer was on the table and she was sound asleep.

Another missed opportunity, I thought. Story of my life.

I got a blanket from the bedroom and realigned her legs to cover her before going back to throw the filthy rags Moses called clothes into the washer. I crawled into bed and felt the crash from the spent adrenalin coming on. All in all, it wasn't a bad night.

I woke up to find the blanket that covered Lexi neatly folded on the couch. On top of it was a note: "You did good tonight. Call me." Ah, Lexi, so economical with words. But she did take her two remaining beers.

I went back to the laundry room to throw Moses's clothes in the dryer. I took them out of the washer and heard a metallic clank. At the bottom of the washer was something that looked like a key. I took it out and looked at it more closely. It was nothing like any key I'd seen before; it had a cylindrical stem about three inches long that had an odd shaped end. It looked like one of the old jailer keys from the cowboy movies my father used to watch. I checked the other pockets for anything else I might have mistakenly washed but found only a faded slip of paper with some smeared writing on it. I did notice that the washing machine appeared to have caused the cuffs of the pants to fray a little more than they were.

Maybe washing these old things wasn't such a great idea, I thought.

I put the clothes in the dryer and turned the setting to "cool," hoping I wouldn't shrink them much. I dressed and put the strange key in my pocket. Then I hustled up to Elmwood Avenue and breakfast at Pano's. There were some drawbacks about Buffalo, winter being prime among them, but no one could ever complain about the quality and variety of the restaurants. Breakfast at Pano's was a must for natives and visitors. I couldn't figure out which I was at the moment but the omelet before me told me it didn't matter. I was almost finished eating when the phone rang. I answered but didn't have time to say anything.

"Your father call yet?"

"Not yet, Lexi," I said. "You know I'd call you if he did."

"I suppose. I just get antsy waiting. Where are you now?"

"I am just finishing breakfast."

"At Pano's?"

"Well, yes, I'm at Pano's. How did you know?"

"Because I'm at the curb outside. You always loved Pano's and, Coe Duffy, you are a creature of habit."

This girl would have made a great detective, I thought, if only I hadn't screwed that up for her.

I paid, tipped handsomely with my newfound wealth, and joined Lexi in the jeep.

"What do we do today?" she said.

I told her about the key I found and how I found it.

"Strange he should just have it in his pocket, isn't it?" she asked.

"Did you find anything else?" Lexi said.

"Just a scrap of paper that had gone through the wash. It had some writing on it but the water had blurred it. I put it on the stove when I left the house. Maybe when it dries out a little, we'll see what it has on it."

Lexi took out her phone and called the hospital to get a status report on Moses.

"No change," she said. "He's still in a coma."

She put her phone away and looked at me.

"Any ideas?"

"A couple, actually," I said. "There was an old Russian we called on one time to open a small safe we found in a storeroom in City

Hall. Kulavich was his name - Mikhail Kulavich. He was a locksmith and an expert in antique locks."

"Did he get the safe open?" Lexi asked.

"He did. It took him about five minutes but he got it open. Nothing inside but some old deeds and papers."

Lexi was fiddling with her phone while I talked. She held it up for me to see.

"Is this the name?"

"Yeah, that's it. Let's go see him and find out what this key might mean."

The address for Kulavich Locksmiths was on South Park Avenue in South Buffalo.

It took us twenty minutes to get to there. We pulled up in front of a rundown building with a weather-beaten sign indicating we were in the right place. We tried the door but it was locked. I pushed a button on the door jamb and a voice came through some kind of speaker.

"Can I help you?" a voice said.

"Yes, Mr. Kulavich. I'm Coe Duffy. I hired you once for a job in the mayor's office."

"Oh yes, Mr. Duffy! I remember. What can I do for you this time? Another safe to crack?" I heard him chuckle a bit.

"Nothing quite so dramatic," I said. "I found an old key that doesn't look like anything I've ever seen before and I was hoping you might help us out."

A buzzer rang and the door lock clicked and we entered a dimly lit space. I could see the old Russian sitting behind a small table. A goose neck lamp brightened the surface in front of him. As we approached, he swept some tools and locks off the table into a box on his lap. He put the box on the floor and looked up for the first time.

"It is nice to see you again," he said with a smile, "and this must be Mrs. Duffy?"

"No sir," Lexi answered quickly. "Not by a long shot. I'm his business partner Lexi Crane."

"It is nice to meet you also," Kulavich said. "Now what have you brought me?"

I took the key out of my pocket and laid it on the table. He took off his glasses and picked up a magnifying glass. He studied the key for all of five minutes, never taking his eyes off of it. Finally, he put down the magnifier and put his spectacles back on.

"Where did you get this, if I might ask?"

"It belongs to a friend who asked us to find out its origin," I said.

"This key is very old, like me," he said with a laugh. "It is actually even older than I am. This type of key and the lock it would open haven't been made for more than a century. This circular barrel would slide into a padlock and the teeth would engage."

"Would it be possible for such a key to open a lock or a door in Central Terminal?" Lexi asked.

"Oh no," he said. "That building was built in the 1920s. Locks and keys like this were used long before the terminal was built. It isn't likely such a lock would be installed in such a new building."

The old man kept turning the key in his hand and looking at it like it was some sort of treasure.

"You wouldn't be willing to part with this key, would you? I could pay you for it."

"I'm sorry, Mr. Kulavich, it is not my property. I'm just trying to help the owner get some idea about its origins."

I held my hand out to retake possession. The old Russian took a while but finally placed it in my palm.

"If your friend has no further use for the key, might I ask that you consider giving it to me?"

"Of course," I said. "If he doesn't want it, it's yours. Thanks for your help. Do I owe you anything?"

"No, sir, you don't owe me a thing. Good day to you both."

We walked out of the shop and got back in the jeep.

"Did you find that as weird as I did?" Lexi asked.

"Hell yeah. For a key that doesn't open anything the guy sure was attached to it."

She started the jeep.

"Where to?"

"It's almost lunch time. I have an old friend out here with a bar. Let's stop and see him."

"Do all your friends own, work in, or frequent bars?" she said.

"Well, I do know one very attractive friend who works at the Historical Society," I said, knowing that was going to get me a punch. And it did.

Dennis Talty and I went all the way back to the playground days when he pitched and I caught but I hadn't seen him in twenty years or so. I heard he bought a neighborhood saloon on the city's south side, not far from the sandlots we used to wear out. We pulled up in front and walked in. If the dictionary had a listing for "neighborhood saloon," it would have a picture of Talty's as an illustration. The place was adorned with Irish paraphernalia, with pictures of various denizens of the pub, an American flag, and a corner of the cramped barroom cleared away for a microphone stand. A sound mixer sitting on a ledge near the corner looked strangely out of place. We took a couple of stools at the bar and I asked the bartender if Dennis was around.

"Hell, man, he's always around," he said. "He's in the back. You want me to get him?"

"Sure, but can we get a couple of Buds first?"

"That's what I'm here for, friend," he said, going into a cooler and pulling out a of couple bottles. "I'll be right back."

He wasn't gone two minutes when he returned with my old friend.

"As I live and breathe," Dennis said," It's Coe-goddamn-Duffy!'

I held my hand out in greeting but he brushed passed it and gave me a bear hug.

"How the fuck are you?" he said, slapping me on the shoulder. I winced a little.

"Still got the bum shoulder?" he asked.

"Not exactly 'still'," I said. "It's the shoulder my friend here keeps punching."

"Lexi, gimme a kiss. It's been way too long."

That surprised me. How did Dennis know Lexi and why had it been too long and why didn't she tell me she knew Talty?

Dennis didn't wait for me to ask.

"Lexi is one of the biggest draws in the place," he said, "at least she was. We haven't seen her in a while."

My face must have told Dennis I had nary a clue about what he was talking about.

"She hasn't told you?" he said. "Lexi sings here on my open mike nights. The people love her."

I had been away too long. I had no idea Lexi could sing.

Dennis pointed to a couple of plaques hanging behind the register.

"We've been voted the best open mike night in the city two years in a row," he said. "First Monday of the month. We really pack them in and Lexi is one of the reasons."

"You sing?" I asked.

"Hell yeah, she sings," Dennis answered for her. "She has a beautiful voice. Sounds like Carole King."

Lexi returned my stare.

"What? Did you think I'd just sit around waiting for your sorry ass to return? I have a life, you know."

"It's just a side of you I never knew existed."

"There's a lot about me you don't know, Coe." She wasn't smiling and I took this as a bad sign.

"Lexi, sing something now," Dennis said. "Let this asshole know what kind of talent you are."

"Come on, Dennis," she said. "There's no music."

"You don't need music with that voice. Please? Let Coe know what he's been missing."

I think that last exhortation struck a respondent chord and Lexi put down her beer and walked to the microphone. The six other patrons in the place stopped their conversations and watched her. Lexi started clapping her hands to set the rhythm and sang.

"Stayed in bed all mornin' just to pass the time There's somethin' wrong here, there can be no denyin'. One of us is changin', or maybe we've just stopped tryin'…"

Lexi continued in a beautiful a capella rendition of one of the most heartbreaking songs in any American songbook. Her eyes never left mine as she sang.

"There'll be good times again for me and you. But we just can't stay together, don't you feel it, too? Still I'm glad for what we had and how I once loved you …"

I had to get out of there before anyone saw my tears welling up. There wasn't a sound in the place until she finished then the prolonged applause came. There weren't many people but they sure as hell were enthusiastic. I headed for the sign designating the men's room before she or anyone else got a look at me. I splashed some water on my eyes. Lexi was killing me.

When I came back she was talking to Dennis and sipping her beer.

"What did I tell you, Coe? Can she sing or what?"

"She sure can, Dennis. She sure as hell can."

Dennis and I talked about old times for half an hour, boring Lexi to tears, I'm sure. When we finished our beer, I stood.

"Dennis, we have to run but I promise I'll be back," I said.

"Who gives a shit if you come back, Coe? Just bring Lexi."

I think Dennis was only half kidding.

We got in the jeep but she didn't start it up.

"What the fuck?" I said. "Why didn't you tell me you knew Dennis, that you knew Talty's, that you could sing?"

"You never asked, Coe. You came back here, thinking it would be like it was in the old days. You never asked me about my life, about what I was doing, anything about me. But then again, it's always about you.

"Well, I'm doing pretty goddamned good, Coe. I have a good

life here. Not a great one but a good one. And don't start asking questions about me now. You didn't want to know before so don't pretend you want to know now."

We sat silently for a minute, just staring out the window.

"You have an extraordinary voice," I said, finally.

"Thanks."

"But your song selection leaves something to desired."

"Dennis likes Carole King."

"So, you sang that for Dennis?"

She stared at me.

"Partly. What do we do now, asshole?"

"Do you have our terminal exploring gear?"

"In the back," she said.

"Let's go meet my friend Louis."

CHAPTER TWENTY-TWO

W<small>E PULLED UP</small> under the terminal marquee and I pried our way into the cavernous lobby. I switched the headlamp on and led the way through the big room to the stairs at the far end.

"Louis! Hey, Louis! It's your friend Coe Duffy!" I yelled. My voice echoed off the stone walls and yielded to quiet. Lexi had her flashlight jerking around the lobby.

"This must have been some building," she said. "This is amazing."

I was about to holler for Louis again when I heard his voice from the shadows.

"Coe, is that you?"

"Yes, Louis, it's me and my friend, Lexi."

Louis appeared from the shadows opposite where I was looking for him.

"Coe, I's real sorry 'bout hitting you with that board," he said.

"I know you are, Louis. All is forgiven. Can you come over here and look at something we found in Moses's clothes?"

Louis shuffled over and bowed to Lexi. I was always amazed at how life had dealt people like Louis such a shitty hand but how strongly guys like him clung to the manners they'd been taught. I knew a lot of well-off people who should have learned that lesson.

"Have you ever seen this, Louis?" I said, holding the old key in my palm.

He studied it closely for a minute.

"Can I hold it, Coe?"

"Sure, Louis. Take a good look." I handed it to him and he held it up to the light coming from my headlamp. His eyes started to tear up.

"I never seen this here key, Coe, but my grandpappy had one like it."

That piqued my interest.

"Do you know where he got the key, Louis?"

"Yessir, I do. He told me he got it out of a lock that held his daddy in chains. He had that lock too. Said he was gonna keep it to remind him how tough his daddy had it."

"You mean your great granddad was a slave, Louis."

"I suppose he was, Mr. Coe. I didn't know him none but my granddaddy said he was a fine, strong man."

"I bet he was, Louis. I bet he was."

He handed back the key and I handed him a five-dollar bill. He took it with a bow and a mumbled thanks.

"You seen my friend Moses?" he asked.

Lexi answered him.

"We were up to see him, Louis, but he's still sleep. We'll go back soon and if he's awake we'll tell him his friend Louis is asking about him."

"That'd be right kindly of you, ma'am."

"Louis, did you ever see anything here in the terminal that looked like it could be opened with a key like this?" I said.

"No sir, I never seen anything like this. The lock my granddaddy had was real old; older than anything I ever seen in here."

"Thanks, Louis. We'll be heading out. You take care of yourself, okay?"

"I'll surely try, sir, and thank you for your kindness."

Two minutes later we were outside standing next to the jeep. Two of the neighborhood hoods were watching us from Memorial Drive. I waved them over to us. As they approached, Lexi let her leather jacket open to reveal the Glock on her belt. An ounce of prevention, someone once said.

"I want you guys to spread the word," I said. "I don't want anyone touching that old man in the terminal, you understand? No one, no how."

One of the guys looked like he didn't take me seriously. I snatched the baton from the back of my belt and snapped it open.

"My friend and I don't give a rat's ass about anything you punks are up to here," I said, firmly. "But one hair on that old man's head get mussed and I'm coming back here and rain a world of hurt down on your heads."

"You be a tough guy with that stick but I bet you ain't shit without it," the punk said. So, I dropped the baton.

"You want to see what I am without it? Bring it."

I knew what the asshole would do so I bent my knees and brought my ass down into almost my catcher's crouch. The guy rushed me as I knew he would. He was about two feet away when I exploded his world. I sprung out of my crouch, bringing my arms inside his. The heels of both my palms drove into his shoulders. If I wanted to kill him, I would have struck the throat. As it was, the force from my hands on his clavicles was enough. I thought I heard one side pop and hoped I'd broken the other collarbone. He didn't even scream. He just flew backwards and moaned loudly.

I looked at his pal to see if he was a threat. He wasn't. He was already backing away.

"Good," I said. "at least one of you has some intelligence. If any one of your posse needs any more proof, just bring them around when I'm here. And after I kick their asses, my friend will call her friends."

"I'll bring the wrath of the Buffalo Police Department down on your asses," Lexi added. "There will be so many cops crawling around this place your nightmares will be in blue."

The standing thug spoke.

"What's that old dude to you?"

"He's a long lost relative of mine from the old country," I said. "Czechoslovakia."

I don't know why, but the dude shook his head as if to say "now, I get it."

"We're clear, right? I leave you alone and you leave him alone. You hurt him and I will hurt you."

We got in the jeep and drove off, heading back toward downtown.

"That was a nice move back there," Lexi said. "You didn't learn that catching in the Mexican League."

"I was working for this guy who spent time in the Dutch army," I said. "He needed me to act as the bouncer some times. He taught me Muay Thai, Thai boxing. That little maneuver is known as a *hanuman dak han*."

"That sure as hell was no boxing move I saw."

"Well, Thai boxing is a little different than ours. It is known as the art of eight limbs – two fists, elbows, knees, and shins. You should try it sometime."

Lexi just smiled.

"What now?" she said. "It seems like we're learning a lot but what we're learning isn't getting us any closer to what we're looking for."

"Not yet it isn't but knowledge is power."

"Spare me the fortune cookie philosophy," she said. "We might be running out of time."

"Let's get some food and go over to Richmond Avenue and talk through what we've found."

Lexi called Pano's and ordered some souvlaki. Fifteen minutes later, I was in and out of the restaurant and we pulled up in front of the Culhane house. We sat at the dining room table and between bites, took stock of what we knew and what we didn't.

"We're pretty sure that not all of the money taken in the City Hall robbery was reported," she said.

"We're looking at Central Terminal as the hiding place for the money but we have a key that probably doesn't match anything in that building."

"That key might not mean anything at all," Lexi said. "It could just be the lone possession of an old homeless guy."

"We also know that a guy with the same last name of the thief is looking for the same thing we are, in the same place," I said, "and that he needs a dentist."

That got a laugh out of her. I liked when she laughed and liked it more when I could make her laugh. But her mood faded as we ate.

"We really don't have shit," she said. "There wasn't anything else in Moses' pants with the key, right?"

"Just the key," I said. "No wait. There was a piece of paper. It went through the wash but there was a little bit of writing that was still legible. I left it on the dryer."

I got up from the table and went into the laundry room. The slip of paper was right where I'd left it. I brought it back and put it in front of Lexi.

"Can you make anything out?"

She smoothed out the wrinkled paper.

"What's this?" she said, point to some letters.

"Em, eye, something …" I could see an 'M' and an 'I' but the rest was too blurred.

Lexi looked at it then held it up to the light.

"It looks like 'm-i-c-h," she said.

I was sounding it out, trying to make some sense of it.

"Mich …Michigan?"

"Could be," she said. "Michigan what?'

"Hell, Lexi, these guys hung at the train terminal. Trains coming from Michigan? Trains going to Michigan?"

"How can we find out?" she said.

"Find out what?"

"What the Michigan connection might be, Coe."

This woman sure knew how to ruin a nice meal. I could sense another call to Sheila McCartan in my future. We finished eating and she helped me dispose of the trash.

"Where you going now?" I asked.

"To the gym. I need to work off some of this frustration."

"Can I come? I could use a little sweat myself."

"I guess so. Grab your gear."

My "gear" consisted of an old Reynosa Broncos T-shirt, a pair of swim trunks, and my beat-up Adidas. It was only a ten-minute ride until we pulled up in front of KC Fitness, Lexi's gym. We went in and a burly redheaded guy grabbed Lexi in a bear hug.

"You brought a friend," he said, extending his hand. "I'm Kevin."

"Nice to meet you, Kevin. I'm Coe."

"You both here to box?" Kevin said.

"Not today," Lexi said. "Coe was showing me some Muay Thai strikes. Do you do that here?"

"You should know better than to ask. Of course, we do."

Kevin saw the clothes in my hand and led the way to the men's locker room.

"*Muay Thai* is some pretty heavy stuff. Are you ex-military?"

"Sort of," I said. "But I started learning while I was working in Mexico."

He just nodded and left me to change. When I came out of the locker room, Kevin led us over to Sebastian, his Muay Thai specialist. Seb asked me to show him what I knew so far. I showed him my spinning elbow, and double elbow strikes and I threw in an axe kick just to show off. Seb nodded and gave me ten minutes of technical advice about my leverage and the torque in my kick. Then he showed us an elbow uppercut that I'd never seen before. When the instruction period was over, I got an idea of how little I actually knew about *Muay Thai*. For forty-five minutes, we practiced what he'd demonstrated on the heavy bags. I thought I could kick but when Lexi spun around and whipped her long leg into the bag, it popped in a way I couldn't duplicate. She had speed, grace, and power where as I was merely a blunt instrument. I was dripping with sweat when Kevin approached.

"Looks like you got a good workout, Coe. I hope Sebastian was a help."

"He was great, Kevin, and I appreciate you letting me workout. Do I owe you anything?"

"Just take care of our girl here," he said with a grin.

"Are you kidding?" I said. "She takes care of me."

We got in the jeep. Lexi had a towel in her back seat and handed it to me.

"Don't drip on my sweet upholstery."

I was about to ask her what sweet upholstery but she was smiling.

"That Thai stuff is pretty effective shit," she said, as she drove. "I was doing *Krav Maga* but I think I like this better."

"It might be better suited to what we're doing around the terminal," I said. "I like elbows and knees instead of punches. No broken fingers this way.

"And if I do say so myself, you have some sweet leg whip on you."

"Yeah, that felt good. You might have actually done some good for me, Coe." She was smiling again.

She dropped me off on Richmond and told me to call her if I heard from my father. I didn't bother to tell her I would be calling Sheila again. No sense in spoiling the mood, I thought.

After a shower and a beer, I reclined in bed trying to make a connection that involved Michigan. I fell asleep before I could.

CHAPTER TWENTY-THREE

Aᖴᴛᴇʀ ᴀ sʜᴏᴡᴇʀ and some coffee, I walked to the Historical Society building. Sheila hadn't yet arrived so I busied myself with some of the exhibits. Then, I walked to the back of the building and looked out at the lake and across the expressway to Hoyt Lake in Delaware Park. In spring, I thought, this must be a beautiful site. It didn't look bad even in the gloom of March.

"That's the Japanese Garden," Sheila said, as she came up behind me, "and Mirror Lake."

"I recall that from my stay in City Hall," I said. "A joint effort with our sister city in Japan, I believe."

"You're right. It has undergone some significant renovation in recent years though. Some Japanese landscape architects came over and worked with our folks to create that beautiful space."

"I bet it is something to behold in the spring," I said.

"It certainly is," Sheila said. "We even have a cherry blossom festival. I love to sit back here and take in the scents. It's quite relaxing."

I turned to face her and thought I could sit back here and take in her scent for a while but I didn't think it would be relaxing.

"What can I do for you today, Coe?"

I told her as we walked to her office.

"A key, Michigan, and the terminal," she said. "Quite a puzzle."

"Yes, it is and I'm having trouble trying to connect the dots."

"Can I see the key?" she asked.

I handed it to her. She studied it for a minute and handed it back.

"This is quite old. Given the age of Central Terminal, I doubt that a lock opened by this key would have been in use."

"You are the second person of that opinion," I said.

"Sorry to have validated bad news," she said. "Is there something else I could do?"

"I'm wondering if the Michigan aspect of the puzzle had something to do with trains coming into the terminal," I said. "I can assume that some traffic heading east to and west from New York City passed through here."

"I think you are assuming correctly," she said. "I can probably get some more definitive information about that if you'd like."

"When I say I would like that, Sheila, I am only assuming that I would. I don't know for certain if that will help or not but I guess I'm just trying to assemble as many facts as I can."

"I can call you this afternoon with what I discover. Speaking of which, you could have called me with your request. You didn't have to come all this way."

"I'm not that far away and besides, the view here is worth the walk."

She smiled and said she'd call but even if she did, I wondered if her information might help connect these scattered dots. It was too late for Pano's and too early for Cole's so I headed back to the Culhane abode and spread things out on the dining room table. Lexi's blueprints were still there but I wasn't sure how they were going to help. The layout of the building was discouraging and the new clues weren't helping either. I wondered if this all was going to be a giant waste of time. Then I realized that wasting time was exactly what I'd been doing in Mexico. I spread the scrap of paper from Moses's pants out and looked at it again. We were assuming the visible letters were spelling 'Michigan' but not even that was a sure thing. I kept thinking the key might be the most important clue but I couldn't connect it to anything else we had. I got up, walked around the house, brewed some coffee and went back to the table to survey the pieces again. We think there was money. We think it was in the big building. We have a key that probably had nothing to do with either of the other two. And we had a piece of half-washed paper that might say "Michigan" on it. Which one of these was not like the other? I mused. The words of an old Simon and Garfunkel tune popped into my head:

"…Michigan seems like a dream to me now …"

I slid the slip of paper to the other side of the table. Michigan was too much of a leap for what we had. I could see no connection that made sense. The trouble was nothing else was making sense either.

I got up again and took another circuit around the house. I was about to sit down again when the phone rang. It was my father.

"Hey dad, find anything interesting?"

"Hell yeah, we did. Just like you guessed. The money that was recovered was less than half of what was stolen!"

Less than half, I thought, that meant there was at least two-hundred grand somewhere.

"Christ, that's a bunch of cash. I don't suppose old Lenny knew anything about where it might be, did he?"

"We're pretty certain he was telling the truth when he told us he didn't know."

That sounded ominous.

"You didn't have hurt him, did you?"

The next voice I heard was Murray's.

"Not much. The guy was a pussy, a bean counter; no stomach for pain. The threat was almost enough to make him spill."

The two of them sounded like they had been to Disneyworld instead of getting information from a reluctant witness. They proceeded to tell me about finding Carlyle and explaining what they wanted. Carlyle feigned ignorance, they said, until Mur-man broke one of his fingers. After that, they couldn't shut the guy up. He got fifty thousand dollars to keep his mouth shut about the total take. Petrelli knew the big boys in the mob weren't going to like his play. He figured there would be some heat and he would ultimately take a fall. His plan was to stash the rest of the money and get to it when he got out of jail. He told Carlyle that was his retirement. Carlyle also knew a good thing when he saw it so he bought into the plan. Of course, all he had to do was play it cool about the total take until the investigation blew over.

"He seemed to gloat over the fact that Marshall Brown was dead," my father said. "He called him a nosy bastard and I didn't think it was too polite to speak ill of the dead."

I could see this one coming.

"So, what did that faux pas cost him?"

"Another finger," my father said. "But we broke it on the same hand so he'd still have one good hand."

"You two are the Mother Teresas of collections. And did Mr. Carlyle express his appreciation to you for your restraint?" I said.

Murray jumped in again.

"To the tune of five hundred a piece."

God, these guys were liking this way too much.

"So, what's still out there?" I asked.

"Lenny says the take was nearly six hundred thousand," my father said. That means there's about three hundred grand floating around somewhere."

"You didn't happen to mention that Petrelli was dead, did you?"

"No," my dad said, "were we supposed to?"

"It doesn't matter," I said. "But you're sure he didn't know where the rest of the money is?"

"Oh yeah," Eddie said. "I told him his nose was next and he started crying. Told us he never spoke to Petrelli after he got paid. We threw some clues out about the terminal building but they got no reaction."

All this confirmed the money part of the puzzle but it didn't get me any closer to where we could find it.

"Thanks guys. I don't have any money to pay you but it seems you got your expenses covered."

"Hell yeah," my father said. "We went to Gulfstream and won a couple grand each."

These two guys were like frat boys. What did Vietnam do to them? I wondered.

"Well, behave yourselves on the way home and thanks again."

I hung up and called Lexi.

"You have to come over and hear this," I said. She gave me the wordless goodbye I'd become used to. Some things were getting clearer but not the most important thing. Where the hell did Petrelli hide the money?

When Lexi came in, I couldn't gauge her reaction.

"So, I was right about the money," she said.

"You, Cletus, whoever," I said. "You were right about the money but we are no closer to figuring out where to look for it."

"But there is money," she said.

That was it, I thought. She didn't know whether the money story was true. Now she had confirmation.

"Yes, Lexi. There is money - a whole lot of money. But we still don't know where it is."

"But we must have been right about the terminal. Why else would that Petrelli asshole show up there?"

"He was there because he doesn't know anything more than we do, except for the existence of the money," I said. "But with his brother dead, we're all at a loss for where to look for it."

Lexi moved over to the dining room table.

"Find anything interesting?" she said.

"No, but I might have found something totally uninteresting. I don't think the Michigan thing has any relevance.

"It's a fact without context. What could Michigan possibly have to do with any of this?"

"And you arrived at this conclusion on your own?"

"What's that supposed to mean?"

"You've got some other people involved in our business and I want to know if this is your idea or if it is coming from another source."

I was getting a little pissed. So far, I had my father and Eddie Murray in the picture and Sheila McCartan. I got a lot of information from Lee Coppola and a little from Mikhail Kulavich. What was she getting at?

"I, myself, arrived at that conclusion based on the disparate pieces of the puzzle on the table. We have a key that is too old to have been of use in the terminal. We have a piece of paper that might say 'Michigan' in it. We have confirmation that way more money was stolen than was turned in. I am struggling to piece this together and I can't figure out where Michigan might fit. If it doesn't fit, I am willing to discard it.

"How's my reasoning so far? And as for the people I brought into our business, those people have been giving us some pretty valuable information."

"Especially Sheila, right?" she said.

I should have figured that was where Lexi was headed.

"Actually, Lexi, Sheila not so much," I said. "Your old pal Cletus put you on the scent of the money. Professor Coppola gave me some inkling the money actually existed. My father and his pal verified the information about the money. The key came from Moses' pants along with the scrap of paper."

I released some of the anger, but not all.

"I didn't get much out of Sheila except some of the mob backstory," I said. "But come to think of it, even that's a little more than you've provided so far."

That just blurted out without much thought. Lexi turned away from the table and slapped me hard across the face. I could taste the blood welling up from a cut inside my mouth.

"You ungrateful sonofabitch," she said. "I'm sorry I called you. I should have known better."

With that she was out the door and before I could say a word. I went to the kitchen sink and spat a mouthful of blood into it. I ran the water and watched it swirl around and disappear down the drain, just like any chance I had with Lexi. The phone rang and snapped me out of my pity party.

"Yeah?" I said

"My," Sheila said, "what an inauspicious greeting."

"I'm sorry, Sheila. You caught me at a bad time."

"I guess I did. I have some information about trains to and from Michigan but I doubt it will help establish the connection you are looking for."

"Perhaps it can help me rule out a connection," I said. "That might be just as useful."

"Well, the Michigan Central Railroad was taken over by the New York Central just after the Civil War and then became part of the Penn Central. As such, it ran one train daily between Detroit and New York City. That train, the Empire State Express, ran through our Central Terminal."

"It stopped in Buffalo for what, half an hour, before heading east to New York and, on the way back west, another half hour on the way to Detroit."

"Did that train use the same track each time?" I said.

"Yes," she said, "it did. Track number seven."

We had been focusing all out attention on the buildings to the exclusion of the tracks. It seemed logical. If the money wasn't where we were looking, look somewhere else. Maybe that was the connection, I thought, the Michigan train track bed.

"Thanks, Sheila, I owe you," I said.

"Yes, Coe, you do." Then she hung up. Doesn't anyone in Buffalo say goodbye anymore, I wondered.

I could see a mark developing on my face where Lexi had slapped me but I didn't think I had time to dwell on that. I needed to check out track seven.

CHAPTER TWENTY-FOUR

I CALLED FOR an Uber and ten minutes later, a cheerful young woman arrived. I gave her the destination and a caveat.

"If you don't want to drive over there, I understand," I told her. "Just let me know now and I'll call for another ride."

"I'm okay with it," she said. "But what do want to go over there for?"

"There's just something I want to see about the old building before it comes down," I said.

"You better look quick" she said. "I heard on the radio that a movie company would be here in a month to start looking at ways to blow it up."

That was new information. Time was growing short. We rode in silence till we pulled up on Memorial Drive.

"Is this okay or do you want to go up to the building?"

"This is great," I said. "If you don't get another call, could you swing by here in about thirty minutes? I'll probably be done exploring by then."

"I can't promise anything but if I'm free, I'll drive by."

I walked up the rise toward the building. The air was still bracing but it wasn't that bitter cold I'd experienced when I arrived in Buffalo, or maybe I was just getting used to it. Much of what I'd seen of the terminal was at night and I didn't get much perspective. From the inside, I saw that the concourse opened to a narrow hallway that had the legend "To Trains" over it. I entered that hallway and walked as far as I could. A plywood sheet nailed across the corridor blocked the path. I used my pry bar to peel back the plywood. When the terminal was built, the long, narrow corridor merged with an elevated platform that spanned the seven tracks. I could see the corridor once went a hundred yards or so down to what appeared to be the track beds. But that wasn't the case now. That platform had been demolished and now it was a twenty-foot drop to ground level. I wasn't about to make that jump. I retraced my route and walked around the grounds outside the tower to the rear where the track beds were. Looking down from the rise upon which the terminal was built, I saw long trails where I assumed the tracks once ran. The rails themselves were gone, either repurposed or sold for scrap. There were seven concrete abutments where the tracks once laid. The now-demolished corridor would have run from the terminal across the tracks. Passengers would peel off the corridor to smaller hallways to get to the right trains. I didn't know which track was number one and therefore didn't know where number seven was so I started at the nearest one and worked out. There were barriers between each track bed, a hundred feet of brick peaked in the middle like long, low pyramids. They were pretty much intact but it didn't take long to see there was nothing like a hiding place among the bricks and nowhere to hide lots of money like three hundred thousand dollars. I headed back up to the rear of the main building with another idea busted. Then I got a different idea of what 'busted' was going to mean. There were half a dozen or so thugs waiting at the top of the rise. They didn't look like Uber drivers.

"Hey fellas," I said. "Do you know when the train to New York City comes by?"

They responded by running down the hill toward me.

One guy was ahead of the pack and coming fast. I grabbed him by the shirt and fell backwards with my feet up in his chest. I pushed up with my feet as I was pulling him forward with my arms. His momentum worked against him and he flew over my head and down toward the track bed. I used the same momentum to roll backwards and jump to my feet but not before I took some glancing kicks around my head and shoulders. I used a spinning kick to the side of the closest knee to disable another attacker and an elbow uppercut to fell another one but the numbers were not on my side and I had, unfortunately, forgotten my baton. I kept moving and weaving to try to deflect as many of the blows as I could but a couple got through. One hit me on the side of my head that was still stitched and that hurt. I knew I had to stay on my feet or risk being stomped unconscious or worse. I slipped a punch thrown at my nose but took it on the cheek. I got a straight right hand to the eye of one of my assailants and he went down but the fists and kicks were coming fast and furious. A punch hit me on the ear and I got dizzy. Another one glanced off my shoulder but with enough force to hurt like hell. I was almost out on my feet when I got put down with a whack on the back of the head. The guy I flipped over my head got back in the fray and hit me with a board. I fell to my knees, but was still lucid enough to know being on the ground might kill me if I stayed down too long. I spun around and snatched the board from my attacker. I jammed the end of it into his groin and he tumbled back down the hill. I brought the other end forward and caught another guy in the balls. I stood up. I was pretty shaky but I was upright and I had a club. The place started spinning around and I knew I was going to lose consciousness and that wasn't a good thing. I took a big swing with the board, hoping to discourage close attacks but succeeded only in make myself dizzier. Everything started to go dark and I thought I might die before ever figuring out this puzzle. I heard the bark of a handgun and knew at once that it wasn't a Glock. That wasn't good, I thought. Cops carry Glocks. I kept waiting for the heat that came with a bullet wound but fell face first on the grass.

"Come on, asshole. Get up."

I felt someone tugging at my arm, trying to get me upright but that cool grass felt so good. I looked up and saw Lexi's frowning face staring down at me. Her frown was the second-best thing I could have seen at that moment. A smile would have been better but, given the circumstances, I could live with the frown, literally live with the frown. I got up to my knees but the landscape was still spinning. I could feel my stomach roiling and I puked on to the grass.

"You got a concussion," she said, always a master of the obvious. "Can you stand? We should really get the hell out of here."

I stood on shaky legs and tried to blink the blurriness out of my eyes.

"Let's go," I said. "I think I can make it."

She held on to my arm and I leaned on her more than I wanted to. I still wanted to be the tough guy who didn't need anything or anyone. We half-walked, half-stumbled to the jeep. I got in and leaned back on the headrest.

"Shit, you're bleeding," Lexi said. "What the fuck is wrong with you, coming down here by yourself?"

"What's wrong with me is that I came back here on this wild goose chase," I said and then I closed my eyes.

When they opened again, I was lying on an examining table under an incredibly bright light. I started to lift my head but realized immediately what a bad idea that was. I looked around as well as I could but didn't see anyone. I closed my eyes again and waited. I'm not sure how much time passed before I heard some voices but when I opened my eyes, the room was a lot more crowded.

"Hello," a woman's voice greeted me. "Nice of you to join us."

"Given the circumstances, it's nice to be joining anyone but angels. Where am I?"

"You are in the emergency room at ECMC," the woman said. "I'm Dr. Fahey. You have some serious head trauma, a few cuts, and a lot of bruises. You also have a few more stitches than you had when you arrived but we're most concerned about your concussion. What happened to you?"

"I'm not exactly sure," I said. "The last thing I remember was trying to get a bunch of East Side kids to accept Jesus Christ as their personal savior."

"I hope you were better at preaching than comedy," the doctor said. "But from the looks of it, you weren't."

"Did someone bring me in? Was there someone with me?"

"Yes. She said she was going to check on a friend but not to let you go until she returned."

"I suppose it's too late to blame all this on her, right?"

"I'm afraid so," she said. "But rather than blame, you might want to assign her credit for bringing you in. According to her account, you weren't faring too well with your preaching."

"Can I sit up, Doc? Lying flat on this table isn't helping my back."

Dr. Fahey helped me to a sitting position then adjusted the table to support my back.

"That's better," I said, "thanks."

"Please, just sit there for a few minutes until you get your bearings. I have to check on some other patients but I'll be back as soon as I can."

For one of the few times in my life, I did as I was told and sat quietly. The spinning in my head had stopped but was replaced by a throbbing headache. I touched the side of my head where the stitches were. I could feel the swelling and it hurt to touch it. A mirror revealed a darkened spot on my face but that wasn't from my new pals at the terminal. My hands looked like they were intact and I felt a pain in my thigh. All in all, I could have been in worse shape.

Lexi walked back into the room as I was taking stock of my injuries.

"You really are a dumb-ass," she said. "What possessed you to go over there by yourself?"

"Because I **was** by myself! Because my fucking partner raised a welt on my face and walked out on me! Because …"

She put her finger to my lips.

"About that," she said softly, "I screwed up and I'm sorry."

Shit, I thought, there goes all the wind I had in my sails. I couldn't be mad at her now.

"How did you know where I was? I'm pretty sure those assholes would still be kicking me if you didn't show up when you did. And what kind of gun was that? It sure as hell didn't sound like a Glock."

"After our little tiff, I called that McCartan woman to get the lay of the land. She told me about the trains to and from Michigan and I figured you'd be dumb enough to go out there alone. I didn't figure you'd go out there unarmed."

I looked in the mirror to check out the bruise from our "little tiff" and hoped she saw me do it.

"What about the gun?"

"My dad's. He brought it home from Vietnam."

"Damn," I said, "a .45, the old M1911. I knew I heard a bigger caliber."

"My dad got off two shots with this," she said. "Two hits. I'll never give this thing up."

"Why the .45 and not the Glock?" I asked.

"In case I had to shoot someone," she said, calmly, "I didn't want the bullet tracing back to my weapon."

Always thinking, my Lexi, I thought.

"Did you have to shoot anyone?"

"No. Just put two in the dirt and that scared them off."

"Too bad. That asshole who hit me from behind needs a round or two. Nothing fatal, just a kneecap or two."

"You pissed them off."

"By walking on the terminal grounds?"

"Not exactly," Lexi said. "Remember that picture you took of that other mook's Timberlands? I gave that to Brett Joseph and he got a forensics team to match them with the bruising on Moses' temple. They busted his ass a couple days ago and he's up on an assault charge."

That was good news but it didn't stop my head from hurting.

"How's Moses doing?"

"No change. The docs aren't optimistic."

I thought about the throbbing in my head and how much worse Moses had been beaten. The stark realization that I could have suffered the same fate really pissed me off. Those punks had a reason to go after me. They just beat Moses because he was there. Someone had to pay for that.

"When can we get out of here?" I said.

"As soon as Dr. Fahey says we can."

Not the answer I wanted but the one I expected. It was an hour and a half before the doctor gave us the okay. They rolled me out of the ER in a wheelchair while Lexi pulled the jeep up. We were heading over to Richmond Avenue when Lexi spoke.

"What did your little excursion uncover?"

I told her of my desire to dismiss Michigan as a relevant piece of information and the role of track seven in the McCartan provided information.

"I needed to check out the track beds to see if there was any place to hide a lot of money. There isn't. Even if the tracks were still operational, there wouldn't be any place to hide a dollar, much less three hundred thousand."

"Your conclusion?" she asked.

"Michigan is off the table."

"Agreed," she said.

How wrong we both were.

CHAPTER TWENTY-FIVE

Lᴇxɪ ᴡᴀʟᴋᴇᴅ ᴍᴇ into the Culhane house and left me there. I sat back on the couch and realized just how sore I was. I propped my head with a pillow and reassessed our clues. We had the key and we had the certainty of money. There was nothing more we could do to deal with the money and that left the key. I found the number for Kulavich Locksmiths and gave it a ring. Mikhail picked up on the third ring.

"Mr. Duffy," he said, "have you called to tell me I might have the key in your possession?"

"Not exactly, Mr. K, but I am calling about the key. What aren't you telling me about it and why do you want it so badly?"

"Can you come out here to see me, so I can tell you in person?"

I told him the sad story about getting my ass kicked and how I was temporarily indisposed.

"I'm sorry to hear that," he said. "But my story and my relation to the key is a sad story also."

His narrative went back some eighty years, just after World War II. Russia had been victorious in the war but was losing the peace to famine, sickness, and despair. The war had taken a horrible toll on Russia. Kulavich had been a soldier and fought against the Nazis.

He fought for three years and the war took him to the banks of the Elbe River in 1945 when the American and Russian armies finally joined up.

"When we reached the river, the Americans were waiting for us," he said. "We were all in great spirits because we knew the war would soon be over. The first night the two armies were together, we were drinking and one of the Americans got rather sentimental with all the vodka. He took a chain off his neck and gave it to me. It had a medal of St. Christopher on it. He told me that it had gotten him through some heavy fighting and he wanted me to have it. I was touched by his gesture and I put the chain around my neck that night."

"Great story, Mr. K, but what has any of this to do with the key?"

"Ah, you Americans," he said, "always so impatient."

Mr. Kulavich's story took him into Berlin where the war finally ended. But for him, another war as just beginning. The Russian army didn't just have soldiers, it had political officers or commissars whose job it was to make sure that the soldiers weren't just sufficiently brave but were also sufficiently communist. Kulavich and some of the soldiers in his unit weren't very fond of their commissar nor he of them. Before their unit was shipped back to the Soviet Union, some of the men were caught raping German girls, the commissar among them. Kulavich reported the rapes to his military commander. But the commissar held a rank equal to that of the commander and he got a pass on the rapes. In reprisal, he reported Kulavich as having "consorted with the Americans in disparaging communism." As evidence, the commissar pointed out the Saint Christopher medal given to him by the American soldier. Despite his distinguished service, Kulavich was sent back home in a prison train, shackled to the floor of the rail car with a chain around his ankle.

"I rode like that for three days," he said. "I shit and pissed my-self many times during that trip. When we reached Russia, another commissar came on the train and released us, saying we'd suffered enough.

"The key that fit the lock on my ankle was very similar to the key you showed me. That's why it is important to me, Mr. Duffy, and as far as I know, it has only value to me as a relic of my treatment."

I had little to say in response so I remained quiet for a minute. When I spoke, I gave Mr. K my assurance.

"In the event this key is mine to give, sir, you may be confident I'll give it to you. And thank you for your service."

"Thank you, Mr. Duffy, and God bless America."

It seemed I'd reached another dead end. I laid back on the pillow and thought about what Kulavich must have gone through. It made my journey seem like a cakewalk.

I got up and wrapped some ice in a towel and put it on the side of my face. My head hurt more but I didn't want to keep looking at the bruise Lexi had left me. I knew we were rapidly approaching the point where we would have to abandon our quest for the stolen money. The few clues we had were going nowhere and I couldn't figure out anywhere to go from here. It seemed like it was there in front of me but I just couldn't see it. I was still searching for it when Lexi called.

"Bijou?" was all she said.

"Sure, but I still look like I got my ass kicked, you know."

"Well, you did, remember?"

"Yeah, I remember. I got my ass kicked twice."

Then I went into the bathroom to take a shower and try to find that missing link that might get us to the cash.

Lexi was at the door an hour later. I wasn't quite ready yet so I beckoned her in.

"You look like hell," she said. "Did you get kicked on the side of your face?"

She couldn't have forgotten hitting me already, I thought.

"No, I didn't get kicked. I got slapped."

"I did that?"

"Hell yeah, you did that," I said, walking back to the bedroom to finish dressing.

When I came back, Lexi was sitting on the couch with her face buried in her hands. She was crying. I'm never going to figure this woman out, I realized. I sat down next to her and put my arm around her.

Why is she crying? I thought. She's the one who hit me.

She put her head on my shoulder and spoke in a very low voice.

"If you weren't such an asshole, I wouldn't have to hit you."

My fault again.

"Come on, Lexi. Splash some water on your face. We don't want Bea thinking I hit you."

'You won't tell her what I did, will you?"

"No killer, your secret is safe with me."

That earned me a punch in the arm.

When we entered the Bijou, Bea was her usual ebullient self, until she saw the lump on the back of my head and the bruising on the side of my face.

"*Mio Dio, abbi pieta di te*? What happened to you, Coe?"

"He ran into a door," Lexi said. "You know what a klutz he is." But she couldn't joke her way passed Bea.

"A door, il mio culo!" I didn't have a clue as to what she was saying but she sounded mad.

"You got mugged, didn't you?" she said. "These damn punks are everywhere. You've got to be more careful, Coe. This city is getting rough."

If she only knew the half of it.

"I'm okay, Bea, really. It only hurts when Lexi smiles."

"Still with the jokes ... you want some wine? I still have some of that special Chianti left."

"That would be great," I said.

Before Bea left she looked at Lexi crossly.

"You have to take better care of him," she said.

Lexi bowed her head and was strangely quiet.

"I think Bea is mad at me," she said.

"You made a bad joke when her favorite customer was suffering," I said.

"I am not above slapping the other side of your face and evening out the bruising," she said. I knew she was joking. Well, I was hoping she was joking.

Bea brought the wine to our table herself and sat down.

"How's my friend Michael?" I asked. Michael was her brother and an old friend now traveling the globe as a gaming casino consultant.

Bea regaled us for the next ten minutes with stories about Hong Kong and Macao and Singapore and all the other places Michael visited. Then she rose and said she was going to check on our dinners.

"But we haven't ordered yet," I said.

"I am making something special for you two. No ordering necessary."

She came back in a few minutes with two steaming plates: osso buco for me and shrimp fra diavolo for Lexi. I think I could have sated my appetite just with the aromas of Bea's cooking but I ate like a condemned man. When I came up for air, Lexi was staring at me.

"You are eating like you are starving," she said. "Can you take a minute to breathe?"

I wiped some sauce off my mouth and smiled.

"The thing I like best about this place is Bea really feeds you."

Lexi smiled back but it was a sad smile.

"You want to give up, don't you?"

Lots of thoughts not involving Italian food were running through my mind and I have to admit that giving up the quest was one of them.

"I don't want to, Lexi, but I'm running out of ideas about where to look. Every time we get what seems like a lead, it goes nowhere. I could have been killed today just disproving a theory. I don't know where to take things from here."

She looked sad. I hated that. She deserved to be happy and I came home with the idea I might help achieve that.

"Do you have any ideas?" I asked.

"That's why I called you. You're the idea man."

She was smiling but I knew that was just camouflage. I started back on my dinner.

"Let me think on it a little more. I have this feeling that the answer is right in front to me but I just can't see it."

She reached over and toughed my bruised face with her soft,

warm hand.

"You're a decent guy, Coe."

I recognized that as damning by faint praise but to feel the touch of her hand, I'd take it. After a few more bites, I signaled my surrender to the food gods by pushing back my chair. I touched my fingertips to my lips and blew a kiss to Bea in the kitchen.

"Magnifico!"

She beamed with her first genuine smile of the night. We boxed up our leftovers and headed toward the door.

Bea called out to Lexi.

"Take better care of him!"

Lexi smiled and we headed toward the jeep.

"See? She's mad at me." Maybe just a little I thought.

When we pulled up in front of the Culhane house, I thought she'd just let me make it to door by myself. This time, she walked me up the front steps and into the living room.

"You going to be okay?" she said.

"Yeah, the pressure on my belly from all that food is making me forget about my headache."

She touched my battered face again and followed it with a kiss on the cheek.

"Get some rest. You look like hell." She smiled and was out the door.

Truth be told, I thought, I probably looked better than I felt. My head, contrary to my assurance to Lexi, was still killing me. I wanted to think of devious and painful ways to pay back some East Side assholes but my mind kept drifting to Michigan. As much as I had dismissed Michigan as salient clue to our mission, it kept popping back into my mind. Every time I thought of Michigan, I heard the Simon and Garfunkel song in my head. Tonight, though, the lyrics went beyond the "Michigan seems like a dream to me now" line and kept repeating these lyrics in my head: "I'm empty and aching and I don't know why." I knew why I was aching but what was this emptiness I was feeling? I leaned back on the couch and closed my eyes but I knew the throbbing wasn't going to let me sleep. I laid there for a long time, trying to make two plus two equal four but I kept coming up with three.

CHAPTER TWENTY-SIX

THE MORNING CAME in its usual shade of gray. I felt a lot more pain than I did yesterday. Now, my body was a Rand-McNally Atlas, mapping out where every kick, club, and punch had landed. A hot shower offered no relief so I tried cold. That was marginally better but I was shivering when I got out. I looked at myself in the mirror as I toweled off. There were red and purple marks all over the place. I made a mental note not to go to the terminal without my baton ever again. Once dressed and fed with cold veal left over from the night before, I looked at the evidence again still arrayed on the dining room table. All I had left was the key and some dollar signs I'd drawn on an index card, signifying that at least I knew there was unclaimed cash somewhere. I figured it was time to bring Sheila in again. She had some resources and some fresh perspectives that Lexi and I were lacking. I waited until ten o'clock, giving her a chance to get settled.

"Sheila, I am rapidly approaching the end of my rope of possibilities," I admitted. "I've got nothing but the certainty there is money left from the robbery and this antique key that I've promised to an old Russian locksmith if I can't place it to something important. I'm desperate for a new perspective on this. I'd hate like hell to leave town without helping Lexi solve this."

"I can see why," Sheila said. "When I spoke to her yesterday she seemed equally as frustrated. You're staying at the Culhane house on Richmond?"

"Yeah, but ..."

"It's Buffalo, Coe," she laughed. "Everybody knows everyone's business. Why don't I come by about seven and see if I can't see something you've missed?"

"Is it all right if Lexi's here?"

Another laugh.

"Sure, it would be fine. It's time she and I met anyway."

I called Lexi and got her voicemail. I left her a message about our meeting with Sheila. I lay on the bed and fell asleep.

I felt a lot better when I woke up, physically anyway. I wanted badly to solve this thing for Lexi. If I had to leave again, I wanted to leave her happy this time. It was almost four o'clock so I turned on the TV and tuned in Nicolle Wallace on MSNBC. I didn't get to watch much before Lexi called.

"I was going to head over to DiTondo's and get some spaghetti parm for dinner. You want to come with or eat in tonight?"

"I'm a little more beat up today than I was yesterday. Can we eat here tonight?"

"Sure. Do you want meatballs?"

"That would be great. We're going to have a visitor tonight to get some new eyes on what we have."

"Let me guess ... does she work for the Historical Society?"

"Come on, Lexi. Sheila could give us a perspective we don't have. She's been pretty good so far. It can't hurt."

"Well, is it okay for me to be there? I wouldn't want to be a third wheel."

"Don't be an ass ..." I had more to say but she ended the call so I watched the last thirty minutes of Wallace before switching over to the local news. There was an interesting story about an arrest that had been made in the brutal beating of a homeless man in the vicinity of the Central Terminal. The police spokesman was talking about some new technology that allowed the police to match the bruises on the homeless man with the boot prints of the perp. When they called him in for questioning, the dummy was wearing the same boots and they had traces of blood in the tread. The blood was a match to the still-unconscious victim. So, it is true – the good guys can win. The five o'clock news was bleeding into the five thirty news when the doorbell rang. I looked around for my baton, found it, and stuffed into the back of my jeans. I went to the door and saw Shamus Culhane smiling through the window.

"Hey, come on in," I said, feeling funny inviting my old friend into his own house.

"Shit, what the hell happened to you? Actually, I know what happened. I ran into Lexi Crane over at DiTondo's and she filled me in. What the fuck are you doing hanging around the terminal?"

"I understand it's going to be gone soon, so I thought I'd take a look around. My father used to tell me stories about the terminal in the old days, after World War II, when my grandfather and most of his pals came home from the war. I thought I'd take look around but didn't think that would be a problem in the daytime. I guess things have changed since I've been gone."

"Yeah, these kids are all in gangs now. The gangs want to control shit that has no value. They are killing each other over stupid shit."

"What about the demo?" I said. "Will that be good or bad for the neighborhood?"

"School is still out on that question," Shamus said. "We had some feelers when I was in the Mayor's office but nothing materialized. You know these developers; they are always willing to trade you a wiener for a ham."

He stood up and looked a lot taller than he had when I worked for him.

"I just wanted to see how the best speechwriter in Buffalo was doing," he said.

"When I run into him, I'll tell him you were asking about him."

He laughed, punched me on the Lexi arm and was out the door.

Good ole Shamus, I thought, rubbing my arm. Does everyone in this town punch?"

The front door had hardly closed before I heard it open again.

"Knock, knock." Lexi had arrived with dinner. It smelled heavenly.

"Come on in," I said, but I needn't have bothered. She walked into the dining room and helped me get plates and glasses. She looked great; not unusually so, but great nonetheless: the long black hair wound up in some kind of arrangement that only women know how to do, her skinny jeans clinging nicely to her shapely legs and giving her butt a nice curve, and those perky swells beneath her vee neck tee. Have I mentioned I really adore this woman?

We ate quietly for a while before Lexi wanted to know on what pretense I wanted Sheila to join us.

"And if you say one word about her tits, I'm going to whack you again but harder," she said.

"Be serious for a minute," I said, "and be honest. If we hadn't found out for sure that there was money somewhere in this city, we would have called off this escapade. But now that we know the money exists, we need a real lead or to call this thing off for good."

"OK," she said, "but what does that have to do with her?"

"Like it or not, Sheila has provided some valuable insights. She has some understanding of this city and between her and her mom, they have a pretty good feel for mob history. This was money stolen by a mobster, returned because the mob wanted it returned, and hidden from the mob by said mobster. So, I believe she can be valuable to us."

"If we find the money and decide to reward her, it comes from your share."

"You know something, Lexi, she hasn't once mentioned the money. She knows that's what we're looking for but she's never even hinted she wanted in on the split."

"She will. Mark my words."

We finished eating and I started to clean up when the doorbell rang. Lexi headed toward the door while I filled the dishwasher.

"Good timing," she said. "There was only enough food for two."

"Come on in," I heard Lexi say. "It's finally nice to put a face with the voice."

"A pleasure to meet you as well, Lexi," Sheila said. Her "Beautiful" perfume wafted around the living room replacing the aroma of spaghetti parmesan and meatballs. This woman would be a temptation hard to ignore, so I was really glad I wasn't alone with Sheila tonight.

"Hello Sheila," I said. "Thank you for coming tonight. We've appreciated everything you've done to help but we're kind of at a dead end."

I proceeded to tell everything we'd learned to date, which wasn't all that much. Then I told her what we didn't know: what possible connection the key might provide and if we really could rule out any connection with our quest and Michigan. I told her what little we'd learned about the key from Louis and from Mikhail Kulavich.

"There seems to be some sentimental attachment with both guys but nothing more than that," I said.

"May I see the key?" Sheila said.

I put it in her palm and she looked at it for a few seconds before speaking.

"I might disagree with your conclusion about the key," she said. "I think you've learned quite a bit."

"How so?" Lexi said.

"Well, two men have identified the key in different centuries but similar circumstances. Your friend Louis connected the key to a lock that once held his great grandfather captive. The locksmith identified a similar key that once held him in chains. What remains is to tie the events together. This key fits a lock that may or not be in the terminal. But from its pedigree and age, it is probably not germane to the question of the terminal in any real sense."

"But the key could be important?" I said.

"That's yet to be determined," Sheila said. "We don't really know enough to include or discount it."

"If it doesn't have any connection, why would Moses hang on to it?" Lexi said. "All he had in his possession was the key and a slip of paper."

"Why, indeed? Sheila said. "Why was the key so important to him? We have to stop looking specifically at the terminal and look at the bigger picture."

"And that picture would be what exactly?" I said.

"The real, true picture that you are trying to uncover, Coe. Where is the money?"

We were heading back to where we'd began, I thought. We have no clearer idea of where the cash is even knowing now that the cash truly does exist.

"Lexi, what else can you tell us about your friend?" Sheila said.

"Moses?"

"No, his brother, Cletus. You began this pursuit based on conversations you had with him, correct?"

"Right. I knew him from City Hall. He shined shoes in the lobby of the building and I got to talking to him one day and we sort of became friends. When he retired, I used to go over to his house on Genesee Street. I brought him roast beef from Bailo's. He loved those sandwiches. When he was fed, he was happy and he'd talk about the days when he started shining shoes. He mentioned something about Lehigh once or twice but I never pressed him on it because I didn't know what he was talking about. He also talked about making the rounds with his shoeshine box. I guess he was talking about the bars downtown but I don't really know. He was a religious guy, I know that. He said he heard two councilmen arguing one time and they were swearing a good bit. Cletus told me he stepped between the two men and told them the next one who took the Lord's name in vain was going to 'feel my righteous wrath.'

Sheila shuffled through a folder in her lap and found what she was looking for. She'd done some research about the history of railroads in Buffalo and brought some notes. She told us the reference to Lehigh was probably a reference to the first major rail terminal in the city. The Lehigh Valley terminal was at the foot of Main Street in downtown. It opened in 1916, more than twenty years before Central Terminal. The Lehigh terminal functioned just thirty-six years, she said. So, it might have been the first place Cletus shined shoes.

"But that knowledge does us no good as the Lehigh Valley Terminal was demolished before the City Hall robbery," she said. "When he spoke of making rounds, Lexi, he might have been referencing heading to the other rail terminals. At one time, there were four downtown."

"That will be great info if I ever get on 'Jeopardy,'" Lexi said.

"It could be useful information if we can provide some context for Cletus and what he might be referencing in his discussions about the money," Sheila said.

She put her notes away and asked Lexi if Cletus had ever mentioned Central Terminal by name. I thought Lexi was running through as many of her conversations with Cletus as she could.

"No. I don't think he ever did. He said the old railroad terminal but he never called it by its name."

"Is that important?" I asked.

"Not yet," Sheila said, "but it might give us more context later on. But that's for another day. I really must be going."

I stood and helped Sheila on with her coat. As I was walking her to the door, Lexi's phone rang.

"I appreciate you coming over tonight, Sheila. Your fresh eyes mean fresh perspective."

"Coe, you know I'll do anything I can to assist." With that, she peeked in the door to see Lexi still absorbed in her phone call. Then she kissed me softly on the cheek and I thought I might get drunk sniffing her perfume. I watched Sheila drive off and went back inside.

'Grab your coat!" Lexi said.

"Why? What's up?"

"Moses just woke up."

Maybe our luck was changing for the better.

CHAPTER TWENTY-SEVEN

I WAS ON helicopter insertions in Afghanistan that weren't as scary as riding with Lexi on an average trip. Tonight, though, there was nothing average about her driving. I have to admit I had my eyes closed for most of the seven-minute drive. If I had to guess I would have pegged her motivation as fifty percent from her joy that Moses finally woke up and fifty percent from her desire to find out the role of the key in our quest. As for me, I was just glad that he was awake. I hadn't been optimistic we'd be getting good news about Moses, so him being awake was a big plus. But a little, tiny bit of me was interested to hear about the key. Lexi was running through the lobby toward the bank of elevators and attracted the attention of a security guard on duty.

"Hey Miss!" he called. "Slow down!"

She flashed him a badge and he waved her on. What the hell kind of badge does she have? I wondered.

We got to our floor and Lexi treated the opening of the elevator door like the starting gun in a fifty-yard dash. She was at the nurses' desk before I got off the elevator. The nurse hugged Lexi like they were long lost buddies reuniting. I followed Lexi to a room and went in. Moses was just finishing a fruit cup. Two empties were on his tray. At least his appetite is back, I thought. Lexi almost spilled his fruit with her hug.

"It's so good to see you, Moses," she said, once she let him go. "We were so worried about you."

"Mighty good to see you, Miss Lexi and you too, Coe. The nurses told me you were here a lot when I was sleeping."

"You're our friend, Moses, and that's what friends do," I said. "I'm so glad you are awake."

I thought I looked bad from my go-round at the terminal. Moses looked worse. But he was a whole lot cleaner now and the big white bandage on the side of his head made him look a little lopsided. Two of his fingers were taped to splints and his left leg was elevated by a couple of pillows.

"What happened to your leg, Moses?" I asked.

"Don't know," he said. "I got hit in the head and knocked down and I don't remember a much after that. That leg sure does hurt, Coe."

It made me want to go back to the terminal tonight and extract a little more payback.

Lexi sat by his bed and gently held his battered hand. I wished it was hard for me to believe that anyone would inflict such injury on such a harmless old man. But my life had gone on too long for that naivete to last long in my head. The simple fact was that there were a lot of two-legged vermin infecting the streets of the world - vermin that deserved to be eliminated.

"Can I get you anything, Moses?" I said.

"I do like them fruit cups, Coe. Could I get another one?

"Of course, Moses. I'll go grab you one right now."

I went out to find a nurse while Lexi sat with Moses. There were a couple of nurses at their station. One went to the refrigerator when I made my request and I asked the other nurse for a prognosis.

"If you asked me yesterday, I would have said there was little chance your friend was ever going to wake up," she said. "But this morning he was wide awake and his appetite hasn't suffered. Sometimes science doesn't have all the answers."

"If he needs anything … anything at all, would you make sure he gets it?" I said. "We're prone to heavy tipping."

She laughed and said we might not have enough money if we had to pay for his meals.

"But that's a good thing, right?"

"So far, it's a great thing," she said. "No tipping allowed though. But don't worry, he'll be well taken care of."

The other nurse came back with three fruit cups and a big smile. I thanked her and headed back to the room. When I got there, Moses's eyes gleamed with joy.

"Mr. Coe, I thank you. This is a real treat."

"Eat hardy, my friend. You're going to need your strength."

We left Moses slurping down the juice from his second fruit cup. He looked like he didn't have a care in the world. It warms your heart to see someone that happy. It reminded me that you didn't need grand gestures to make someone happy, just a little kindness.

Lexi dropped me off about midnight. Neither of us had mentioned the key or anything about it to Moses. We were too happy he was back among the living. It was just before dawn when I got her call. Moses was dead. The docs think it might have been an embolism while he was asleep. The nurse who called said the three empty fruit cups were stacked on his night stand. At least he died happy, I thought. Then, for the first time in a long time, I cried. I called my friend Anthony Amigone, Sr, one of Buffalo's finest funeral directors, and a friend from my days in City Hall. I told him the circumstances and he said he'd take care of it. I told him I'd take care of it but Dan told me "I said I would take care of it" and that was that. Lexi was a wreck.

"We just saw him yesterday," she said between sobs. "He looked and sounded good, now he's gone?"

She had come over to Richmond Avenue and sat on the couch. I guided her head on to my shoulder.

"The nurse said his leg had taken a beating from a bat or pipe or something like that," I said. "She said that an embolism from that trauma probably hit his lungs in his sleep. She said she knew it was no consolation but that he probably died peacefully."

Lexi pulled her head up straight.

"I know some motherfuckers who aren't going to die very peacefully," she said.

"All in good time," I said. "All in good time. Why don't you call your detective and let him know his assault became a homicide?"

"I'm going down to headquarters to tell him in person. Want to come?"

"No, I'm going to stay here for a while. I don't feel like going anywhere. Call me if you need me but don't go near the terminal without me."

She had a troubling look on her face.

"I mean it, Lexi. Don't go down there without me. It won't be helpful if you need backup and I have to Uber."

"Got it," was all she said. She gave me a peck on the cheek and was out the door.

Part of my brain was still processing the death of our friend. The other part was processing the loss of what seemed to be the last remaining chance we had of determining if Moses' key had anything to do with our quest. We'd counted on Moses for some information that now would never be forthcoming. This would be a great place for this story to end. There was little chance we'd get much further than we were and every promising turn seemed to dead end. The only thing keeping me in the game was Lexi. With little else to do, I called Sheila to give her the sad news.

"Oh Coe, I'm so sorry for your loss. I know you genuinely liked the man but he was also one of your last lifelines, wasn't he?"

"Lifelines?" I said.

"One of your last real sources," she said. "I didn't mean to be crass."

"I don't think you were, Sheila, and you are right. Part of me was hoping we would get a clue from Moses. I'm really stumped now about where to go."

She was quiet for a minute than made an offer.

"I know your friend was a poor man, Coe, so if you need financial help with his burial, I am in a position to help."

"That's very kind and most generous of you, Sheila, but a friend of mine is handling everything."

"You have some great friends, Coe. That's one of life's greatest accomplishments. I hope you will consider me as a friend, as well."

"Of course, I do. You have proven to be one of my truest and best friends, Sheila, and I appreciate that."

"I'm glad because I think of you that way also."

She went on to say that she agreed with me that something important was dangling in our faces but we just couldn't see it.

"We may just be coming at this thing from the wrong perspective. I've been giving this a lot of thought and I share your frustration. It would seem like the three of us should be able to make some headway."

"I agree," I said, "but right now, I think it's more like the two of us. Lexi is very angry at the moment and I am afraid she's focusing most of her attention on retribution for Moses. But she'll have her head in the game again soon."

Then I told Sheila the story of Lexi's father's murder at the hands of some street punks and her subsequent decision to become a police officer, mostly to avenge her father's death.

"Sheila, you are one of the brightest people I know but Lexi is right there with you. She was a genius, a great athlete, and a stunning woman. She could have been a doctor or lawyer or investment banker or just about anything she wanted. She was that smart."

"Well, who knows, Coe? She might aspire to greatness again once she sees this project through. But you should stop blaming yourself for the decisions she's made."

That threw me for a loop.

"How do you know what decisions she's made and what role I might have played?

"How many times must I tell you? This is Buffalo, Coe. Everyone knows everyone else's business."

"As long as you know the story, you know she was right and I was wrong and she tried to save me by giving up something she loved."

"Sounds like she gave up one thing but wound up losing two things. Stop blaming yourself. We are all big boys and girls now and we make our own way. Furthermore, something tells me she still cares a lot about you."

"Really?" I said. "I must have missed that part."

"Then you are blind. Don't you see how protective she is of you? How much she stiffens up around me because she thinks of me as her competition? Surely, you must have recognized that."

Now that Sheila mentioned it, that might account for Lexi's suspicions about Sheila. No wonder I couldn't figure out the clues about the money. I couldn't even read Lexi.

I changed the subject.

"Lexi thinks you are in this for a share of the money," I said. That struck Sheila as funny.

"Coe, the last thing I need in this world is more money. How do you think I can afford to work for a non-profit? Lexi and I will talk. I like a challenge as much as the next person and this search you two are on is certainly the most challenging puzzle I've encountered in a while."

"Well, the terminal isn't going to be standing much longer so let's hope our three heads come up with a solution pretty quick. Call me if you think of anything. In the meantime, I'm going to try to keep Lexi out of trouble."

"Good luck with that," she said. "Lexi strikes me as rather single-minded."

We said good-bye and I had the feeling we were further from and not closer to some answers.

I called Lexi but it went straight to voicemail. I told her I wanted to know the plan to extract retribution and thought that might get a response. It did. She called me ten minutes later.

"I want to go back there tonight," she said. "I had a conversation with some of my cop friends. We have a bit of a plan."

"What time?" I said.

"I'll pick you up at ten. Don't forget the baton. I might let you lead the orchestra tonight." She got a little chuckle out of that.

"I might have the baton," I said, "but you are always the maestro."

We hung up and I looked around the Culhane house for something else suitable to crack a few skulls. I found it in the hall closet. It was one of those small souvenir bats from a Buffalo Bison game. It was solid, concealable, and easily handled. I had time to get in a decent run so I headed out south on Richmond and ran pretty hard to Symphony Circle and then I took an easy jog back. Back inside, I sat on the floor and cranked out a hundred crunches and twenty push-ups. I felt like I did before a big game: lots of adrenalin beginning to pump and that nervous anticipation that was part of the preparation. There was nothing to do now but to wait for the honk of the jeep horn. I closed my eyes and tried to think about the next step in our quest but all I could see in my mind was Moses being stomped and beaten by a gang of thugs.

Lexi was as punctual as ever and we were cruising toward the terminal at Lexi's usual speed. She talked as she drove east on Broadway.

"Different avenue of approach tonight," she said. "We're going to come in from the north, down Curtiss Street and behind the terminal. There's less chance of early warning."

"Frankly, I don't give a shit if they see me coming from a mile away," I said.

"My guys told me something is going on over here tonight. Either they heard about Moses or they figure you are coming back.

Whatever it is, I want to take a few precautions."

Lexi made a hard right off Broadway and stayed to the right where Memorial Drive and Curtiss split. She pulled over on Curtiss and faced me.

"We go in right at ten thirty," she said, "and we have a maximum of twenty minutes."

I looked at her with a puzzled look on my face.

"About ten thirty-five, the boys in blue are going to get call about a gang fight at the terminal and they are going to show up *en masse*. They'll probably be here in ten minutes after the call. It would be good if we were gone by then."

I didn't question her. I didn't think I would need more than fifteen minutes to inflict the kind of pain I had in mind for the killers of my friend but I could certainly stretch it out if need be.

Lexi drove slowly along the street.

"Are you carrying?" I asked her.

"No," she said. "If this doesn't go the way I want it to go, I don't want to get shot with my own gun."

That made sense but I had no intention of letting this go any way but the way I wanted it. As she drove, Lexi slipped on some gloves.

"Weighted?" I said.

"You bet. Eight ounces of steel shot in each glove."

We were almost at the rear of the terminal.

"Say together," she said. "We watch each other's back. I don't want one of the headaches like you got."

"I don't need another one myself," I said.

We got out of the jeep and walked around to the back of the terminal. It looked like Lexi's intelligence report was right. There were at least a dozen guys. This could get interesting, I thought. Baton in one pocket and the bat in the other; I was ready to rock n' roll.

When you get into something like this there is no point in subtlety. We were moving on them and they were advancing on us. I checked to make sure we weren't getting flanked but these punks weren't much on tactics. We were about two feet apart when we stopped.

"Who's in charge here?" I said, drawing a puzzled look from Lexi.

A very large guy stepped forward into my kill zone.

"I am ..." he started to say, but before he could I jabbed the butt end of the bat into his throat. He gurgled like he wanted to say something but I didn't let him. I smacked him over the ear with the bat and he keeled over and just like that it was on. I grabbed the baton from my pocket and snapped it to full length and started twirling with my arms of wood and steel. I don't know how many I took down but I did like the twin sounds of the bat thwacking on one side and the baton scything through the air on the other. I cleared a path and took a look at Lexi. She was whipping those weighed gloves in sharp, crisp punches. One punch and someone would go down. There was half a dozen or so laying in the grass in various states of disrepair. We probably could have walked away at that point but Moses was dead and these fuckers killed him. I wasn't going to kill them but I was going to make good and goddam sure they didn't forget this night. A guy took a swing at Lexi that she parried with her left arm redirecting it over her shoulder while driving her right palm into the dude's chin. He stumbled backward but Lexi moved like she was dancing with him. She got in close and faked a right hand. Then she whirled with her left and caught the guy on right side of his face. Something cracked. His eyes rolled. He went down.

I wanted to just stand back and watch her work but every couple of seconds one or two of the braver guys in the group would move on me. I faked one with the bat. He took the bait. Then I got the baton around on his knee. The sound of stainless-steel cracking a knee cap is frightening, more so for the recipient than the hitter, but it makes an impression on both. Fighting is mostly inflecting pain. But it's also about enduring it. Rarely does anyone get through a fight like this without taking hits. As I dropped the guy with my baton to his knee, I took a pretty hard punch to the stitched left side of my face. I got that flash of pain that stabs one's eyes in an explosion of white and instinctively spun in that direction. My attacker was still in range and he got the bat in the gut. Then I kicked him square in the balls with my left leg. As he bent over, my right knee came up to meet his face. I'm not sure where I got him but I got him. That was enough. He rocked back and went down. Lexi was in her boxer's stance, bouncing on the balls of her feet. I moved to cover her back but was just a little slow.

"Behind you!" I yelled.

She responded like she'd been in this position before. An attacker was over her left shoulder so she opened her stance by moving her left leg back. The mook kept coming and she slid her leg behind his right leg. As he charged, she whipped her left elbow around and caught him squarely on the nose. Then she brought her right leg around to face him and hit him in the nose again, this time with eight ounces of shot in her glove. I heard the crack. Then I heard the moan. Then the guy dropped like he'd been shot. But her movement to defend against the rear attack left her vulnerable to the thug she was originally squared up with. He caught her with a solid shot to the ear before I could jab the baton into his eye. He screamed and fell back but not before Lexi caught him on the collar bone with what the Thai call a *sok sap* but we called a downward elbow strike. As the guy crumpled to his left, Lexi used her right leg to spin and jam hard into his left knee. I got too caught up in watching her work. I took a hard shot to the cheek. A normal guy would retreat after taking such a punch but the well-trained guy attacks through his pain. As he was advancing to follow up on his sucker punch, I caught him with a straight right hand, the hand still clutching the baton. He reeled back. I was already advancing. I got him on the right side of the head with the bat and added a kick to the balls. I looked over at Lexi and she was still bouncing and weaving and assessing the situation. No one was closer than ten feet so they weren't threats. I broke into a sprint toward the biggest cluster of punks and they bolted.

"It would appear our work here is done," she said.

"Not quite."

I wandered around the battle scene smacking my bat and baton on every leg. I swung hard, wanting to inflect maximum damage.

Lexi was quiet until we started back to the jeep.

"What was that all about?" she said.

"The nurse said Moses died from an embolism. I looked that up. Most embolisms start in the legs and travel to the lungs. I just wanted to make sure those clots get a running start on these assholes."

"Good plan," was all she said. We got back in the jeep.

She made a U-turn and drove out the way we'd come. We were almost to Broadway when we heard the cacophony of multiple sirens.

"Almost on time," I said, but Lexi didn't respond. Her right ear was badly swollen.

I signaled to her to pull over the curb.

"Your ear looks bad," I said.

"You should see your eye," she said, and we both laughed.

We stopped at a 7-Eleven and I got a twelve pack of Bud. We drove home in silence, allowing the adrenalin to wane and heart rates to get back to normal. As we walked up the stairs to the Culhane house, Lexi took my hand.

"Good work tonight," she said and she was right.

CHAPTER TWENTY–EIGHT

Adrenaline is a two-edged sword. During times of stress, it can heighten strength and awareness. It can even mitigate the effects of pain, temporarily – the key word there being "temporarily." When the adrenaline levels go back to normal, so does everything else, like pain. I was going through the crash I always felt after high stress periods like combat or like the fight we'd just experienced. Now that things were leveling out, I had a throbbing headache to go along with my left eye that was swelling shut. I could tell by the way Lexi was slumped on the couch that she was going through something similar. I went to the kitchen and came back with a couple of Ziploc bags full of ice. I put one against her swollen ear and she winced.

"Are you dizzy?" I asked her.

"No. Just sore as hell. I must have been hit a few times more than I thought. I feel like I got run over by a car."

"I know the feeling. My head is throbbing like a mother."

"Does your eye hurt?"

"Not really but it is swelling shut, I can tell."

"Yeah, it is and it looks like hell," she said with a laugh.

"And that's funny to you?" I said, trying and failing to look serious. "What the hell is wrong with us?"

And we both started laughing. I always find that Budweiser is effective in minimizing the effects of an adrenaline come-down so, we sat together on the couch and drank some beer while we recounted the effort to avenge Moses.

"You hit a lot harder than you did when I arrested you," she said.

"When you arrested me, I wasn't really trying to hurt that dickhead. I was just trying to make a point."

We both got a laugh out of that. It felt good to hear her laugh. It felt even better that I had something to do with her laughter.

"You going to call your cop friends to see what the damage was?" I said.

"That can wait till tomorrow. Hand me another beer."

We sat silently on the couch, sipping our beer until Lexi put her head in my lap and fell asleep. I stayed awake with the ice on my eye for one more beer.

What we did was exceptionally stupid, I thought, but still it felt damned good. I hoped Moses was smiling, wherever he was.

•••

In the morning, my aches and pains remained but Lexi was gone. I wasn't surprised at either development. I cleaned up the living room and took a twenty-minute shower, first letting the hot water wash over me and then switching to cold to get my heart started pumping again. Despite my first aid efforts of the previous night, my eye was now completely swollen shut. I was considering whether or not I should take a run with only one good eye when Lexi called.

"Hey, did you hear from the friends in blue?" I said.

"Yeah; first thing this morning. They have seven in custody. Another four are in the hospital. One of them is in serious condition with a probable concussion and broken collarbone. Three were treated and went to jail with minor injuries.

"Damn," I said. "I thought we were better than that." That got a bit of a chuckle out of her.

"My detective friend wanted to know what happened to their legs. Well, actually he wanted to know 'what the fuck happened to their legs?'"

"Did you clue him in?"

"No. They're holding the mooks on assault charges but they will probably get released later. The charges are really thin."

"I bet, like non-existing thin. How's your ear?"

"Very sore and very swollen but otherwise, okay. How's the eye?"

"It's closed and looks like hell but it doesn't hurt and I can see pretty well out of the other one." I lied about it not hurting.

"What's on the agenda for today?" she said.

"I was thinking about going for a run to loosen up some of these tight, sore places on my body. How about you?"

"I'm laying low today. I need some rest."

"Okay, I'll … "but she'd already hung up.

I decided against the run and did some stretching instead. I was starting to feel better when my phone rang. It was Sheila.

"Hi, Sheila. How's it going?"

"I'm fine," she said, "but how about you?"

"What is that supposed to mean?"

"Well, I understand there was quite a dust-up at Central Terminal last night; lots of injuries and some arrests. I'm hoping that you aren't in either category."

I was about to ask her how she knew but I remembered her catch phrase: this is Buffalo, blah, blah, blah.

"I am happy to say that I am not in the latter category and only on the superficial side of the former."

"As pleased as I am to hear that, I'm calling about something else."

She went on to say that she'd been doing some serious thinking about our mystery and that she had a few thoughts she wanted to share with me. She wanted me to go to her office. There was no polite way to say no. She recognized we'd hit a dead end in our search and was spending her own time and brain power trying to find new avenues of approach to pursue. I told her I'd see her in thirty minutes. I checked my eye again to see if the swelling might have magically disappeared. It hadn't and I still looked like I went ten rounds with Mike Tyson. I got dressed and hoofed it down to the Historical Society building. Sheila was waiting for me in the lobby. She took one look and just said "holy shit." That was only the second time I'd heard her curse so I knew I looked worse to others than I did to myself. She raised her hand to touch my eye but I pulled back out of reach.

"Easy, lady, that's not stage makeup," I laughed.

"Oh my God, Coe, I thought you said your injuries were superficial."

"Well, they are, comparatively. You should see the other guy." My humor was lost on her. She led me down the stairs to her office, holding my arm all the way down. She needn't have but it felt nice to enjoy her concern. Once again, she took the chair next to me instead of sitting behind her desk and gave me her insights.

"I've been looking at your problem and like you, I've reached a dead end," she said. "So, I concluded that the quest must end or that other avenues of approach must be found and since neither you nor Lexi seem ready to give up, I have opted for the second approach."

"What other else is there?" I said. "We have a couple of disparate clues that have led us nowhere."

"Exactly," she said. "So, I'm thinking you or we need to look at things from a different perspective."

My look must have given away my less-than-enthusiastic embrace of where we were heading.

"Open your mind. Step back from what you're focused on and see what might be instead of what is."

I thought I should be lying on a couch listening to this analysis but Sheila wouldn't be dissuaded.

"Look at the evidence again, Coe. You have the word of a dying man that money exists and was stashed somewhere. You've verified that the money does exist. You have a key but it's too old to fit in anything in Central Terminal where your search is focused. Finally, you have a slip of paper that seems to have the word Michigan written on it."

I was sorry to admit that's a pretty thin inventory of clues, I thought.

Sheila went on.

"Forget about the money for the moment and forget about Central Terminal since that has been a consistent dead end. What do we know about the key? Where might Michigan fit in with what we know about the key?"

She had obviously spent more time on the key than we had. Perhaps we were too focused on payback to think about solving the mystery.

"That was a question, Coe. What do we know?"

"We know that it's old," I said. "We don't know what it might have been used for."

"I asked what do we know, not what don't we know. We don't know a whole lot so let's pay attention to what we know."

I was getting a little irritated but I played along.

"We know that the Russian locksmith wanted the key."

She perked up now that I was playing along.

"That's right! Why is the key important to him?"

"It reminded him of a bad time in his life," I said.

"What was bad about that time in his life?" she said.

I felt like I was playing a parlor game.

"He was a prisoner in chains."

"Exactly! Now who else had some comments about the key?"

I had to think for a minute before it struck me.

"Louis," I said. "Louis said something about his great granddaddy being …" Then it hit me.

"…about being a slave and in chains!"

"Right! Both men related the key to some sort of captivity because similar keys locked their chains."

"Damn," I said. "Are we on to something?"

"I'm not sure but with your assent, I'd like to call a friend of mine to get some input from her."

"I'll take as much help as we can get, Sheila."

"Good. I'll call her this afternoon and let you know after I've made contact."

She reached up again and this time I let her touch my damaged eye.

"You must take better care of yourself, Coe."

She gave me a rueful smile and I knew I had to get out of there before I did something I'd regret.

When I made it back to Richmond Avenue I felt much better than I did when I left. I wanted to call Lexi and let her know about the new direction we might take but thought I'd save it for dinner. It would cheer her up and I liked it when she was happy. I started to do some yoga but quit early on when dipping my head caused my eye to act up. I decided Lexi's course of action, that being no action, was the best recourse so I laid on the couch and let a bunch of thoughts run through my head. Were we actually getting closer to some resolution? Could we actually find the money? What do we do if we did? I closed my eyes and let myself drift off.

When they opened again, the last glimmer of light was fading beyond the Niagara River and would soon dip below the Canadian horizon across it. I couldn't see it from here but I had seen many times before - the last vestige of the day hanging on in a last brilliant blast of red and gold when Lexi called.

"Do you feel like going out tonight?" she said.

"Not really. I look like hell with this eye and I don't want to answer any questions about it. But I'll go out if you want."

"No, I feel the same. My ear is not suitable for public viewing. Pizza and wings from LaNova?"

"Sounds good to me. I'll call in the order."

"Naw, I'll pick it up on my way. Do you have beer?"

"Is Coe Duffy clutch with men on base?"

"Do you want me to get some?"

"Very funny. I have beer, Lexi."

She showed up at my door with the chow and a badly swollen ear. She handed me the boxes and made for the kitchen.

"I'll get the beer. You get some plates and napkins."

The bag was overflowing with napkins so I grabbed a couple plates and set them on the dining room table. Smelling the pizza and chicken reminded me I hadn't eaten yet today. I sat down and got ready to tell her my big news. She beat me to it.

"Coe, we've got to talk," she said. Any guy who has ever heard those words knows what's coming after them isn't going to be good.

I sat silent, desperate to eat but needing to show my attentiveness.

"I think I might have gotten us out over our skis," she said. "I got so juiced about this notion of money lying around waiting to be found, I think I lost perspective. I've been thinking about this all afternoon so don't try to talk me out of it but I think we should give up this wild goose chase."

I remained silent, biting my tongue, dying to tell her we were back on track, just a different track but I continued to listen.

"Look at us," she said. "We're beat up. We just put a bunch of teenagers in the hospital. We're running around like headless chickens pretending we know what we're doing but we don't and we never did. I called you back here on a fool's errand, Coe, and I'm sorry."

As much as I enjoyed hearing her apologize, I hated seeing her look so defeated. I was about to give her my news when the doorbell rang.

Lexi looked at me and asked if I was expecting anyone.

I waited until I got out of punching range and told her I hired some male strippers to cheer her up. I opened the door and there stood Sheila with another woman I'd never seen.

"Coe, I'm sorry for coming over unannounced," Sheila said, "but we have some news that I couldn't wait to share."

"Don't be silly. You are always welcome here, isn't she, Lexi."

Lexi gave Sheila a wry smile and said "sure."

"Forgive my manners, Coe, this is the friend I was telling you about this afternoon. Meet Imogene Hayes."

"Hello Imogene. It's very nice to meet you. This is my friend and confidante, Lexi Crane."

Lexi smiled, a little.

"Please come and join us. Lexi was just telling me how she thinks we should shut down our search for the missing money."

Sheila was settling into her chair when I said that.

"What!" she said. "Quit now?" Then she looked at me with a knowing smiling.

"You haven't told her yet, have you?"

"I was about to when you and Ms. Hayes arrived," I said. "But now that you are here why don't you tell her?"

"Tell me what, dammit? Somebody tell me something," Lexi said.

Imogene was looking at our chicken wings with great interest.

"Would you care for some wings, Imogene?" I said, ever the gracious host.

"Sure …"

Lexi snatched away the box of wings.

"Nobody eats until somebody tells me what's going on. And just who the hell are you, Imogene?"

Sheila answered while Imogene was still eying the wings.

"Imogene is one of the Historical Society staff who specializes in Buffalo's history as an important stop along the Underground Railroad back in the days of slavery."

Lexi wasn't satisfied.

"And she's here because …?"

"Coe and I had a brainstorming session… oh my Lord, what happened to your ear, Lexi?"

"O dear God! Coe Duffy! Tell me right now what the hell is going on!"

"As Sheila was saying, Lexi, she and I sat down this afternoon to talk about the knowns in our puzzle." Lexi had the look of impatience she gets just before she punches me and I was still way too sore to be punched.

"We've been dwelling on what we don't know, Lexi," Sheila said, "instead of delving into what we do know."

"Like what do we know about this key?" I said. "There was much we didn't know about it but we reduced the discussion to whom it was important and why."

Lexi was getting interested.

"We know that two men had some interest in the key: Mikhail Kulavich and Moses's friend Louis," Sheila said. "Both men had that interest because of something common to both – being chained in captivity."

Lexi wasn't there yet but I could see her start to process. She absently pulled a wing from the box and offered one to Imogene.

"Mr. Kulavich recognized the key as similar to the one that locked his shackle," Sheila said, "and Louis knew that his great granddaddy had also been shackled … "

"As a slave!" I blurted out. "Our mistake has been looking for a door the key would unlock. What it might unlock is a padlock that secured shackles."

Imogene reached for another wing as Lexi spoke.

"And this gets us where?" she said. And here, I was as lost as Lexi for I had no clue where it got us.

Sheila motioned toward the box of wings. Apparently, no one had eaten today. I slid the box over to her. She motioned to her staffer and Imogene began.

"Well, it got Sheila to come to me because I specialize in Buffalo's 19th century history," she said, "but I was lost until Sheila told me about the other clue."

"The other clue?" Lexi said, taking back control of the wings.

"Yeah," Imogene said. "The scrap of paper that had m-i-c-h on it."

I was as eager as Lexi to see where this was going.

"When you take the data about key and add it to the scrap of paper there is only one salient connection to be made – the Michigan Avenue Baptist Church."

"The church was one of the last stops on the Underground Railroad," Sheila said. "With Canada just across the river, Buffalo was the terminus of the railroad. I believe that's what Lexi's friend was trying to tell her. The 'terminus of the railroad,' not the terminal.

Sonofabitch, I thought, the "other railroad."

"What's our next step?' Lexi said.

"Take your key to someone I know at the church," Imogene said, between nibbles on the wing bone. "If she can give us some idea of the efficacy of the key as fitting a lock of the type that shackled slaves, we'll know we're on to something."

I looked at Lexi and saw a gleam I hadn't seen in way too long.

She was energized again.

"You can be assured we'll be discrete in contacting the church," Sheila said. "We can do so because of our historical context."

"What should Coe and I do?" Lexi asked.

Sheila smiled that incredible smile.

"You both should heal, Lexi. Heal and wait. We will contact you as soon as we have something verifiable."

I slid the wing box over to me only to find one wing left and Imogene trying vainly to wipe her mouth free of the barbecue sauce.

Sheila took the opportunity to speak to Lexi and I alone.

"Imogene, why don't you use the rest room to get rid of the sauce?"

When Imogene left, Sheila spoke to us in a quiet voice.

"That disgusting little man called me again," she said.

"Petrelli?" Lexi asked.

"Yes. He wants to meet with me but I loathe him and his awful leering eyes."

"We've got to find out what he wants," I said.

"Or better yet, what he knows," Lexi said.

"Could you meet with him to see what he wants?" I said.

Sheila didn't look happy but she agreed that it was a good thing to do.

"If he so much as lays a hand on me ..." Sheila started.

"I'll guarantee he never touches anything again," Lexi said.

"Okay, I'll call him back and tell him to come to the office in the next day or two."

Imogene returned from the bathroom without the scarlet ring around her mouth. Sheila rose and asked for the key then led Imogene to the door. When they were gone, Lexi joined me on the couch.

"What do you think?" I said.

"I am pretty pissed off that I led us down the wrong rabbit hole," she said, before whacking me on the arm. "That's for not telling me we were heading in a new direction."

She was quiet for a while before asking me what I thought.

"It makes sense," I said, "and it gives us a shot at finding the money. But I still have some questions that need to be resolved."

"What do we do in the meantime?"

"You heard the lady. We heal."

I put my arm around her shoulder and fed her a piece of pizza. We fell asleep like that, with her slice falling on her chest.

CHAPTER TWENTY-NINE

SHEILA, ON THE other hand, was a bit more restive. She dropped Imogene at her car back at the Historical Society and after her colleague drove off, she called her mother.

"Hello darling, how's the search going?" Marsha McCartan said.

"Lots of progress, mother, I'm happy to say. The Duffy lad is as bright as you thought."

"Delightful. I'm pleased to hear that. If I'm going to make an erroneous assessment about someone, I prefer that I underestimate them. What's next?"

"Well, there is a bit of a hiccup," Sheila said. "That nasty Petrelli creep wants to see me again."

"Well, I suggest you see him," her mother said. "These Neanderthals are nothing if not persistent."

"The man is a pig, mother. Last time I met him, I wanted to have my office fumigated."

"I encountered many like him in my life. Their saving grace is their vapid stupidity and their gullibility. Use that against him. You can steer men like that in any direction you wish."

Sheila thought for a second about her mother's last statement and a plan was born.

"Thank you, mother. I think I know just what to do with Mr.

Petrelli."

"I'm sure you do, dear. Be sure to keep me informed."

"Good night, mother."

Sheila pulled out of the parking lot with a gleam in her eye. I know exactly what to do with this pig, she thought.

I woke up on the couch, alone again. Lexi must have left before dawn because I could see some light filtering through the normally drab sky and some large patches of blue up there. I wondered if Spring was about to make an appearance. I pushed Spring out of my mind to consider where we were now on our mission. Sheila and her hungry friend had given us new hope of finding it. That hope also extended our deadline. If the money wasn't in Central Terminal, we had more time to search. But where do we go from here, I wondered. I figured I would think better with bacon and eggs and some coffee at Pano's. I showered, got dressed and headed up to Elmwood Avenue. Spring popped back into my mind along the way. The air was warming, if not exactly warm, and the sky was bright blue. It was a good day to be in Buffalo. Twenty minutes later, I decided it was also a good day to be at Pano's. I sat at a window and let the smells of bacon and my coffee warm my soul. I was on my second cup when I heard the knock on the window. Lexi had pressed her nose to the glass like a kid looking in the old A.M.&A.'s Christmas window. Now my heart and soul were warm. She came in and sat across from me. The first thing she did was take a piece of my bacon.

"You were up early," I said, pulling my plate back from her reach.

"Yeah, I like waking up in my place." I didn't move it far enough as she snatched the remaining two slices of bacon and a piece of toast off my plate. I gave up and pushed the plate over to her. I signaled to the waitress for another order.

"Damn thoughtful of you, Coe," she said

"The least I could do for my partner in crime." At least I kept my coffee.

Lexi gobbled the breakfast down like she hadn't eaten in weeks. When she came up for air, the waitress was placing my breakfast before me.

"So, what do you think?" Lexi said, snatching yet another piece of bacon off my plate.

"I think the next time that dainty little hand reaches across the table, I'm going to stick a fork in it."

"Seriously," she said, "what do you think?"

"I think we are on the verge of something," I said. "Everything I heard last night makes sense. We were spinning our wheels at Central Terminal. There was way too much to search and all that gang bullshit to deal with every time we went over there, so I would be happy if that building is off the table."

"What about Sheila and her sidekick?"

"What about them?" I said.

"You still think Sheila's motives are pure?"

"If you mean do I think she's only in this for cash, the answer is no. I take her at her word."

"You think that she's taken such an intense interest in the search out of the goodness of her heart?"

"Yes, I do and you don't?"

"I guess I'm just naturally suspicious. I'm not used to people cooperating without ulterior motives."

"All I can say is that she's been great so far. Without her, we might still be prowling the terminal. She helped me think through the issue with the key. She brought in an expert on the Underground Railroad and she says she's not interested in the money. So, I believe her."

"What's her motive? Is she hot for you?"

I wanted to say she might be but I didn't want to get punched.

"You are forgetting the connection between her mother and my father. That might be it."

"I'm going to keep an eye on her, regardless," she said.

And while Lexi was ruminating about Sheila, Sheila was doing us another solid.

THE voice on Sheila's intercom alerted her that Petrelli was waiting to see her. She had security bring him down. She sat behind her desk. He entered the office with his arm in a sling.

"Oh dear, did that nasty mouth of yours get you in trouble, Mr. Petrelli?"

He just snarled at her.

"Let's make this quick," she said. "The less time you spend here the better."

"You got a smart mouth on you. That's going to get you in trouble someday," he said.

"Perhaps," Sheila said, "but not today. What do you want?"

"I think you know what I want. I want to know where the dough my brother stashed is."

"And I would know this how, exactly?"

"Cuz your mother knew all the bosses and they must have told her about the cash. So, if you don't know where it is, ask her," Petrelli said.

"And why would I want to do that?"

Petrelli shifted in his seat and pulled his soiled sport coat back to reveal a pistol sticking out of his belt.

"Because it would be good for your health. That's why."

"Oh dear, Mr. Petrelli, is that supposed to scare me?" Sheila said. Then she pulled her own gun, a Smith & Wesson SD9VE, and placed it on the desk.

"Mine's newer and has more bullets, I assure you. I've got 16 in the clip to go with the one in the chamber."

Petrelli's eyes widened but he kept the menacing expression on his face.

"But in the interest of peace and harmony - and never seeing your ugly face again - I will share a bit of information with you. I am not exactly sure where the money is but I do know it's on the 9th floor of the Central Terminal tower.

"Now kindly get your filthy ass out of my office so I can have that chair replaced. If you ever come back here again, I won't be so accommodating."

Petrelli rose and started to say something but thought better of it when Sheila's hand touched her pistol. He mumbled something as he left but well out of Sheila's hearing. She smiled to herself as she put the gun in her drawer.

Mother was right about people like him, she thought.

IMOGENE called while Lexi and I were discussing Sheila. She wanted to know if either or both of us wanted to join her on a trip to the Underground Railroad Museum in Niagara Falls. I wasn't up for it but Lexi said she'd go. Ten minutes later, Imogene pulled up to Pano's in a Mini Cooper. I thought that would be a deal-breaker for Lexi but she was strangely amenable to riding in Imogene's car.

"And here I thought you were married to that jeep," I whispered to her as we left Pano's.

"I'm going to find out what these chicks are up to, helping us like they are," Lexi said. Then she slid into the passenger seat and away they went, while I headed back to Casa Culhane to do a little snooping of my own.

I got on the Internet and Googled "Buffalo and the Underground Railroad." There was a surprising amount of data to be found. I went through several websites and took in all the information. I'd lived in Buffalo most of my life and been a city official for some of it and I never knew the rich history of Buffalo's role in helping runaway slaves make it to freedom in Canada. It did make sense, of course, with Canada being so close but it surprised me to learn about the people and places that helped fugitive slaves to freedom. The data about Broderick Park struck a chord and with time on my hands I Uber-ed over there. You couldn't get any closer to Canada than from the Park. It was on an island attached to the city proper by a lift bridge over the Black Rock ship canal. The island was no more than fifty yards or so wide. The Niagara River swept passed on the west side of it and the Black Rock Channel drifted by on the east. Canada looked like an easy swim but the river current let me know it would be harder than it appeared. Runaways were often housed at locations around the city then brought to the island where they could be loaded on to a ferry to take them to freedom. I took advantage of the warming Spring air to explore. There was a historical marker noting the significance of the island to the freedom movement and the beginning of what a sign told me was a "freedom garden." I walked north to the stone breakwater separating the still water of the canal from the fast-flowing Niagara and walked a hundred feet or so along the wall. The speed of the Niagara was hypnotizing. I watched the flow for a minute or two and knew that trying to swim across the river would be next to impossible. It was only twenty-odd miles upstream where the river cascaded over Niagara Falls. I was headed back toward the parking area when a man with a young boy approached me.

"Are you from Buffalo, sir?" the man said.

"Yes, I am."

"My son would like to ask you a question," the man said.

"Of course," I replied, "and I hope I'm able to answer it."

"Well, sir, could you please tell me why this place is called Buffalo? I haven't seen any buffalo anywhere," the boy said.

I got a laugh at that but it wasn't an unusual question.

"Young man, Buffalo was not named for an animal," I said. "It was named for this" and I pointed to the river.

The lad looked confused.

"Some of the first people who came here a long time ago were French and they saw the river and they called it '*beau fleuve*.' That means beautiful river. Over time, people mispronounced the French word and it became Buffalo.

"So, we are not named for the bison, the correct name for buffalo, but for this beautiful river."

The boy looked disappointed.

"We do have some bison at our zoo," I said, "and it's not far away."

The boy cheered up with that and I gave the father directions to Delaware Park and the zoo. Thirty minutes later, I was back on Richmond Avenue hoping Lexi had a more exciting time of it than I had. I was on my second Bud when Lexi came bursting through the door.

"Don't tell me," I said, "that was an imitation of a no-knock warrant."

"Don't be an ass," she said. "I'm glad you are here."

"Well, I don't know where else I would be, except maybe Cole's."

"I got a call from my contact at police headquarters who told me word is circulating around the Broadway-Fillmore Avenue area that the two white fucks who've been beating the shit out of the mooks over there are coming back tonight. I thought you might be planning something on your own."

"And you were worried about me?" I said.

"No way. I thought you might have all the fun yourself." Lexi was smiling and that made me smile.

"I've got no clue about what your contact told you. I have no plans to go back over there unless it's to watch it be exploded."

"That's a relief. I'm not sure my ear is ready for another encounter."

She sat down next to me on the couch and took my beer.

"Learn anything new at the museum?" I said.

"Cool place, but no, nothing new. Imogene showed the key to the curator lady there and she absolutely identified it as being a potential match to the locks that shackled slaves. She showed me a couple of big-ass padlocks like those that would be opened by a key like this. She also said she wanted it after we were finished with it."

"Did you tell the nice lady the key was already spoken for?"

"I did and she offered me money for it."

"Save her name and number," I said. "It might be the only revenue-producing part of this caper."

That got a laugh out of her.

"She also schooled me on some terminology about keys," Lexi said, taking the key from her pocket. "This round part here is called a barrel. The thing on the end that fits into a lock is the bit and this part where you hold the key to turn it is called the bow."

I clapped my approval.

"Anything stand out about our key?" I said.

"Just one thing, besides the fact that it is so old."

"And what might that be?"

"These numbers on the barrel." She held it close to my good eye. "See them? I think it's one-one-four-oh."

"Hmm … did the curator have any idea what those numbers might signify?"

"Just some guesses. She thought the number might have corresponded to a certain lock, either on a shackle or a door or a cell."

"Thus, the key is another dead end?" I said.

"For now," she said. "The curator did tell us that many of the homes in East Buffalo had tunnels or dugouts to hide the slaves should people from the south come looking for them. She said they had some hiding places near the ferry to Canada, just in case the bounty hunters staked out the ferry."

"Bounty hunters?" I said.

"Bounty hunters would come up north here to try to find runaways and collect on them."

"Shitty way to make a living," I said.

"Enough history," Lexi said. "I'm hungry."

"Do you want to take a ride?" I said. "We could head out to Lackawanna to the Mulberry for dinner."

"Do you still have cash left from your terminal score?"

"Yeah, quite a bit, in fact."

"Then let's go," Lexi said.

A few minutes later, we were on the Scajaquada Expressway heading toward the Niagara River. Buffalo has a lot of Native American words scattered throughout the area. We then hit the New York State Thruway and took it to the Skyway Bridge and onto Route 5 heading south. We passed the rusting skeleton of the Bethlehem Steel plant. It once employed some twenty thousand people and was one of the biggest plants in the Bethlehem system. During World War II, it was the largest steel-producing plant in the world. When it shut down, it threw the entire region into an economic downturn that took more than two decades to climb out of. The Mulberry used to be a gin mill where the steel plant workers would come every Friday to cash their paychecks and drink. It is located in a neighborhood of houses aptly called Bethlehem Park, as they were built to provide housing for plant workers. Some enterprising guys bought the place and turned it into a great place for Italian food and good conversation. I hadn't been there in five years, but walking through the door made me feel like I'd never left. The memorabilia and photographs on the wall were there to remind one of Mulberry Street in New York City. Newer additions to the walls were autographed jerseys of Buffalo Bills players. It was one of those places that made even strangers feel at home.

It took me five full minutes to shake hands, renew acquaintances and introduce Lexi around. It had been quite a while since I'd seen the owners, Joe Jerge and Tim Eberle and even longer since I'd seen my favorite waitress, Brenda. We had a couple of beers at the bar and then sat down at a table to order dinner. I took a calculated risk and advised Lexi not to order the lasagna.

"The portion is so big, you'll eat it for a week," I told her.

When Brenda came by, I knew exactly what Lexi would say.

"I'll have the lasagna, please."

"Spaghetti and meatballs for me."

Lexi sat quietly for a minute, taking in the ambiance.

"This place is cool," she said finally.

Our food came out and Lexi's eyes grew almost as big as my meatball. She waited until the waitress left the table and then spoke.

"Holy shit, I'll be eating this for a week."

I laughed and told her, simply, "I know."

"Your meatball looks like something I pitched when I played softball," she said, grinning.

"I like this place," I said. "They feed you."

We ate quietly and happily for a long time, until it was time to ask for take-home boxes. We grabbed a cannoli and a tiramisu to go and staggered out to the jeep, overloaded with food. Once we were strapped in, Lexi leaned over and took my bruised face in her hands and kissed me long and soft on the lips.

"Thanks," she said. "This was very nice."

I leaned back in for another taste of those lips but her hand on my chest stopped me.

"Don't get carried away," she said. "Wait till after dessert."

"I thought you were dessert."

We both laughed as she drove away back to Richmond Avenue. We went into the house and I started a pot of coffee. Lexi the romantic was once again Lexi the sleuth.

"What do you think about the key?" she said.

I should have told her the key was the furthest thing from my mind but I didn't want to get punched.

"I'm thinking that the key took the focus away from the terminal but I'm not sure how it helps beyond that."

"Do you think that church on Michigan Avenue has anything to do with any of this?"

"Lexi, I don't know yet. I think we need more information before we start heading off in another direction right now. But I do think we have made a lot of headway since we started."

"Maybe," was all she said as she turned the television on. We sat silently for a while, pretending to be interested in what was on. Then I went out to the kitchen to get the coffee and dessert.

"I don't think I could eat another crumb," she said. I agreed. I was stuffed.

We were drinking the coffee when Lexi's phone rang. She answered it.

"No, we didn't go anywhere near the terminal tonight," she said. "It's not any of your business, but we were out in Lackawanna having dinner. Yeah, a couple dozen people can verify that! What the fuck are you talking about?"

She listened for a minute, then clicked off without a word.

"What was that all about?" I said.

"One of my guys at police headquarters wanted to know if we

had been at Central Terminal tonight?"

"Why?"

"I'm not sure ..."

The breaking news banner flashed across the TV screen. A reporter stood on location and gave a report that a gang war shootout had taken place at Central Terminal and there were multiple fatalities.

"What the fuck?" I said.

"Jesus, that's why my friend wanted to know if we were there."

The reporter continued talking but was saying essentially the same thing over and over: "When we get more information from Buffalo police, we'll be sure to pass it on." The backdrop was lots of flashing lights and wailing sirens. The reporter came back on.

"There goes another ambulance," she said. "That's four that have left the scene in just the last five minutes ..."

"Christ, those bangers didn't have guns when we were there," I said.

"Well, they had guns this time. What the hell went down over there?"

I grabbed my phone and called Culhane. If anyone outside of police headquarters would know what happened, he would. He answered on the second ring.

"Shamus, what the hell is going on? I just heard about a shootout at the terminal on television."

"I'm not sure yet. I'll call you back." The line went dead.

I was trying to get my head around the new developments even as I was counting us lucky. We laid some pain on the gangbangers without any real damage to us but if I had known they had guns, things might have been different. For the first time since I'd known her, Lexi looked shaken. I put my arm around her shoulders and she let me pull her in closer.

"That could have been us, "she said, "in those ambulances."

"Could have been but wasn't," I said. "What the hell happened over there?"

A swirl of thoughts were whipping around in my mind: When did guns come into play? Did we cause this? Who was shooting who? As pissed off as those punks had been at Lexi and I, we never had to deal with guns. Or was this something that was going on without any connection to us? I couldn't figure it out; - not yet anyway. My phone rang. I hoped it was Culhane but the caller ID said it wasn't.

"Hi Sheila."

"Coe, you and Lexi weren't at the terminal tonight, were you?"

"No. We were at dinner far from the terminal."

"Thank goodness. I just learned of some terrible violence over there and I had the worst feeling that you were involved."

"We just saw the news on TV" I said. "We are blown away. We had some scrapes over there but nothing involving guns."

"I understand people were killed," she said. "How awful."

"You don't know who was killed, do you?" I was thinking about my friend Louis.

"No, I don't know any more than I've seen on television. But I am glad you weren't anywhere near there."

"Me too," I said. "A black eye is one thing. Another bullet wound is something else."

"Another?" Sheila said. "You mean you've already been shot?"

"Well, yeah. I got shot in Afghanistan a few years back."

"You have to take better care of yourself, Coe," she said. "I must go. Mother is on the other line."

While I was on my phone, Lexi was working hers, or trying to anyway. She wasn't having much luck connecting with her cop contacts. I knew that by the way she kept muttering under her breath each time her call went to voicemail.

The television coverage now preempted the scheduled programming. A young male reporter looked stricken as he gazed into the camera.

"The scene here is one of bloody carnage," he said. I knew he had no idea what real "bloody carnage" looked like.

"Police tell me there are four confirmed dead and three more in grave condition."

You don't have "carnage" until you've got double digit body bags. The kid was eating this up – covering a mass shooting.

"This is your big chance, kid," I mumbled at the screen. "Don't blow it. Keep giving facts."

Lexi finally got through to one of her contacts. I was getting only bits and pieces from hearing her side of the conversation.

"Wow… no shit… six dead… TV is reporting four… yeah, I know they don't know shit… helicopter… that much brass… sounds like you'll have your hands full all night… okay, go to work… thanks."

"What do we know?" I said.

"Shit like this, there's always a lot of confusion," she said. "But it seems like the gang over there got into a shoot-out with another group inside the terminal tower. My guy said there were shell casings all up and down a stairwell. The bodies started up there and were scattered down the stairs, like the fight started on an upper floor and went down.

"He said there were at least a hundred rounds fired, judging from the brass. The body count is six, not the four that guy is reporting but they don't know if two other guys are going to make it. They've got a bird up with thermal imaging to see if there are any other casualties in or around the building."

"They aren't doing a sweep yet?" I asked.

"They are trying to get more lights inside. They don't want to be stumbling around in the dark."

"Makes sense," I said, 'but nothing else does. If it was a gang thing, why not just shoot it out on the street? They didn't need to go inside, in the dark. And since when do these punks have guns and all that ammo? We never saw them with guns. We'd be dead if they had them when we rousted them."

"Correction," Lexi said, grinning. "You'd be dead. I was packing."

Good point, I thought.

"Something about this whole thing doesn't make sense," I said.

"Criminals don't always make sense," she said. "Sometimes, the shit just hits the fan."

I still wasn't buying it. We watched the TV coverage for an hour or so but didn't learn much more than Lexi's cop buddy told her. I figured we'd just have to wait till the morning to find out more.

"Do you still have my pajamas here?" she said.

"Yeah, why? You want to take them home?"

"No, pal. I want to sleep in them. You get one look at my sexy underwear and I'd have to shoot you. I figure I'd be safe in flannel."

I went to the bedroom and pulled her pjs from under a pillow. The old tee shirt she's slept in before was still there too. I left them on the bed and went to the bathroom to brush my teeth. When I came back to the bedroom, I thought she still might have to shoot me. It didn't matter what she wore, Lexi was still the sexiest woman I have ever laid eyes on. The pajama bottom couldn't hide the soft curve of her butt and the shirt just made her breasts look more enticing. She must have seen the lust in my eyes.

"Do I have to sleep with the .45 under the pillow, you pervert?" But she was smiling. That was almost as sexy and her curves. I crawled into bed and spooned with her. She felt warm and soft and so good ... until she started snoring.

I awoke to the sound of her shower. Her sleep wear was folded neatly on her pillow. I figured she woke up before I did so I wouldn't have the chance to try to persuade her that morning sex is great sex. She came out of the bathroom fully dressed, drying her hair.

"Pano's?" I said.

"Nope. I'm heading downtown to see what more I can find out about the battle last night. I'll call you if I find anything out."

"Okay," I said, not liking it all that much. But what else could I say?

Her hair was still damp when she kissed me and when out the door.

I came out of the shower ten minutes later and saw that I had missed a call. It was Sheila's number. I called her back and she picked up on the first ring.

"Are you doing anything important right now?" she said.

"I'm not even doing anything unimportant," I said. "What's up?"

"I'd rather not tell you over the phone and I have a breakfast meeting in a few minutes. Might you join me in say, thirty minutes or so?"

"At your office?"

"No, Coe. I'm actually at the Tim Horton's on Niagara Street, near West Ferry. Do you know it?"

"Not really, but the Uber driver will. I'll see you in a bit."

When the driver dropped me off, I saw the back of her perfectly coiffed head facing the door while she stared out at the Niagara River hustling on down to Niagara Falls. It made me a little jumpy, seeing her sitting like that with her back to the door. I had to see all the doors when I sat down.

"Good morning, Sheila," I said, before she turned around.

"It is, Coe. Such a good morning." She turned to face me and offered her cheek, which I gladly kissed.

"So nice to see you in such a good mood. What's the occasion?"

"I was just sitting here, watching the river and the current. It's almost hypnotic."

"I know. I was down here yesterday and I walked out on the break wall. Look at it long enough and it almost sucks you in."

"What were you doing out there?" she said.

"I had time to kill and never knew about Buffalo's history as a refuge for fugitive slaves so I thought I'd come out and see the new park."

"It is quite impressive, the history and the park," she said. "Did Imogene report back on her trip to the Niagara Falls museum?"

"Lexi took a ride with her and she filled me in. I now know more about keys than I ever thought I would but there wasn't much more."

"Lexi told you about the inscribed numbers on the key?"

"Yeah, she did ... one-one-four-zero ... the numbers don't mean anything to me or to Imogene or to Lexi or to the curator in the museum."

"Maybe you'll find some connection with the number," she said. "In the meantime, I have to tell you something I learned from my mother this morning. One of the people killed in that terrible fight at Central Terminal was none other than Max Petrelli."

"What!?"

"Yes, mother heard this morning that Petrelli had taken some of his crew to the terminal and while inside some of the local toughs confronted them. The rest is still unfolding but Petrelli's body was found this morning on the ninth floor of the tower. He'd been shot several times."

I was stunned into silence. What the hell was that moron doing in the tower? What did he think he'd find up there? I could only assume he was still looking for the same thing Lexi and I were looking for but he apparently didn't have new information we did. But what brought him up into the tower?

"Are you okay, Coe? You looked perplexed."

"Yes, to both, Sheila. I am okay and I am very perplexed. What the hell made Petrelli and his goons go up into the tower in the darkness of night? Why did the locals open fire on him? Lexi and I had been there twice and kicked some serious ass but no one ever showed a gun. Why the escalation to a shoot-out now?

"This thing keeps getting weirder and weirder."

"Well, I am not happy anyone is dead but I am glad I won't have to deal with that horrid little man anymore."

With that, Sheila leaned over and kissed my cheek and gathered her stuff.

"Thank you for meeting me here, Coe. Can I drop you off somewhere?"

Now, I was the one staring out at the current.

"Coe?"

"No, thanks, Sheila. I'm going to take a little walk. I'll be fine but thanks anyway."

She smiled and was out the door. I wasn't far behind her.

CHAPTER THIRTY

I STARTED WALKING north on Niagara Street, paralleling the river. It was a pleasant day in Buffalo and I thought the fresh air might give me some time to sort out all the bullshit swirling around recent developments. I hadn't heard from Lexi so I didn't have the cop perspective yet but Sheila had thrown me for a loop.

Petrelli was searching for his brother's money, just like we were. But what made him go up into the tower? We were focused on the terminal for a long time but we never ventured beyond the lobby and the baggage building. What was he doing up there? Had we missed something? Should we still be focused on Central Terminal? All these thoughts were running through my head while I walked.

I was approaching West Ferry where the lift bridge takes foot and car traffic over to Bird Island and Broderick Park when I stepped on a stone and started to roll my ankle. I caught it before it went all the way over but still went down on one knee. I recalled the excruciating pain of sprained ankles that were part and parcel of being a jock. I was relieved that I didn't have to go through that again. I stood and staring me in the face was a street sign that indicated I was at the corner of Gull Street and standing in front of a street address. I could hardly believe it. But it was in big silver numbers right there on the building façade … 1140. I needed more perspective so I walked down the hundred feet or so of Gull Street. It dead ended on the cusp of a steep drop off that went down to a rail bed. Down the slope, across the tracks, beyond the state Thruway, and across the canal was the island where the fugitive slaves could board the ferry to Canada.

Damn, I thought, could this be the 1140 on the key?

I went back to Niagara Street and turned left to West Ferry and across the bridge. I walked through the park along the same route I'd taken the day before. The river raced by, gray and swift. I made a little jog to the right and walked through the parking area. At the end of it, there was a little roundabout that allowed cars to turn north and head back to the bridge. But I wasn't interested in heading back to the bridge. I looked to the east, toward Niagara Street, and saw the back of 1140 Niagara Street. I walked to the right of the roundabout and walked over a manhole cover. Nothing jumped out at me but I had a feeling the address and the key might be adding up to something. I walked around for a few more minutes and decided another pair of eyes might help. I called Lexi but it went straight to voicemail.

"Meet me at the Culhane place when you get this message. I might be onto something."

I ended the call and walked up to Niagara Street and headed north. Thirty minutes later, I was back to Richmond Avenue. The jeep was already there. Lexi got out and looked white as winter time snow.

"You okay?" I said.

"Let's go inside." There was some urgency in her voice.

We were no sooner in the door when Lexi put her arms around me. This is a surprise, I thought. She should have lingered longer in bed this morning. She pulled back as though she could hear my thoughts. I made a mental note to think more quietly in the future.

"That shoot-out last night was meant for us," she said.

"Bullshit," I said, leading her to the couch. "How could it be for us? We weren't anywhere near there."

We sat down and she looked at me with some real concern in her eyes.

"My guy at headquarters said that during questioning, a couple of the bangers they brought in said they were told the white dude and the bitch were going to be prowling around in the tower," she said. "I guess we made quite an impression on them because that's why the guns got involved. They were looking to do us some serious harm, Coe."

If this was true, this was some serious shit, I knew. But who would have told them we would be at the terminal last night? Why would someone have told them? Could it have been Petrelli? And if it was him, how did he wind up dead?

"Did your guy tell you one of the casualties was Max Petrelli?" I said.

"No! He said three white guys got iced and three of the thugs but he didn't give me names."

"Sheila told me this morning. She said she heard it from her mother."

"What the hell was Petrelli doing there?" she said. "And what was he doing in the tower? As lost as we were, we weren't dumb enough to go up there."

We sat quietly for a minute, trying to frame our own scenarios.

Lexi broke the ice.

"Maybe Petrelli gets the idea he knows where the money is," she said, "so he decides to throw the gangbangers off by telling them we're on the way. He's already made contact at least once we know of. While their attention is diverted, Max and his boys sneak into the terminal and go upstairs to where he thinks the money is. In the meantime, the thugs downstairs get impatient and figure Max has screwed them with bad intel. Then they go into the terminal to find Petrelli and all hell breaks loose?"

"Make as much sense as anything else," I said. "But who gives Max the tip that the money is in the tower?"

"Anyone who thinks the money is still in the tower," Lexi said, not helping me much.

"Did your guy tell you anything else of interest?" I said.

"Only that the spent brass made the O.K. Corral look like child's play. We could have been killed up there, Coe."

"Hell yeah, we could have. We would have waltzed in there with a baton and weighted gloves and ran into a platoon armed with Glocks and God knows what else."

"The cops got seventeen guns off the locals and nine off the Petrelli dudes," Lexi said. Then she must have remembered why she was here in the first place.

"Did you have something you wanted to tell me?" she said.

For the next ten minutes I filled her in on my discoveries along the Niagara River.

"So," I summed up, "one-one-four-oh Niagara Street could be a coincidence or it could mean something because behind that address is about where the ferry took the runaways to Canada."

"Why do you think the money would be there? It's not likely the other Petrelli would give two shits about the Underground Railroad."

"I don't know," I said. "That keeps eating away at me. We seem to be making connections that were not likely made by the original thief. We started at Central Terminal and now we're at the Underground Railroad. It seems like a big-assed leap to me. But we might as well take a look, don't you think?"

"What have we got to lose?"

We decided we would take a ride to Bird Island that night to reconnoiter.

I thought I might finally have some use for the night vision scope I bought. The sky was that too-beautiful-for-a-name color that blended the pink of the setting sun with the darkening blue of the springtime sky when we drove up Richmond to Forest and over to Niagara for a five-minute drive south. I told Lexi to go by West Ferry so she could see the stainless steel 1140 on the building. I made her drive around to the back so she could get the same perspective I had earlier in the day. Once back in the jeep, we headed over the Ferry Street bridge and onto the island. She made a left and drove along to the parking area near the southern end of Bird Island. We parked and got out. We walked over to the fence separating us from the river.

"It's pretty flat and way too open to be hiding much of anything," I said.

"You are a master of the obvious," Lexi said as she headed toward the roundabout. She circled it before stepping into it. She looked around and came back out on the pavement.

"What's that?" she said, pointing to the man hole.

"Is that a Jeopardy question? It's a manhole cover."

'What's under it?"

"A sewer, I would imagine," I said.

She stood on the steel cover and bent down to get a closer look.

"It doesn't look like this has been moved in a while," she said. "And don't imagine, Coe. Discover."

As we were talking a security guard was making his rounds.

"'Evening, folks. You come to see the sun go down?"

"Yeah, my friend here is from out of town so I was giving him a little history of our fair city," Lexi said, cheerfully.

The guard tipped his hat and drove around the roundabout and headed back north.

"We need to get down in this hole," Lexi said.

"Now? And who is 'we'?"

"We is you and no, not now, but soon."

We were on our way to see Bea at the Bijou when she told me her plan.

CHAPTER THIRTY-ONE

Early the next morning we headed out to South Buffalo and McKay's Work Clothes where I got outfitted with spiffy navy-blue coveralls. Lexi also made me get work boots I would probably never wear again and a bulky tool bag for which I had nary a tool. My father once told me not to keep too many tools around as people would then expect that you know how to use them. I also got a hard hat.

"You don't look like a worker if you wear top-siders with your coveralls," she noted. "As for the bag, if you need it to bring things out of the hole, the bag helps – assuming you find something worth bringing out."

I hated it when she was right.

As for Lexi, she had swapped her ubiquitous jeans and T-shirts for a gray business suit and equipped herself with an official-looking clipboard. I had almost forgotten how beautiful Lexi was. She accentuated her femininity. She caught me staring a couple of times and those stares earned me a couple of punches.

"Knock it off! You act like you've never seen a stunningly beautiful woman in business attire before," she said. But she was smiling and that made me smile.

I had a few concerns about our choice of vehicle but Lexi dismissed them.

"With any luck, they'll be looking at me, not the jeep," she said and she did have a point.

I suggested I undertake my exploration at night but Lexi was right again.

"You ever see union guys work in manholes at night?" she said. "You'll attract less attention during daylight."

We got out to the island about mid-morning. I stuffed the night scope in the tool bag before I got out of the jeep. Lexi put out some traffic cones she had left from her police days, and I used the pry bar that had been so handy at Central Terminal to pop the manhole cover. I turned on my headlamp and started down the ladder inside the manhole. I thought I went down about ten feet. I was facing north when I got to the bottom of the ladder. I could hear the rushing of the river on my left. I turned to move south and took the out the scope. I took two steps before I realized my blunder. Night vision scopes work by amplifying ambient light at night like stars or moonlight. There wasn't much ambient light at the bottom of a manhole so the scope was useless. The beam on my headlamp would have to suffice. The hole I was in wasn't actually a sewer. It was more of a tube, just a space carved out of the subsurface rock. I saw some boxes I figured must have something to do with the street lighting up above. I continually refocused the beam, first to floor of the hole, then to the front. I walked about ten yards and saw the south wall straight ahead. I walked as far as I could and turned around to see what lay ahead to the north. I heard the squeak of a rat and pivoted away from it. I bumped hard into the east wall of the cave and felt something give. I refocused the light and saw that the wall was actually just a canvas curtain but it was colored to blend in with the rock. I moved the curtain to the side revealing a piece of plywood. It, too, was shaded like the rock and would be virtually invisible to anyone curious enough to be in the hole. I moved the plywood carefully and saw several matching travel bags neatly arrayed on the rock floor. My heart was pounding as I opened the first bag. Jackpot. It was filled with cash - but not just cash, shrink-wrapped cash. I opened another, then another. They were all the same. Packs of $100 bills shrink-wrapped, I assumed, to seal out the moisture in the hole. I was a little wobbly when I made it back to the ladder.

"Find anything down there, Chet?" Lexi yelled.

I picked up on the idea she was trying to convince someone of our legitimacy.

"Just some condensation, Joyce. You know, the kind we find down here all the time."

"Do you need anything from the jeep?"

"There's another bag in the jeep, Joyce. Could you throw that down?"

I heard voices talking, then Lexi saying good-bye.

"How's it going down there?" she said, softly this time.

"Beyond our wildest dreams," I said. "I'm going to hand some bags up to you if it is safe."

"No one here right now," she said.

I carried one of the cash bags to the top rung of the ladder.

"Don't look inside yet" I said. "It's all cash. I think there are six bags."

I carried all six up to Lexi, then threw the night vision scope in the tool bag and moved everything back where I'd found it. Then, I kicked a rat off my boot and came to the surface.

Lexi had taken the bags to the jeep and stacked them on the back seat. She sat in the driver's seat, looking stunned with six carpet bags full of one hundred-dollar bills stacked in the back.

"Well, Joyce," I said, louder than I needed to, "That's a wrap here. Let's go."

She didn't move for a minute, then looked at me and smiled.

"Okay, Chet. We're outta here."

Then it must have hit her that we actually found the money. She started giggling, then broke into a full-throated laugh that made me laugh. We didn't stop laughing until we got to the Culhane house and carried the bags into the house. Lexi went to the bathroom when Shamus knocked on the door. I opened the door for him and he hugged me.

"Just wondering how long you intend to hang around," he said. "I got a realtor who wants to start showing the place. I told him I'd let him know when he could get in here."

"I don't think I'll be here a whole lot longer, my friend," I said. "I'll be out of your hair in a few days."

"No sweat, Coe. You know you can stay as long as you need to," he said. "Hey, did you hear about the shit at the terminal last night?"

"Just what we saw on the news. Was it a gang war or some shit like that?"

"I don't think so. Three wise guy wanna-be's got whacked by the local gang. Nobody can figure what the hell was going on."

Lexi came out and even Shamus was impressed.

"Damn, girl, you look great," he said. "You two getting ready for Halloween or something? Coe looks like he's going to work and you look like a princess."

Lexi laughed.

"Hey, you guys going on a trip? Those carpet bags are beautiful."

"We might be, Shamus," I said. "would your wife like a couple of those bags? We got them for a steal."

Lexi started laughing and said she would empty a couple and give them to Shamus. She headed to the bedroom and came back with two empty bags. She handed them to Shamus.

"You two look like you are having too much fun. Take it easy and thanks for these. Kathryn will love them."

Shamus shook my hand and was out the door.

Lexi put her arms around my neck.

"We got them for a steal … Coe Duffy, you are an asshole." Then she kissed me, really kissed me, really, really kissed me. I picked her up and started to carry her into the bedroom. She wiggled free.

"Let's count first." She was grinning from ear to ear.

We hit nine hundred thousand dollars before she didn't want to count any more. Then, I did what I've been hankering to do since I got back to Buffalo. But we were a little out of practice, so we did it all again. Still, it took one more time to get it right. Then we dozed off, surrounded by shrink-wrapped one hundred-dollar bills.

EPILOGUE

It was one of those luxuriant spring mornings that almost make you forget about the Buffalo winter. A cloudless blue sky was the backdrop for fat green buds on the trees across the city. I was standing on the balcony of Marsha McCartan's posh apartment, looking out over the city I once called home and just might again. I think Lexi was too overcome with the thrill of victory to be asking herself the same questions I was asking. The search for those answers led me to visit Marsha.

"Why did you do it?" I said.

"Whatever do you mean, Coe?" she said with a smile.

"That's just the first question. I have a bunch more," I said, smiling back.

"As beautiful as it out here," she said, "let' go inside and discuss this further."

We moved to a luxurious sofa. I ran my hand over the soft, fine leather. Marsha poured coffee from shiny silver service into china cups.

"That's Wexler leather," she said, smiling. "You can probably afford one now."

We sipped and sat back.

"You are without your partner, Coe," Marsha said. "Does that mean you are the only one with unanswered questions?"

"I don't know, Ms. McCartan," I said. "I think Lexi will be more inquisitive once the joy of newfound wealth fades."

"Please, Coe, you must call me Marsha."

"After what you've done for us, I'll call you anything you want, Marsha."

"And what is it you think I've done for you?"

"Pretty much everything," I said. "And by you, I mean, of course, you and Sheila."

I could see so much of Sheila in her mother's face. The elder McCartan remained an absolutely beautiful woman and I couldn't quite understand how my father's faults led to them breaking apart. She looked into my eyes but stayed silent.

"Well, let me tell you how I think everything played out and you tell me if I'm right, okay?" I said.

She continued to stare.

"I think the story Lexi got was true. There was money unreported from the City Hall theft and it may have once actually been stashed somewhere in Central Terminal. The thief was familiar with the terminal and he probably felt comfortable hiding it there. Somewhere along the way, though, the money got moved from the terminal and hidden somewhere else. But Lexi placed too much credence in the word of her friend Cletus and Cletus may have been telling her straight – that the money was in the terminal. Lexi being Lexi was undeterred whenever I told her the task of scouring the tower and the outbuildings was too much for the two of us. Even when the street punks got in our way, she was determined to see things through."

I looked at her and could see a hint of a smile starting to form. Marsha was paying close attention, so I went on.

"Whoever moved the money then faced the harder task of moving us away from our focus on the terminal. Magically, a key and a scrap of paper appeared among the possessions of Cletus's brother, Moses. We tried but couldn't make heads or tails of that new evidence. Then a very helpful and insightful woman gets involved and starts by dropping clues and interpreting some of that evidence. Finally, she brings along a colleague to lend credence to the new tale being spun, a colleague who really likes chicken wings, I might add."

Now, Marsha had a full smile.

"The key we've assigned as an important clue takes on added significance when a number is found on the barrel of it. Right after the number is discovered, I am invited to a coffee shop on Niagara Street, a couple blocks from a street address that corresponds to the number etched on the key. I see some connection but it is finally Lexi who sees the manhole on Bird Island as significant."

Marsha took a sip of her coffee so I drank some as well before I continued.

"Then we find nearly a million dollars shrink-wrapped and stuffed in carpet bags."

"Is there a question coming soon, Coe?" she said, "because your narrative paints a very neat and concise picture of developments."

"But too neat and too concise, Marsha. First, there is no way the City Hall thief was going to shrink wrap the cash. I don't even know if shrink-wrapping was around at the time of the robbery.

"Second, if the money was hidden in Central Terminal, it didn't need to be shrink-wrapped. It only needed to be sealed like that to protect it from something like the moisture beneath Bird Island.

"Third, a typical thief would never have stuffed the cash in carpet bags that probably cost a hundred bucks apiece. Only someone with impeccable taste, someone who might buy a Wexler sofa, would do that."

I drank more coffee and saw the gleam in her eye.

"So, the question now is, why did you do it?"

"You assume I did it," she said.

"You and a helper or two," I said. "Sheila had to be involved but I still don't get why you did it."

Marsha was quiet for a minute and put down her cup.

"There is only one thing I can't fit into the puzzle. The shootout. It was pretty obvious that we were the intended targets but we had moved off the terminal as the hiding place already."

"You were not the intended targets, Coe," she said. "The intended target was dealt with as hoped."

I must have looked confused.

"That was all Sheila's doing. She despised Max Petrelli. She gave him false information about the cash being on the ninth floor of the tower. She also knew how much the locals wanted to get some payback for what you and Lexi had done. So, she combined the two elements: getting Petrelli and company into the tower where they would be in a confined space, and telling the locals it would be you and Lexi who would be there."

"Then nature took its course," I said. "How did Sheila get word to the neighborhood?"

"Your Lexi is not the only one with connections in the police department," she said. "A well-placed word to an informant was all it took."

These two women were very clever, I thought.

"How about the money? There was much more money in the bags we found than was left over from the robbery."

"Perhaps it was left by your fairy godmother, by someone who has been watching you for a very long time - someone who was heartbroken when your career in city government ended. Who saw fit to intervene with an understanding judge? Someone who even followed your baseball career south of the border."

It was beginning to make sense.

"And someone who decided to help me out financially?" I said.

She nodded.

"But you're more than a fairy godmother mother, aren't you?"

"Your father and I were quite involved for a time and it's true, I am your mother. I'm sorry I lied about that earlier."

"And the money?"

"I knew things weren't going great for you and I knew you wouldn't accept any handout from me, even if you knew I was your mother."

She went on to say she had heard all the same rumors about cash being squirreled away in the terminal. She, like Lexi, got antsy when the word came down about the impending demolition. Her friend, Gabe DelNegro, told her he had an idea about where it could be. Gabe was too old to do any exploring himself, so Marsha gave him a few thousand dollars for the information. She and Sheila went into the baggage house one night and grabbed the stash. Then they devised the plan to move the money and lay some bread crumbs.

"So, Sheila is …"

"… your half-sister," Marsha smiled.

"Holy shit, I was lusting after my half-sister?"

That brought on full laughter.

"Sheila told me how unmerciful she was in teasing you but she said you were always a gentleman."

"Yeah, but I didn't always want to be."

We both laughed at that.

"Does my father know?" I said.

"Yes," Marsha said, her smile gone. "You know better than anyone else that life throws you curveballs. Sometimes things don't always work out the way you'd like but they do, eventually, work out. I gave birth to you and nurtured you as long as I could but I couldn't be a mother to you. Josh filled a dual role with you admirably. I threw a few hundred thousand in the bags in atonement for my failures as a mother."

What could I say? What could I do? She was mom. I slid over on the couch and gave her a hug. We were in that embrace when Sheila came in.

"And I thought I was the object of your affection," she said, laughing. Then she turned to her mother.

"Did he figure it out?"

"Most of it," Marsha said.

"See?" Sheila smiled. "I told you he was smarter than he looked."

Then she came over and gave me a hug.

"If you are really smart, you'll let mother invest some of your newfound wealth. She's quite good you know."

Looking at this apartment, I knew that to be true even though so much of this story seemed too good to be true.

I told my new family it was time for me to leave.

"Where are you headed?" Sheila said.

"I need to get out to South Buffalo. I made a promise to Mikhail Kulavich I have to keep."

"I'll give you a ride, Coe," Sheila said. "Then, maybe we can go look for a car for you."

"Damn nice of you, sis. Damn nice."

ACKNOWLEDGEMENTS

If you've never written a work of this length, making up stuff and weaving it with real stuff, you won't know how many people are part and parcel of the finished product.

Mike Del Nagro, my friend and editor, is the red pen behind the art of this book. Thanks, Mike, for your professional talent and friendship.

Lee Coppola, who has had as many jobs as I have, gave me the background on the City Hall robbery. Lee, the retired dean of the Journalism School at my beloved St. Bonaventure, a former investigative reporter and U.S. attorney was a Godsend. My dear friend Sal Martoche added some valuable information about the City Hall robbery.

I relied on some on-line research about the underground railroad and Buffalo's proud past in it. I also found some great pictures and information about Central Terminal on the website centralterminal.org. I got some helpful information about the city treasury robbery on the website bpdthenandnow.com … my special thanks to those whose labors created those websites.

Thanks to Bea Montione and her brother Michael Militello, two great friends and proprietors of one of our favorite restaurants, the Bijou. My gratitude also goes to Kevin Cunningham, a great fitness trainer and greater friend and owner of KC Fitness. Cole's has been a favorite watering hole since I was old enough to drink legally and the Shatzel family are among Buffalo's best hosts. The bartender in the book is named for two of Cole's all-time favorite bartenders, Donny Pappas and Joe Lang, both of whom have passed on but will never be forgotten. My friendship with Dennis Talty began in grammar school and continues to this day. Dennis owns Talty's Tavern that does, in fact, have the best "open mic" night in Buffalo to showcase both new and established musical talent. Eddie Brady's is a standout bar in downtown and Eddie is one of Buffalo's nicest guys. Joe Jerge and Tim Eberle at the Mulberry are masters at the art of hospitality and great food. Readers of my first novel, *For No Good Reason*, will recognize my semi-fictional hero from that book – Josh Duffy. His sidekick in this book – Eddie Murray – is real and a fellow Vietnam veteran and a graduate of St. Bonaventure University and a genuinely great guy. Anthony Amigone and his family have been long time friends and Dan Crawford is, in reality, our travel agent par excellence, and a fine man. Brett Joseph is actually Joe Brett, another Bona grad who once pitched a doubleheader for the Bonnies in a blizzard, but that's another story.

I could never write a book about Buffalo without a mention of Jim Litz who was combat veteran and one of the gentlest souls I ever knew who has also passed on.

One of my oldest and best friends, Mike Kull, is the basis for Mikhail Kulavich. Mike is, of course, a Bona guy. He isn't a locksmith but he is Russian.

The rest of the names are figments of my imagination.

ABOUT THE AUTHOR

This is Steve Banko's second novel. His first, *For No Good Reason*, was published in 2016.

Steve spent more than two decades as a speechwriter and professional communicator. He has also spoken to audiences across the country on the issues of war and peace. His non-fiction work has been included in several anthologies and periodicals.

His essay, "Love Must Survive War," was judged the nation's best patriotic essay at the VA Creative Arts Festival in 2019. He repeated that feat with his 2020 essay, "Purple Hearts and Purple Minds," which deals with the moral wounds of war.

Steve served 16 months in combat in Vietnam where he was wounded six times. His awards for heroism included the Silver Star, the nation's third highest decoration for valor, and four Purple Hearts.

Steve lives with his wife, Shirley, in South Buffalo NY and North Ft. Myers FL